D0640697

The Gingerbread Spy

JJ TONER

Other books by JJ Toner

The Black Orchestra

The Wings of the Eagle

A Postcard from Hamburg

The Serpent's Egg

Houdini's Handcuffs, a police thriller featuring DI Ben Jordan

Find Emily, The second DI Jordan thriller

JJ Toner writes short stories and novels. His background is in mathematics. He lives in Ireland with his wife and youngest son.

www.JJToner.com

ACKNOWLEDGEMENTS

Thanks to all my proofreaders, Helen Baggott, Marion Kummerow, Paul T. Lynch, Peter O'Boyle, Susan Offord Jones, Jason Orpwood, Fred Stowell, Pam Toner and Pamela Wilkinson. I am indebted to Anya Kelleye for an inspired cover design, to the Flying Boat museum at Foynes, and to Flavio the real life Good Samaritan in Lisbon airport. A special thanks to Pam, Roisin, Kaitlin and Joshua for the Gingerbread men.

The Gingerbread Spy

Part 1 – London

Chapter 1

February 1944

Major Robertson sat hunched over his desk. "We've got a problem, Kurt. The radio vans in north London picked up a rogue transmission last night. The boffins haven't been able to decode it fully yet – the signal was a short one – but the call-sign is *LBK*."

Kurt Müller said, "That's Lebkuchen – Gingerbread in English. It's not a call-sign I recognise, sir."

The major attempted a sour smile. "The timing couldn't be worse. This Gingerbread could easily derail Operation Overlord. And if Overlord fails, thousands of Allied servicemen will lose their lives."

Kurt was running one of the German agents in the Double Cross programme. As preparations for D-Day intensified, the British relied more and more on the programme to deceive the German high command about their invasion plans.

The major sat back heavily in his chair, hands tucked under his armpits. "Until yesterday I was confident that we had rounded up every last Abwehr agent in Britain. They are all so ill-equipped and badly trained, picking them up is like shelling peas. I can't see how we could have missed one."

And yet you have, thought Kurt.

Chapter 2

A few days earlier

Kurt shivered in his leather jacket as he turned into Perrymead Street. Only one in every three of the street lamps in Fulham was lit. Blanketed in a thick London fog, everything looked grey – the lamp posts, the houses, the trees. Even the black cars appeared grey, sliding in and out of the pools of shimmering lamplight. Distant foghorns sounded from the river, while seagulls cried overhead, like the voices of dead children.

He picked up a copy of the *Daily Mirror* from the newsagents, before following the stubs of the iron railings to number 12. He lifted the doorknocker.

Harry Locke, the elderly guard, opened the door immediately. "That's quite a peasouper, sir."

Kurt stepped inside, and Harry closed the door.

"Is Arnold about?"

Harry grinned toothlessly. "He's in the bathroom. Been in there for hours. I expect he's trying to scrub the swastikas from his hairy arse."

Kurt wasn't in the humour for Harry's wisecracks. That one wasn't even original. Picking up on Kurt's mood, the guard wiped the grin from his face. "The kettle's on, sir." He handed Kurt a brown envelope, sealed with wax, and returned to his station in the front parlour.

Kurt took a book and a paper pad from a shelf in the kitchen and placed them on the table with the newspaper. He made coffee with milk. There was sugar. He took a spoonful. Then he cut himself a slice of fresh bread and added a generous sheen of salted butter. He sat at the table, opened the envelope, and read the outgoing signal for the day from the Wireless Board of the Double Cross 'Twenty' Committee.

He found the code word for the day from the book – *Gone With the Wind* – and created the substitution matrix on his paper pad. Then he added Arnold's Abwehr call-sign to the front of the signal and encoded it.

Arnold made an appearance at 7:30 dressed in his red silk dressing gown, holding a lighted cigarette between his thumb and middle finger. He was a German to his hair roots, and clearly considered himself a cut above everyone in Britain. He picked up the newspaper. Propping himself against the sink, he spoke in heavily accented English. "I don't know why you buy this rubbish, Kevin. Are there no better newspapers out there?"

Arnold wore his lank hair swept across his forehead much like Hitler's. He was ten years younger than his beloved Führer though, and sported a pencil moustache. The British had given him the working name of Arnold; his real name was Paul Hoffmeister. Kurt was pretty sure that everyone in this make-believe world had been given false names. Harry and Clarence, the two ancient guards, Hendriks the cleaner. He couldn't even be sure that Partridge was the cook's real name. Kurt went by the name Kevin O'Reilly.

Arnold's one and only job was to transmit signals to the Abwehr in Hamburg. Kurt could have transmitted these himself, but Arnold's handler in Hamburg would know the 'fist' of his agent, and would recognize any attempt at transmission by another operator. This fact alone was keeping the double agent alive. Forced to operate against his own government every day, his continued existence hung on his usefulness to the British war effort. As the spymaster, Tar Robertson, was fond of saying, 'His coat hung on a shoogly peg'.

Kurt unlocked the door to the back parlour. He went inside, and switched on Arnold's Telefunken r/t set.

It took a few minutes to warm up. Normally, Arnold would fill this waiting period with mindless chatter, but today he had little to say. He sucked on his cigarette and exhaled a cloud of smoke. "I swear the cook must be Irish. Today's meal was a miserable pork stew. It was mostly vegetables."

Kurt raised a questioning eyebrow. Mrs Partridge was pure cockney. Tapping his pencil impatiently on his pad, he sipped his coffee. Real coffee with sugar! Arnold was better fed than most Londoners.

Arnold was hard to like, but Kurt felt sorry for him. Following capture and interrogation by Tin Eye Stephens in the London Cage, he had been given a stark choice: work for the British Secret

Intelligence Service as a double agent, or go directly to the gallows.

His life was comfortable. Two domestic servants came in daily to cook and clean for him. But he was guarded day and night, and he could never leave the building unaccompanied. 12 Perrymead Street may not have had barred windows, but it was still very much a prison.

The transmitter hummed. When the clock on the wall reached 7:40, they received two incoming signals. Kurt wrote the Morse sequence on his pad. The terminating code, *Ende*, told him there was nothing more.

Kurt yielded his stool to Arnold and watched as the agent keyed in the outgoing coded signal.

"What was in that signal?" said Arnold.

"A weather report."

Arnold curled his lip in disgust. "How many days is that?"

"What do you mean?"

Arnold jumped to his feet, knocking his stool to the floor. He raised his voice, switching to German. "All I ever get to transmit is stupid weather reports. How long since I transmitted anything important?"

Kurt was startled, but he replied in a quiet voice, designed to calm his agent, "I'm sure weather reports are important."

Arnold took a step closer to Kurt, waving his arms about. "You think every captured Abwehr agent in London is sending signals about the weather? What sort of *Dummkopf* do you take me for? Don't you think the high command in Berlin will want information about the positioning of British and American troops and equipment? How else will they know where and when the invasion of Europe will start?"

"I'm sure the British know what they're doing. Don't you think the Abwehr would smell a rat if every agent in the programme sent details about troop movements every day?"

"Why, how many agents have been turned like me?"

"I have no idea, Arnold. There must be a few. There's really nothing to worry about."

Arnold's colour deepened. "You have no idea what my life is like, have you? Try to imagine what it feels like to be a puppet of a foreign power, a traitor to the Fatherland. I'm no better than a fly stuck to a flypaper. And what do I have to look forward to? What do you think the British will do with me when I'm no longer useful to them?" His voice rose with every beat.

Harry appeared, brandishing his rifle.

Kurt waved him away. "Lower your weapon, Harry. You're liable to poke someone's eye out with that."

"I heard raised voices, shouting – in German."

"Everything's under control," said Kurt.

Harry returned to his station, mumbling under his breath.

"I don't have answers to any of your questions," said Kurt to his smouldering double agent. "My advice to you is to carry on as you are. Take each day as a gift and be thankful that you're still alive."

Arnold flounced out of the room. Kurt switched off the radio and set about deciphering the two incoming signals. The first informed Arnold that his Swiss bank account had been topped up by £100. MI5 would be pleased. The second signal translated:

INVESTIGATE MOSQUITO AIRCRAFT PRODUCTION BELIEVED RELOCATED FROM HATFIELD

The cover the Abwehr had given Arnold was as a Swedish ball bearing salesman. A field trip to an aircraft factory was a credible option.

Kurt slid the sheet with the two signals into the newspaper before leaving the back parlour, locking the door carefully.

The double agent was loitering in the hallway. Kurt showed him the first decoded signal.

Arnold's face was still red from his earlier tantrum, but he gave Kurt a watery smile. "My friends in Hamburg are happy with my work, at least."

"So it would seem."

Kurt stepped toward the front door, but Arnold moved into his path. "Could you ask our masters one question for me?"

"What question?"

"I'd like to know how many Abwehr men have been recruited by British Intelligence."

The question puzzled Kurt. "Why is that important?"

Arnold's wave of the hand suggested it was a trivial matter, but the tremor in his voice said otherwise. "The size of the deception operation might give me some notion how safe I am."

"You have the major's assurances..."

The tremor in Arnold's voice intensified. "He gave me his word as a gentleman that I would be returned to Germany once the War is over. But how do I know I can trust him?"

"I still don't see how the number of Abwehr agents in the programme has any bearing on the endgame, but I will ask your question if the opportunity presents itself."

"That's all I ask, thank you." Arnold stepped aside.

Kurt stuck his head into the front parlour to say goodbye to Harry.

Harry gave him a 3-fingered scouts' salute. "See you tomorrow, sir."

Chapter 3

Princess Alexandra Military Hospital Millbank, London

Lina Smit removed her coat and changed into her uniform. She stowed her clothes in her locker and took a last look in the mirror before leaving the changing room, and making her way to Matron's office.

Matron's office was empty. Lina couldn't recall a day when Matron was not at her desk, handing out assignments to the nurses at the start of the evening shift. Where could she be?

Sounds of activity drew Lina to the hospital's main concourse, where she found three nurses and the two porters rushing about in frenzied activity. Matron stood at the centre, directing operations like a traffic policeman.

Lina stopped Julie Parker, one of the nurses, as she passed. "What's happening?"

"Talk to Matron." And Julie was gone.

Lina approached Matron.

Matron said, "We've had instructions from the Emergency Medical Service to get ready for an influx of new casualties. A serious bombing raid is expected over the weekend. We're reorganizing the hospital. Help the porters."

Dan and Martin, the two porters, were busy wheeling occupied beds about. Dan said, "We're moving patients from two orthopaedic wards into the psych wards. I need you to fetch empty beds from the basement."

The basement. This was the one part of the hospital that Lina hated. It scared her. It gave her the shivers just thinking about it. The morgue was down there, and sometimes she thought it might be haunted by evil spirits, but that wasn't the complete explanation for her fear of the place. During the German invasion of Holland in 1940, she had been trapped for three days in a basement in Rhenen. She still bore the mental scars of those three days.

Dan was old enough to be her father, but she fluttered her eyelashes at him. "Couldn't I help move the patients?"

"Martin and I can handle that," said Dan. "We need empty beds for St Mary's and St Mark's. Shake a leg."

Dragging her feet, she headed down the corridor toward the service elevator. She grabbed Julie by the arm as she rushed past. "Where are you going, Julie? Can I help you with whatever you're doing?"

"I'm fetching new beds from the basement," said Julie.

Lina groaned. "I don't want to go down there."

Julie knew how Lina felt about the basement. She gave a hollow laugh. "Remember the first rule of nursing."

"I know I should do what I'm told, but I really hate the basement."

"Come with me," said Julie. "We'll go together."

"I can't."

"Of course you can." Julie pulled her toward the elevator. "There's nothing to be afraid of."

Lina shuddered, but she allowed Julie to steer her inside the elevator. "Why are we doing this, Julie?"

"Because we've been told to."

"No, I mean I don't understand why they need our little hospital. None of it makes any sense. Millbank is too small to handle a large number of casualties. We don't even have an emergency department, for heaven's sake."

Julie replied, "There's been talk of big numbers of bombers on the way from Germany over the weekend. We have to be able to take in some of the less seriously injured." She pressed the button on the panel, and then, as the doors swung closed, she stepped out, leaving Lina on her own in the elevator.

Lina stifled a scream. She stabbed at the buttons, but the elevator was already on its way down...

The elevator doors slid open. She stayed where she was, hoping the doors would close, but they remained open. She stepped forward and peered into the corridor. A ripple of cold air, like a ghostly breath, caressed her cheeks. A murmur of distant voices reached her ears, but she couldn't make out any words. Were the dead awake, and talking amongst themselves? Worst of all was the smell, not the usual hospital mixture of disinfectant and cleaner; this was a faint smell unique to the basement, a smell of death and despair.

Rattling sounds and footsteps echoed along the corridor, coming toward her. Terrified, she stabbed at the buttons again, and shrank back into the elevator. The doors began to close, but, before they came together, a hand reached in, forcing them open again.

Julie's friend, Nurse Kathy Benson, pushed an empty bed into the elevator. "Hold the doors open while I fetch another bed."

Lina held the bed across the line of the doors while Kathy hurried away up the corridor. When she arrived back with a second bed, the two of them took the elevator up to the ground floor.

"Where's Julie?" said Kathy.

"She played a trick on me. She sent me down in the elevator on my own."

Kathy's response to that was a deliberate lie. "I expect she had something more important to do."

"Who else is down there?" said Lina.

"What do you mean? There was only me."

"I heard voices."

Kathy smiled her wicked smile. "You must have imagined it."

Lina shivered.

At the ground floor, they rolled the two beds out of the elevator. Lina would have been happy to wheel hers to one of the wards, but Dan took it from her. "Go back down and bring up some more," he said.

This time, Lina held the elevator doors open until Kathy joined her. They rode down together. In the basement, they left the elevator together, and made their way along the corridor to a storage area where Lina found a figure in a white coat.

It was Joost van Dijk, the hospital's clinical psychologist, preparing beds for deployment in the wards.

Relief flooded Lina's mind. Joost was Dutch, like Lina. She considered him a friend, perhaps her only friend in the hospital. She laughed out loud, and the sound of her laughter, like the braying of a donkey, echoed from the walls.

Kathy smirked, but Joost smiled at Lina, and her fears receded. "*Goede middag, Lina.*"

"*Goede middag, Doctor.*"

He switched back to English. "Take these two beds and come back for two more. That should be enough."

"Very good, Doctor," said Lina.

It had felt good to converse in their shared tongue, even if only for a moment, but a sideways glance at a tight-lipped Kathy sounded a warning in her head. The young nurse was clearly fuming at the intimacy of the exchange.

At lunch in the canteen, she joined a table occupied by Kathy, Julie and two other nurses. They barely acknowledged her as she sat down, and she found herself excluded from the conversation. That suited Lina fine. She had no great desire to converse with people who obviously hated her.

As they stood up to leave, Kathy looked down at Lina. "Are you still with that Irishman?"

"Yes."

"I'm curious. How did you two meet?"

"It was at that big Thanksgiving party the Americans threw, you remember."

"Who introduced you?" said Julie.

"I can't remember. I was with a group of Dutch people. I expect it was one of them."

"The tulip brigade!" Julie snorted to Kathy, and they flounced off.

Chapter 4

Plunging into the fog, Kurt crossed the road to the Pelican Café. His contact, an MI5 courier, known to Kurt only as 'John', was sitting at his usual place by the window, a teapot, cup and saucer, together with his hat, and a copy of the *Daily Mirror* on the table in front of him.

Kurt sat down, placing his newspaper beside John's.

"What would you like?" John spoke with an upper class accent, and carried a permanent look of hood-eyed boredom.

The girl behind the counter hurried over and placed a fresh cup and saucer on the table in front of Kurt.

Standing a smidgen closer to Kurt than was necessary, she smiled. "That's quite a bad one, but I think it's lifting."

They made eye contact. She had large crystal blue eyes, and perfect teeth, like a Hollywood actress. "You couldn't see your hand in front of your face, earlier," said Kurt.

"What can I get you? A fresh pot of tea, perhaps?"

"Nothing for me," said Kurt.

John dismissed her with a wave of his hand. "Thank you, Miss."

She smiled at Kurt some more, and moved away, her hips swaying.

Kurt and John shared a short, desultory exchange about the weather. Then John picked up Kurt's newspaper, put on his hat, and left the café.

Kurt ran his eyes over the *Daily Mirror* headlines. The Anzio campaign was going well, although the enemy was holding out in the monastery at Monte Cassino, which was under almost constant aerial bombardment. A second article carried news of a huge bombing raid on Berlin, two nights earlier. Aided by a diversionary raid over Frankfurt, over 1,000 bombers had dropped 2,500 tons of high explosives on the capital in a 30-minute raid. According to the report, the city was still burning 24 hours later. Kurt read that article twice, and shivered. He had friends in Berlin.

He put the newspaper down and scratched an itch behind his left ear. Arnold was worried about what would happen to him when the Allies won the War. Perhaps he was right to worry, but there had been no mention of the other possible outcome. If Germany won the War, Arnold would face certain death as a traitor – and so would Kurt.

Arnold was a pompous ass, but he was an educated pompous ass. It was difficult to understand how people like him had fallen so completely under the spell of the Führer. And there were millions like him. What was it about that angry, ranting, dyspeptic 54-year-old that had captivated most of the adult population of Germany?

Through the window, the fog was thinning. He could make out vague shapes of people moving about on the far pavement.

A beautiful, red MG PA Midget drew up outside. A tall man in a trench coat and fedora climbed out, stepped into the café, and sat at Kurt's table.

The stranger removed his hat, revealing a head of red hair. He held out a hand.

Kurt was immediately on his guard. He ignored the hand. "Do I know you?"

"My name's Greg Ellis. I'm in the same business as you." His boyish face lit up with a smile. "We both work for Tar Robertson. We need to talk."

"What about?"

Ellis pointed at the empty cup on the table. "Are you finished here, Kevin? I could walk with you."

Kurt's heart jumped in his chest. "How do you know my name?"

"I've been in the game a lot longer than you. Come on, we can't talk here."

Kurt's instinct was to tell this stranger to go the hell, but his curiosity had been aroused, and there was something engaging in Ellis's manner, an indefinable, infectious enthusiasm. Kurt waved goodbye to the waitress and followed Ellis into the fog. Ellis turned north. They walked together briskly onto a green area, dark and deserted in the cold, damp air.

Ellis kept his hands jammed in his pockets. Kurt envied the man his trench coat and hat. His own short leather jacket was fine as far as it went, but the damp seeped through his trousers. "Where are we going?"

"I thought we could walk about the common. We can talk in comfort here without being overheard."

They strolled on together, following an east-west path. The fog was still thick enough to diffuse the lights from the houses on the north side of the common, creating strange, ghostlike effects.

"How did you find me?'

"Does it matter?"

Kurt stopped. "Tell me how you found me."

Ellis turned back to face him with a broad grin. "It wasn't difficult. I followed John."

They resumed their walk.

"What did you want to talk about?"

It was Ellis who stopped this time. "I needed to ask you a question. How have you been getting on with your man? What's his designation?"

The hairs bristled on Kurt's neck. "I don't think we should discuss that."

"My man is F17. At least, he was."

"What do you mean? He was?"

"Not important," said Ellis. "Just tell me you haven't noticed anything strange, recently."

"Like what?"

"Anything, anything at all."

"No, I don't think so. Why do you ask?"

A cloud passed over Ellis's face. "My man's been blown."

"That's unfortunate. What happened?"

"When I turned up as usual on Tuesday, he was gone. The house was empty. He was blown. Out of the blue, with no warning."

They reached the edge of the common and turned back.

"You spoke to someone about it?"

"There was no discussion. Not before or after. I got a short note in the post. It said my man's cover was compromised. They would let me know when – if – they needed my services again."

"Bad luck."

"Luck had nothing to do with it, old son. His cover was blown on purpose. It was Tar Robertson's decision."

"You're sure of your facts? How can you know that?"

"Believe me, it was obvious. The evidence is irrefutable."

"Why would Major Robertson blow your man's cover? Wasn't he pulling his weight?"

Ellis shrugged. "The material he was given to transmit became less and less important. Nothing but weather reports at the end."

That hit the mark with Kurt. "I don't believe Major Robertson would sanction anything like that."

Ellis produced a packet of Navy Cut. He offered them to Kurt.

Kurt declined. Ellis shook the packet under Kurt's nose. "Go ahead, take one. Stick it behind your ear for later."

"I don't smoke."

Ellis took a cigarette from the packet, tapped both ends on the box, and lit it with a lighter. The light from the flame lasted no more than two seconds, but it revealed Ellis as he really was, a man older than his looks, more careworn than fresh-faced.

Kurt took a moment to gather his thoughts. "I find it hard to believe that Major Robertson would deliberately betray one of his own agents."

Ellis drew on his cigarette. "How well do you know Tar Robertson?"

Kurt made no reply, and Ellis barrelled on, punctuating his delivery with the hand holding the cigarette. "He began his career in a one-man operation, investigating strange lights and carrier pigeons. Did you know that?"

"No."

"It's true. That was in thirty-nine. The Secret Service was based in Wormwood Scrubs prison at that time. Then he ran a double agent called SNOW. That was a disaster. Unmitigated. Have you heard those stories?"

Kurt shook his head.

"SNOW was a Welshman working for the Germans. He offered to double for us. Robertson was assigned as his case officer. SNOW roped in a string of others sympathetic to the Germans, before his cover was blown. Robertson gave him complete freedom to roam around the country spying on all sorts of military installations..."

"Unaccompanied?"

"Completely. The idea was to let him operate as a real spy would, and then doctor his reports to the Krauts. This was in 1940 and 1941. He was given a car with limitless petrol coupons. He collected a lot of intelligence on the Royal Navy, its bases and ships. He even photographed the entire east coast radar defence system and gave the pictures to the enemy."

"Robertson didn't prevent that?"

"No one's sure what happened, but SNOW was allowed to fly back and forth to meet his Abwehr contact in Portugal. My guess is that he pulled the wool over Robertson's eyes and carried the pictures with him. Could easily have cost us the Battle of Britain. If it wasn't for our brave Spitfire pilots we'd all be speaking German by now."

"So SNOW was actually working for the Germans?"

"He was working for both sides at the same time, old boy, and both sides paid him handsomely for his services. Then the Jerries asked him to recruit a Welsh nationalist who might be persuaded to raise a stink..."

Kurt laughed. "A Welsh nationalist."

"I know. It sounds crazy, but the Nazis thought there were enough extreme nationalists in Wales to conduct a campaign of sabotage. They tried the same thing with the IRA in Ireland, of course. SNOW recruited some Welsh nutter, and gave him to the Germans."

"And MI5 swallowed it?"

"Hook, line and sinker."

"Giving SNOW more cash, I suppose."

"You've got it. SNOW ran his Welsh saboteur, so he was given control of all the money."

They turned back toward Ellis's car.

"You say Major Robertson ran this fiasco?"

"He did. In fact, he was promoted. He sits on the XX Committee, so he's involved in all major decisions to do with the Double Cross."

"I thought that was the job of the London Controlling Section," said Kurt.

"The XX or 'Twenty' Committee reports to the LCS," Ellis replied. "To be fair to Tar, he's grown into the job since the early days, but can you imagine the complexity of his job, running an army of double agents?"

"An army? How many are we talking about?"

"I don't have a figure, Kevin. My guess would be a couple of dozen, at least. It's certainly a lot of agents."

Kurt chewed that over for a few moments. Then he said, "What do you want me to do?"

"Not a thing, old boy. I just wanted to check whether your man was still operating, and to warn you about what might be coming down the tracks."

Out of all that Ellis had told him, Kurt articulated his worst fear. "What will become of your man?"

They arrived back at the MG. Ellis dropped his cigarette on the path, crushing it under his shoe. "Robertson had no more use for him." He jumped into the car.

His engine started with an enthusiastic roar. "I'd be willing to bet he's been hanged already," he shouted.

Kurt stood and watched the MG drive away until it was swallowed by the fog.

Chapter 5

Whitehall, London

The façade of the War Office building in Whitehall was scarred from the recent bombing. Many of its windows had been blown out and hastily boarded up. In a smoke-filled meeting room on the fourth floor, eight men sat around a table. These were the members of the secret London Controlling Section of MI5, charged with running the military deception programme in parallel with the preparations for the coming invasion of mainland Europe.

Lieutenant Colonel Bill Baumer of the US War Plans Division sat at the far end of the table. As the sole representative of the US forces in Britain, he felt like a teenager at a toddler's birthday party. Or better yet, an eagle in a nest of sparrowhawks.

Colonel John Bevan, Controlling Officer, was in the chair. He called the meeting to order. "Gentlemen, first a word of welcome to our latest recruit, Major Gordon Clark. Until the appointment of a permanent replacement, Gordon is standing in for Colonel Macintyre, who is indisposed, as I'm sure you all know."

"What's the word on Victor? How is he?" said the representative of the Intelligence Service, Kim Philby.

"He has been transferred to the Royal Military Hospital, in Millbank. He will receive the best of care from the psychiatric team there."

"Can we rely on his silence? I mean, shouldn't we be concerned about what he might disclose?" said Flight Lieutenant Wheatley.

Bevan replied, "Victor is well aware of the need for discretion. I'm sure we have nothing to worry about on that score."

An army colonel said, "With all due respect, sir, the colonel is seriously disturbed. Given what is at stake, we must avoid complacency."

The murmur from the members signalled their agreement.

"And what of the young man that he attacked?" said Baumer.

Colonel Bevan held up a hand for silence. "Complacency is not an issue. Victor is in a military hospital, after all. And the young lieutenant is recovering well in another hospital. His injuries are not life-threatening. Now, to business." He ran his eyes over those present. "I have convened this meeting today to consider just one single item: the revision of Operation Mespot proposed by Lieutenant Colonel Strangeways of General Montgomery's R-Force." He opened a bulky briefcase and pulled out seven copies of a document labelled MOST SECRET. "I must stress the extremely sensitive nature of the contents of this report. The documents are numbered. Each number has been assigned to an individual in this room by name. There are just two more copies of the plan in existence. I have one, the second has been dispatched to the prime minister's office." He checked his watch. "Once you have read the report, the meeting proper will commence, in, let's say, 40 minutes. Under no circumstances must the report leave this room, and all seven copies must be returned to me intact at the close of business. Any questions?"

There were no questions. Each member of the committee received his numbered copy of the report, and Colonel Bevan left the room.

Bill Baumer opened the report. The first page contained an executive summary. And it blew his mind. Whoever this Strangeways was, he sure had an inventive imagination! Baumer wasn't at all convinced about this deception lark. It was a very British way of waging war. But he could see how this new plan could confuse the enemy, and if it kept Rommel and his panzers out of the theatre of war, even for a single day, it would save US servicemen's lives.

Baumer turned to the man on his left. "We haven't met, I think. My name's Bill Baumer."

"Harold Philby. People call me Kim. Standing in for Major Cowgill, SIS." He extended a hand and Baumer shook it.

Forty minutes later, Bevan returned to find the meeting in uproar.

"Gentlemen, I take it you have all read and digested the report."

"It's preposterous, Colonel. We are being asked to build our deception strategy around an entirely fictional US army," said Philby.

"Under the command of Old Blood and Guts!" said Major Clark.

The Royal Navy representative said, "Who is going to create and coordinate all the unit-to-unit chatter between these imaginary armies?"

"J. C. Masterman and Major Robertson of the Twenty Committee will handle all those details. That will be the least of our worries, Commander," said Bevan.

Bill Baumer cleared his throat, and everyone fell silent. "I believe the plan has merit, but it may be difficult to persuade General Patton to play his part. I could be wrong, but I really can't imagine the general leading a phantom army. May I ask whether his involvement is an indispensable element of the plan?"

"No part of the plan is set in stone, including the participation of General Patton," Bevan replied. "But the plan should be considered in its entirety. Every element contributes to the whole. I suggest we go around the table for individual reactions. May we start with you, Flight Lieutenant Wheatley?"

#

What followed was two hours of heated debate. Baumer said very little, preferring to watch and listen as the others fought out their sectional interests.

As lunchtime approached, Bevan was called out of the meeting to take a telephone call. When he returned, he tapped a glass with his pen for silence. "That phone call was from Chartwell. The prime minister has read the report and has moved to endorse the new plan. He urges us all to put our weight behind it and to commit our best effort to make it a resounding success. He has suggested just one change, however. From today, the plan will be called Operation Fortitude."

The meeting concluded on that note. All seven copies of the document were returned to Bevan's briefcase, and the members dispersed.

Chapter 6

As soon as Lina and Kathy arrived back on the ground floor of the hospital, they realized there was something seriously strange going on. The two porters and all the nurses had vanished, and there were raised voices coming from the psych wards, now crammed with patients. Kathy and Lina hurried toward the noises.

St Dymphna's psych ward was in uproar. Three young doctors and the two porters confronted six of the psych patients, standing defiant behind a makeshift barricade of empty beds and chairs. The patients yelled obscenities at the doctors. The doctors looked powerless to bring the situation under control.

One of the patients, an army colonel called Victor, had climbed onto his bed. He looked ridiculous bouncing up and down on the bed like a child in his dressing gown and slippers, brandishing a portable urinal, and bellowing orders to the other patients. "Arm yourselves, men, form a line. Don't let any more of the beggars in. Prepare to repel boarders."

Matron stepped forward. "There's no need for this, Victor, the hospital is being prepared for an inrush of new patients—"

That was all she managed to say. One of the patients dashed forward and laid her out cold with a blow to the head from a bedpan. Two young doctors pulled Matron to safety.

Lina ran back to the service staircase and down to the basement store where she'd left Joost. The psychologist wasn't there.

"Doctor, where are you?" Her voice echoed through the empty corridor.

Joost appeared in a doorway. "What's going on, Lina?"

"You're needed upstairs, Doctor. There's trouble in St Dymphna's ward."

The psychologist grabbed his bag. They met at the doors to the elevator. He pressed the button, and while they waited for the elevator to arrive, she told him what she'd seen in the ward.

"Doesn't surprise me," he said. "Victor is seriously unstable. In his mind he still commands his regiment. He will see the disruption to the hospital as a military attack."

By the time the elevator doors had swung open on the ground floor, Joost had prepared a strong sedative in a syringe. He hid it in the pocket of his lab coat. He grabbed a large envelope from Matron's office, before he and Lina advanced to the door of the ward. They had to step around a dazed Matron, who lay across the doorway, where one of the other doctors was attending to her injury.

"Keep the enemy out!" shouted Victor. "We must hold our position, to the last man, if necessary."

"I'm coming in, Colonel," shouted Joost. The hubbub died. Joost waved the envelope high above his head. "I have an important dispatch for you from regimental headquarters."

"Who signed the dispatch?" said the colonel.

"General Bernard Montgomery, himself," said Joost.

"Pass it through," roared Victor.

"Not possible, Colonel. It's top secret. My instructions are to place it in your hands."

Victor waved his bedpan. "Let him pass."

The men at the barricades stood aside, moving the beds to make a passage through, and the psychologist entered the ward. Lina slipped in behind him. They stopped at the foot of Victor's bed.

Squatting down, Victor lowered an outstretched hand toward the envelope, and before Lina could blink, the doctor had pulled the syringe from his pocket and injected it into the large muscle of Victor's forearm. The sedative took effect quickly. Victor roared incoherently, something about betrayal and fifth columnists, before slipping unconscious from the bed into Joost's arms.

The barricade was dismantled after that. Joost administered mild sedatives to the psych patients, and calm was restored to the hospital.

Chapter 7

Thursday – Friday February 17-18, 1944

Kurt hurried home to number 7 Radipole Road, Fulham. The flat was empty, dark and cold, but there was a surprise waiting for him on the mat. The postman had delivered a postcard postmarked Dublin, signed by Gudrun. The sight of her signature sent goosebumps down his spine.

We all miss you. Hoping you'll be able to visit us soon. Anna sends her love. All my love, Gudrun.

He flipped the card over, propping it up on the mantelpiece behind his one remaining bottle of Irish whiskey. The picture showed Nelson's Pillar on O'Connell Street, Dublin. He set about making a fire, using some newspaper, sticks and a few pieces of anthracite.

There wasn't a lot to eat in the larder. Porridge, egg powder, a few miserable looking vegetables.

Once he had a fire going, he picked up the postcard and read it again. He thought about dropping it into the flames. When Lina saw it, there could be a scene. It would be so much easier to dispose of it now. But something wouldn't let him. He put it back on the mantelpiece and started the gas ring.

He made a frittata using two tablespoonsful of egg powder and half of the vegetables. They were stale and the taste of the egg powder barely tolerable. He made tea and drank it black. They had no milk, and no sugar. You could get milk in the shops, but outside of the meagre daily allowance, sugar was only available for a crazy price on the black market. Turned Abwehr agents were the only ones who could get sugar – and coffee – for nothing.

He turned his mind to what Ellis had told him. If the Double Cross programme was really running a couple of dozen Abwehr agents, it was a massive undertaking. Each one would be set up in a house with a case officer, a couple of guards and a couple of domestics – at least 5 support staff. Multiplying that by 24 made 120 people.

The administration workload must be huge, keeping track of the signals – in and out – a full-time job. The content of the transmissions would have to include some real information mixed in with any misinformation they wanted to send. The Abwehr were no fools.

And what to make of Ellis's account of Major Robertson's chequered history. Was it believable? Why would an officer responsible for such an obvious disaster as the SNOW affair be promoted and then given control of 24 double agents?

Kurt considered his own position in all this. When he first offered to work for the British Intelligence Services, he might easily have been taken as a German spy and made to operate as a double agent like Arnold and the others. The British could have executed him. He shuddered at the memory of how close he'd come under interrogation in the London Cage by a sadistic bastard called Cartwright.

And how secure was Arnold's position? Transmitting weather reports suggested his contribution was not highly valued by the British. Ellis's man had been blown and – if Ellis was to be believed – executed, while sending out similar reports. Arnold was obviously at risk. In the long run, he was probably doomed. Major Robertson's assurances weren't worth a tuppenny damn. Trapped by the cut-throat British, engaged in treason against the Nazis, Arnold had no hope of survival.

Lina arrived home well after midnight. She handed him a parcel containing four ounces of minced meat. While slipping out of her coat, she began to tell him about her day. "We had to set up the hospital to receive incoming wounded. A major Luftwaffe raid is expected in the next few days."

"I didn't think Millbank was that sort of hospital," he said.

"It isn't, but we have spare beds and X-ray equipment. We can handle minor injuries. We will be ready to play our part when the bombs start to fall."

"How have you been getting on with the other nurses?"

Her nose wrinkled as if she'd picked up a bad smell. "Much the same as usual. And Matron sent me down to the basement. Everyone knows how much I hate it down there."

"Did you object?"

"No, Kevin, nurses don't object to Matron's orders. We obey them without question. I went down there and had a really bad time. If Joost hadn't been there I would have died of fright."

"Joost?"

"The psychologist. Remember, I told you about him. He's Dutch."

Kurt remembered.

Spotting the postcard on the mantelpiece, she grabbed it, flipped it over, and read it. She replaced it without comment.

"One of the patients started a mini-revolution. He took over his ward and ordered the men to build a barricade. Matron tried to intervene but they knocked her unconscious with a bedpan."

Kurt laughed.

"It wasn't funny, Kevin. Those bedpans are heavy. She could have been seriously injured. She wasn't, but she could have been."

"Sounds like a riot."

"Not quite, but close enough. Victor's a senior officer. Joost had to handle him with kid gloves. It took great skill to get close enough so that Joost could administer a sedative. He handled the situation really well, as always."

"Well done, Joost!" This Joost could do no wrong in Lina's eyes, and he could work miracles with the patients, apparently.

Kurt's sarcasm was lost on Lina. "I see you've eaten. Did you leave some vegetables for me?"

He grabbed her around the waist and pulled her close. "Of course. Don't I always look after you?" She gave him a peck on the cheek and pushed away from him, but he clung to her for a moment longer, his face buried in her hair. "I missed you."

Lina kissed him again, on the lips this time, and broke free of his grasp.

She started the gas ring. "What sort of day did you have?"

He laughed mirthlessly. "I was leafing through some memories before you arrived."

"Ah! So that's it. I understand."

"My life in London is so different from what it was in Dublin. Sometimes it's difficult to shake the notion that I'm on a different planet – you know?"

She looked deep into his eyes. There were tears in hers. "We each have to live with our histories. We have all made commitments in the past. All we can do is live our lives, moment by moment. You mustn't blame yourself for any of it."

Lina had no idea what was on his mind, but her words were well meant. He smiled at her.

By 2 a.m. they were in bed, Kurt lying on his back, listening to Lina's steady breathing beside him. In his mind he reviewed his own shameful actions since the beginning of the War. He had killed several times, with little thought, and no regrets. Two SS men in Ireland, a Gestapo informer on a train, a factory guard, a German aristocrat.

And now living with Lina in her flat was adding to his shame...

Chapter 8

Friday February 18, 1944

ℱar away, the air raid sirens started, the local sirens picking up the cry within seconds. At first Lina thought maybe they were testing them and they would stop soon. But they kept going. London hadn't been bombed for three years. Perhaps it was a false alarm. But there were more of them now, spread all over the city. The rumour must be true. Was the London Blitz going to start all over again? She tumbled from the bed and looked out the window. Powerful searchlights crisscrossed the sky.

Kurt climbed out of the bed with a groan.

They dressed quickly, put on their coats and hurried to the Anderson shelter in the back garden. As they joined their scared neighbours in the shelter, the drone of approaching aircraft and the thump of distant ack-ack reached them. It was really happening! The Luftwaffe was back to avenge the bombing of Berlin, Bremen and Hamburg.

Inside the shelter, the families of number 7 Radipole Road huddled together, listening to the dull *crump* of exploding bombs in the distance, and then the horrific crashes as they fell on the streets all around them. The shelter was cold and cramped, with nine people, including three young children, in a space designed for six.

As the noises increased, the children cried in terror. Kurt and Lina did their best to help keep them calm. Lina's only consolation was that it wasn't raining. The shelter was far from waterproof.

Two hours later, they emerged to scenes of devastation. Fulham had taken a pasting. One third of the houses on Radipole Road had been reduced to burning rubble, with a fire crew in attendance. Several windows in number 7 had been shattered, but the house, and its neighbour, had been spared. Numbers 9 and 10 hadn't been so lucky. The front walls had been sliced off, exposing everything inside, like a macabre doll's house.

Kurt joined a civil defence team clearing rubble in search of survivors. Lina set out for the hospital.

#

It took her an hour to walk to the hospital. The Tube was closed and there were no buses.

Nothing reminded Lina of the War more than the sight and sound of an ambulance dashing through the London streets. The Royal Military Hospital, being more of a rehabilitation or nursing home, would receive occasional incoming wounded from the other acute hospitals, but never in large numbers. This morning was different. Three ambulances stood nose to tail in an ominous line at the hospital entrance. The sight sent shivers through her body. The Blitz had truly returned to London.

She entered the hospital, weaving her way around beds and stretchers laden with patients cluttering the corridors. There were obvious injuries, a woman's hand here, a man's leg there, an old man with a head bandage like a turban, a child with his arm in a sling, and three men staring vacantly into space.

Several of the patients called for help as she passed.

"Nurse, when will I see a doctor?"

"My bandage is leaking, Sister."

She responded as well as she could with reassurances.

"The doctor will get to you as soon as he can."

"I will change your bandage in a short while."

The men with the vacant looks made no demands. They were obvious candidates for the skilled attention of Doctor van Dijk, the psychologist.

Nurse Julie Parker confronted her in the nurses' changing room. "What kept you?"

"The Tubes aren't running. I got here as quickly as I could. Where should I start?"

"Help the others. Clear up all the discarded bandages and soiled bedding."

Lina bit her tongue. There were patients in pain, people in need of her nursing skills, but she was to clean up after the others? She found a canvas bag and hurried to complete the task she'd been set. The other nurses, busily tending to the sick, sneered at her. Kathy Benson threw a blanket on the floor at Lina's feet. "Pick it up. It's got blood on it."

Kathy was younger than Lina, and she had less experience, but Lina didn't grumble. She placed the bloodied blanket in her bag. Then she fetched a clean one from the linen cabinet and placed it on the bed at the patient's feet.

"Did I ask for that?" said Kathy.

Lina was dumbfounded by Kathy's reaction. "What's the matter with it?"

Kathy ignored her, and Lina picked up the clean blanket to return it to the linen cabinet.

"Leave it!" snapped Kathy. "Get on with what you're supposed to be doing."

Lina had always felt like an outsider amongst her colleagues. She assumed it was because she was the only one who had managed to establish a bond with Doctor van Dijk. He was never anything but professional in his dealings with the nurses. They saw him as aloof and unapproachable. It was only because she and he were both refugees from Occupied Holland that she had a special relationship with him.

She found Matron attending a young man with a serious-looking abdominal wound.

"What have you been doing?" said Matron.

She showed Matron her canvas bag. "Julie asked me to tidy up after the others."

Matron said, "I have a more important job for you. I want you to make a list of patients that have been marked by the doctors for transfer to one of the general hospitals." She pointed to a red sticker on her patient's chart. "Red is for Guy's Hospital, Yellow is for King's College, Blue for Charing Cross. When you have a list of four for one hospital, I want you to arrange with the ambulance crews to transfer the patients. Each group of four should include no more than two stretcher cases."

This was a job for a porter, but there was no time to argue. Lina set about the task immediately.

As she worked, she caught sly glances and the occasional snide comment from the other nurses. It seemed she was not good enough for normal nurses' duties. Lina continued doggedly with the task she'd been set, but her heart was bleeding.

By 10 a.m. 28 patients had been moved from the corridors and wards of Millbank Hospital to the other general hospitals, according to the coloured stickers on their charts. Lina was hoping to take a break, even if only for a glass of water. But a new intake of injured put paid to that idea.

She worked on through the afternoon and into the night. Any patients that lacked physical injuries and whose chart hadn't been marked with a sticker, Lina interviewed. If they appeared dazed or disoriented, she allocated them to the care of Joost van Dijk. Joost was the one person in the hospital that appreciated her efforts. Providing him with new patients was her way of thanking him.

#

As the sun was rising over a battered London, Lina and Kevin met up again at number 7 Radipole Road. Both fell into bed, exhausted, but Lina couldn't sleep. She got out of bed and made tea. When Kurt asked what was troubling her, it all came out. She told him about the harsh treatment she'd received at the hands of the other nurses.

"Why would they treat you like that in the middle of an emergency?" he said.

"They take delight in making me feel small. I'm not sure why. It might be because I'm not fully trained." She stamped her foot. "Is it my fault that the Germans invaded my country before I could complete my training?"

Kurt put an arm around her shoulders. "I'm sure you're just as good a nurse as any of them."

Lina was grateful for his support, but Kevin was in no position to judge her nursing skills. Her confidence had taken a severe battering from the way her colleagues had treated her. And when Matron had sidelined her from normal nursing tasks that only made matters worse.

The nurses were jealous of Kevin – that was obvious. Young men were in short supply. But she suspected that the problem was more fundamental than that. She was Dutch. She was not one of them. Nothing she did or said could change that, and they would never let her forget it.

She kept these thoughts to herself.

#

On Saturday and Sunday nights, the bombers came again, in larger numbers each night. Central London bore the brunt of the attack, and Fulham was spared further destruction.

Kurt and two of his neighbours visited the houses that remained standing on Radipole Road and helped the residents to board up their shattered windows.

Lina did her bit by putting in long shifts at the hospital, enduring her continuing purgatory with stoicism and a healthy dose of Dutch stubbornness.

Chapter 9

Monday February 21, 1944

Early on Monday morning, Kurt walked from the flat to Perrymead Street. The fog had lifted, and the air temperature was close to freezing. The streets were strangely quiet after the Luftwaffe attack of the weekend.

Perrymead Street had got off lightly. A couple of houses at the far end of the street had lost their front walls, and a civil defence team was busy dismantling what was left.

He knocked on the door of number 12. Clarence, the day guard, opened the door. "It's brass monkeys out there, sir."

Kurt stepped inside, and Clarence closed the door. "You should get yourself a better weasel."

"Translation?"

Clarence grinned. "Weasel and stoat – coat. There's a pot of sticky on the go in the kitchen."

Kurt knew what that was: sticky toffee – coffee. "Do we have any milk? And is Arnold up?"

"There's a fresh pint in the kitchen, sir. His majesty's not up yet. He drank a couple of Aristotles of plonk last night. He's probably still elephants."

"Anything from Dispatch?"

"Diddly squat today, sir."

"Better tell Arnold I'm here, although I don't think I'll be needing him."

Clarence stomped up the stairs to the bedrooms.

The cook was in the kitchen, preparing a meal. "You're early, Mrs Partridge. Making something special today, are you?"

Her jowls wobbled as she laughed. "Didn't get a lot of sleep last night. I've some catching up to do. I thought I'd leave something cold in the larder for 'is nibs. How are you, sir?"

Kurt used a phrase she'd taught him. "I'm in the pink, Mrs P, in the pink."

She chuckled. "There's a fresh pot on the stove. Help yourself."

Kurt checked his watch. He had only 15 minutes to get the radio ready.

"Thanks, Mrs Partridge, but I'm running a bit late."

He took *Gone With the Wind* and his notepad from the kitchen shelf, before unlocking the back parlour.

The radio hummed as it warmed up. At 7:40 precisely, an incoming signal began. Kurt wrote down the Morse characters. At the *Ende* code, he switched off the radio and set about deciphering the signal.

By the time Arnold made an appearance in his red silk dressing gown, Kurt had deciphered the incoming signal. In translation it read:

BY ALL MEANS AVAILABLE SEEK INTEL ON OPERATION OVERLORD

Arnold yawned. "Anything of interest, Kevin?"

"Nothing, apart from Hermann Göring sending his bombers over to keep us all awake for three nights in a row."

Arnold gave a sly smile. "Sorry about that."

"You're not needed. You can go back to bed. But before you go, I have some news. I asked a colleague how many Abwehr agents have been turned."

"Yes?"

"He thought it could be as many as 24."

Arnold's reaction was to turn on his heel and walk away without another word. Kurt couldn't fathom the spy's thinking on the subject.

As he was leaving the house, he passed the cleaner on his way in. Pieter Hendriks's unruly hair did little to inspire confidence in his skills as a cleaner. Kurt smiled at him.

Hendriks returned the smile. "*Goedemorgen*, Kevin."

"Good morning, Pieter."

Kurt ordered a pot of tea in the café. John arrived and picked up the incoming Abwehr signal by the usual method. The courier remained standing. As he turned to leave, Kurt said, "Don't you want a cup?"

"More tea? No thanks. I'm already awash with the stuff."

Me too, thought Kurt. "Can I ask you a question?"

"Shoot."

"How many pick-ups do you do in a day?"

"What do you mean?"

"How many case officers do you collect from?"

"Three or four. Why?"

"I was trying to work out how many there were all together."

John glanced around the café. He lowered his voice. "I'm not the only one doing this. There are lots more like me."

"How many?"

"I have no idea. What's behind all these questions?"

"I was just curious. My man's designation suggests there might be nine in total."

"How do you work that out?"

"His designation is C3. If the first agent is A1, then there could be three As, three Bs and three Cs, making nine in total."

He waved a dismissive hand. "It doesn't work anything like that. Tin Eye Stephens gives them the numbers. They don't all make it out of the London Cage."

Chapter 10

Tuesday February 22, 1944

On Monday night, the Luftwaffe paid another visit to London. Kurt and Lina spent two uncomfortable hours in the Anderson shelter, before putting in extra shifts in civil defence and hospital duties.

On Tuesday morning, they got up early. Lina had a rare day off, and they planned a trip to the shops.

The postman delivered a small brown envelope embossed with the government insignia and addressed to Kevin O'Reilly. Kurt recognised Madge Butterworth's loopy handwriting on the envelope. The letter inside contained a terse instruction to report immediately to Major Robertson's office.

Lina emerged from the bedroom, fully dressed. She offered to make breakfast. "We don't have much, but I could do some egg powder."

He said, "I'm needed in the office."

"But what about our plans? I've been waiting weeks for a day off work."

"Sorry, Lina." He showed her the letter. "You go to the shops. I'll catch up with you as quick as I can."

They agreed to meet at Tottenham Court Road at noon.

He took the Tube to Charing Cross, and presented himself at an inconspicuous door at a windy corner of Bedford Street. A brass plate on the wall said these were the premises of Overland Logistics Limited. He rang the doorbell.

"Yes?" Madge's voice on the intercom.

"Kevin O'Reilly to see Thomas."

"Just one second."

He had to wait several seconds in the icy wind before the door buzzed. He pushed it open and climbed the stairs.

Madge smiled at him. "The major has someone with him at the moment. You'll have to wait. It shouldn't be long. He knows you're here."

He returned her smile. "You look like a ray of sunshine, as usual."
She blushed and patted her hair.

He strolled into the waiting room, where he spent the time looking out the window at the comings and goings in the street below. Nobody seeing the sight could have doubted that the country was at war. There were rickety bicycles everywhere, and not many cars. There wasn't much left of the next street in view, and a pall of smoke hovered over the city to the east.

"The major will see you now, Kurt."

Kurt had seen no one leave. As soon as he entered Major Robertson's office, he ran his eyes over the four walls looking for a second exit. Unless it was hidden in the right-hand wall behind the large rubber plant with the variegated leaves, there was none.

Tar Robertson sat behind his desk, a single file open in front of him. He waved Kurt into a seat. "So how have you been getting on with your agent?" Robertson consulted the file. "C3 isn't it?"

"His name's Arnold, sir, and he's been no trouble—"

"I see his expenses have been going up. Is there any particular reason for that?"

Kurt was at a loss for an answer. "I can't say, Major. He's hardly living the high life..."

"He's now one of our most costly agents. He smokes a lot, and I see he enjoys a good bottle of wine."

"The Abwehr has been generous—"

"Indeed, but compared to the others in the programme, his costs are high. Certainly in the top quartile."

Is that why Ellis's man has been terminated, because he was costing too much to run?

"I expect boredom has a lot to do with it, sir."

"Boredom?"

"Yes, sir. He's idle most of his time, and when he is called upon to use his radio, he's sending just one encrypted signal each day. Also, we seem to be transmitting nothing but weather reports these days."

The major pursed his lips. "I see. Well, happily we have an opportunity to do something about that. You received a signal last week asking for information about Mosquito aircraft production. We will need to reply to that. A field trip is called for, I think. Take your man to Hatfield. I'll supply a car. Let him see the factory for himself. Once you've done that, you can get your man to compose a signal. We'll vet it before transmission, of course."

"Yes, sir."

He closed the file, set it to one side and leaned forward. "I'm told you've been asking questions about the number of agents in the programme."

Kurt's momentary surprise was washed away by realisation that, of course, John would have reported their conversation.

"I was curious. I did a rudimentary calculation..."

"What are you, some kind of mathematician?"

"Yes, sir. I do have a maths degree from Trinity College."

He blinked. "Cambridge?"

"Trinity College Dublin."

"I see, well please curb your curiosity. The number of men in the programme is not something you need to be concerned about."

"The last incoming signal mentioned Operation Overlord. I wondered if that was something I should know about."

He straightened his back. "Operation Overlord is the name given to the plans for the upcoming Allied invasion of mainland Europe."

"I take it that is top secret?"

"The *details* of the plan are most secret, of course, but the name of the operation is not. It leaked out weeks ago through the Russians. The Nazis are well aware that we are planning an invasion." He stood up. "You don't need to know any more than that, Müller. As soon as you do, I will see that you are informed. Now get out of here. Just do your job."

Chapter 11

Picking through his memory of the meeting and Major Robertson's demeanour, Kurt came to the conclusion that Ellis's reading of the situation was probably accurate. Robertson had blown Ellis's Abwehr agent deliberately, because he was costing too much, or for some other nefarious reason. But had he disposed of the agent? Was he cruel enough to have a man hanged simply because he was of no more use to the Service? That was hard to judge, but the British had demonstrated a tendency to ruthlessness in the past. Kurt had witnessed first-hand the heartless annihilation of the ancient city of Hamburg. The British had no qualms about killing tens of thousands of civilians. Would they hesitate before hanging a self-confessed spy?

Kurt's experience of the abysmally poor training given to Abwehr agents made such action even more unforgivable. The Abwehr contained many members of the Black Orchestra, the secret German resistance organisation. Under Admiral Canaris and Generalmajor Oster, every agent sent overseas was singularly trained and equipped with one primary objective – to fail.

Kurt's repeated attempts to get the British Intelligence Services to take this idea on board had failed.

#

Kurt and Lina met in Tottenham Court Road. True to form, he was late. They paid pennies for an off-ration meal, and spent a couple of hours wandering through street markets and second-hand clothes shops. Lina bought a handbag that had seen better days.

When Kurt objected to the price, she said, "It's leather, Kurt. I'll get a lot of years' use out of it."

Kurt showed her where the stitching was coming apart.

She paid for the bag and they moved on. What did men know about fashion accessories?

"You could have haggled," he said.

She ignored him.

36

#

Kurt arrived at Perrymead Street in the early evening. The fog of the previous week had been replaced with a light mist. The foghorns were silent, and the tide was out. The acrid odours of the river filled his lungs.

The guard that opened the door was not his usual ebullient self. "You've heard the news about Pieter Hendriks, I suppose, sir."

"No. What news?"

Harry studied his toecaps. "He's been replaced by a new man, name of Henk Janssen."

"Any reason given?"

"No, sir. I was rather hoping you might have heard something. The new man is a bit of a pain in the arse, to be honest."

"Oh?"

"I think he's had his sense of humour surgically removed." Harry's hangdog look told the whole story. The long hours of guard duty were miserable enough. Having no one to share a joke with, from time to time, would make them infinitely worse.

"Sorry to hear it. Do we know what happened to Hendriks? Maybe he's off sick."

"I haven't heard a dickey bird, sir, but my guess is that they found something better for him to do."

"Let's hope you're wrong, Harry. Maybe he will come back in a few days. Anything from dispatch?"

Harry handed over the dispatch envelope, and went upstairs to wake Arnold. Kurt fetched his pad and Margaret Mitchell's classic novel from the kitchen. Then he opened the back parlour and set about coding the outgoing signal – another weather report.

While waiting for the transmission time, Kurt ran his eyes over the newspaper. Queen Wilhelmina of the Netherlands had suffered a 'targeted' attack during the overnight air raid. Six bombs were dropped on the queen's home in South Mimms, Hertfordshire, killing two of her guards. The queen herself narrowly escaped injury. And there were reports that someone had fired flares to guide the bombers to her home. The local police had initiated a criminal enquiry into the incident.

Arnold made an appearance in time to transmit the outgoing signal. When the incoming signal arrived, Kurt wrote it down. Later, when he had decoded it, it read in translation:

URGENT ANY INFORMATION ON USAF AIRFIELDS IN SOUTHERN ENGLAND

Kurt slipped it into his copy of the *Daily Mirror*. Arnold's cover would allow him to travel anywhere in the southern counties, but every time he opened his mouth he risked being arrested by the police or shot by the army. According to his cover story, he was from Stockholm, but he spoke English with an accent that was pure Munich.

Arnold showed no interest in the content of the signal. "Did you get an answer to my question?" His eyes opened wide in anticipation of good news.

"Not a definite answer, yet, no. 24 is still my best estimate. Why does it matter how many there are?"

The agent's eyelids resumed their rest position. "It is important to me. Tell me you will try to get a more definite figure?"

"If I get the chance – yes, Arnold."

Kurt said goodbye to Arnold and Harry, and made his way to the café across the road. John was waiting for him at the usual table by the window.

"No need to order tea," he said. "There's a cup left in the pot."

The waitress sashayed over with a spare cup and saucer. Kurt marvelled at her reading of the situation, which verged on a sixth sense, and her eyelashes, which were longer than usual.

John filled Kurt's cup. "I have a message for you from the office. A car will pick you and your man up at ten o'clock tomorrow morning. Your field trip has been approved."

The tea was cold and black as tar.

Chapter 12

RSHA, Prinz-Albrecht Strasse 8, Berlin

Walter Schellenberg, head of SD-Ausland, took a seat in Heinrich Himmler's office.

Himmler peered at him through his rimless spectacles, as if inspecting one of his chickens. "How's Ernst getting on in the Abwehr hot seat?"

The Reichsführer-SS wore a double-breasted navy blue suit. Schellenberg was dressed in his SS uniform – Himmler always insisted on it. "It's too early to make a judgement, sir, he's been in charge only three days."

Himmler grunted. "I take it we still have nothing to use against von Neumann."

"Nothing yet, sir, but I have men working on it."

"What about that Spanish farrago? Those false papers found on the body of that British major. What was his name?"

"William Martin." Schellenberg winced at the memory. Seen in hindsight, it was nothing but a cheap 3-card trick, but he and his men had been fooled just as much as Canaris and his Abwehr.

"Some of that shit should have rubbed off on the Abwehr, surely."

"It probably did, but that's ancient history now, sir, since Sicily has fallen."

Himmler pulled a handkerchief from a desk drawer, removed his glasses, and began to polish them. "Wasn't there something else?"

"We've been receiving a lot of contradictory information about the Allies' invasion plan from the Abwehr intelligence networks in England, Spain, Portugal, and elsewhere."

"Is any of that reliable?"

"Some of it, perhaps. The difficulty is sifting the wheat from the chaff, and the stakes couldn't be higher."

Himmler jammed his glasses onto his nose, wrapping the arms around his ears. "The public prosecutor has announced the date for Oster's trial."

"Yes, sir. I'm sure he will be found guilty. The evidence against him is strong. But we need to nail Admiral Canaris."

"The admiral is destined for the end of a rope eventually, believe me."

Schellenberg held his tongue. It was common knowledge that Himmler used a stargazer to help him predict the future.

"In the meantime, I expect you to do your job. Ernst has been sending me unsettling reports about you."

Schellenberg placed one gloved hand on top of the other on his thigh. "Unsettling, how?"

"He accuses you of insubordination, of keeping information from him. He says you run SD-Ausland like a private fiefdom, as if it wasn't part of his RSHA."

"He said all that?" Schellenberg placed a hint of a contemptuous smile on his lips, implying that he doubted Ernst Kaltenbrunner could string that many words together.

"All that and more. You must learn to work with others, Walter."

Outwardly, Schellenberg appeared calm, unimpressed, dismissive of his superior's reprimands. Inwardly, this exchange had bitten deep. Following the assassination of Reinhard Heydrich, Walter Schellenberg couldn't see anyone in the combined security services that could deny him the job. The appointment of Ernst Kaltenbrunner had been an unpleasant shock. It made no sense. The man was a failed Austrian lawyer, a senior police officer with no knowledge of international espionage.

"He knows so little of counter-intelligence," said Schellenberg, "I find it difficult to talk to him."

Judging by the way he sat up in his chair, the implied flattery was not lost on Himmler.

"Nevertheless, I urge you to make an effort to communicate better with him. He is your boss, after all."

"Of course, sir, but you know yourself how unapproachable he is."

"If you're referring to his smoking habit and his bad teeth, I have ordered him to have something done about that."

"That is good to hear, Herr Reichsführer."

"Meanwhile, we must find a way to further discredit what remains of the Abwehr. Redouble your efforts on General Neumann."

"As you wish, sir."

Schellenberg was dismissed. Outside the Reichsführer's office, he removed his gloves and loosened his collar. Himmler was badly mistaken if he thought von Neumann could be unseated from the Abwehr. The general was too tight with all of the three principals in the Oberkommando der Wehrmacht: Admiral Dönitz of the Kriegsmarine, Field Marshal Göring of the Luftwaffe, and the supreme commander of the army, Adolf Hitler.

Chapter 13

Wednesday February 23, 1944

The bombing continued on Tuesday night, and on Wednesday morning a driver arrived to collect Kurt and Arnold for their field trip.

The car was an unmarked Volvo PV36 Carioca, the height of luxury. The driver was dressed in civvies. Kurt appreciated these subtle touches, the attention to detail.

Arnold's 'samples' were in a heavy suitcase. The driver had to help him lift it into the boot.

The journey to Hatfield took an hour, during which the double agent smoked incessantly.

Kurt opened his window to dispel the smoke, but this introduced a blast of icy air that kept the internal temperature below comfort levels. Kurt glared at him.

"Sorry." Arnold wound down his window and threw his cigarette out. Within a couple of minutes, to Kurt's dismay, he had lit a fresh one.

The de Havilland factory and aerodrome were completely surrounded by high wire fencing, with armed sentries at the entrance gates. The driver took them around the perimeter. Kurt attempted to assess the level of activity, but it was difficult to tell whether the factory was still operating normally or not. There were lots of people moving about – many in overalls. They all looked busy.

Kurt tapped the driver on the shoulder. "This is hopeless. Find us a pub where we can get some lunch."

The driver dropped them off at the Eight Bells Inn and went off to find somewhere to park the car.

"Leave the talking to me," said Kurt as they stepped inside.

They took a table near the door. Kurt went to the bar. He ordered cottage pie and ale for the two of them. While the barmaid pulled the ale, he lingered, engaging her in a little casual conversation.

"It's years since I was here last. How's business these days?"

"Been here before, have you?"

"Years ago." He cast his eyes around the pub. "Not much has changed."

"You're not wrong. You up from London?"

"Fulham. Just up for the day."

"Got some business in the town, have you?"

Arnold appeared by his side. "We are from Sweden. We sell ball bearings. We were wishing to talk with someone at the factory." Kurt had to admit that Arnold's Swedish accent was surprisingly convincing.

The barmaid's eyes narrowed. "From Sweden, are you? I thought you looked foreign."

Kurt pushed Arnold toward the table. Arnold returned to his seat, muttering to himself.

"Arnold is Swedish. I'm not. His English is not the Mae West."

The barmaid giggled.

Kurt pressed on. "I heard that the factory has moved."

"Who told you that?"

"Heard it on the grapevine. Is it not true?"

"The way I heard it, they're planning to move, but it'll take a few weeks."

"Where are they moving to, do you know?"

"I've no idea. Why don't you ask them at the gate?"

He gave her a grin. "Good idea. I'll do that after the pie and ale."

The driver joined them. He ordered a pint of cider and the fish and chips. Kurt paid the bill for all three meals.

They ate in silence. The bar filled up. By the time they'd finished, the place was packed with a noisy, boisterous crowd. A tall man with a crew cut hovered close by, a pint glass in his hand, poised to claim the table as soon as they left.

Kurt smiled at him. He stood up, signalling to the others that it was time to leave. They stepped out into the sunshine, and were immediately confronted by three police constables.

The tall man with the crew cut stood behind them in the doorway. "You're all under arrest," he said.

Chapter 14

They were bundled into a paddy wagon and driven to the local police station.

Arnold looked close to panic. "Should I explain who I am?"

Kurt shook his head. "Just stick to your cover story. Leave the explaining to me. Once they contact the office, they will have to let us go."

"That could take a while," said the driver. "What do I tell them?"

"Tell them the truth. You are an army driver assigned to accompany a Swedish businessman on a sales trip. You have paperwork to support that story?"

The driver nodded.

On arrival at the police station they were separated. Kurt was taken to an interview room equipped with a table and four chairs.

He sat there for an hour before anything happened. Then the door opened. The tall man with the crew cut came in, followed by a police constable in uniform. Crew Cut placed a file on the table and took a seat facing Kurt. The constable sat beside Crew Cut.

"My name is Detective Inspector Haskins. This is Constable Fry. You have identity papers?"

Kurt handed over his identity and business cards.

"You are Kevin O'Reilly?"

"I am."

"You work as a Liaison Officer for Overland Logistics Limited, with an address in Bedford Street, central London. Is that correct?"

"Yes. Look, Inspector, we can cut all this short if you ring the telephone number on my card. Ask to speak with Thomas Robertson. He will explain everything."

"I dare say he will. You must think we're all bumpkins in the country, that we'll swallow anything."

This was not going to be easy. Crew Cut had a dogged look about him that suggested he was prepared to spend all night interrogating his three suspects, if necessary. The kudos to be gained from capturing a spy was nothing compared to the adulation he would receive if he broke a whole nest of the beggars! Constable Fry's eyes were closed.

Kurt spoke slowly, keeping his voice low and even. "Well, Inspector, I work for a government agency. I can't say any more without breaking the Official Secrets Act, but the answers to all your questions are at the end of a telephone at that number."

Inspector Haskins's reaction was straight from pantomime. "The Official Secrets Act! Well, well, what do you think of that, Constable?"

The constable's eyelids opened a crack. "I wish I had a penny for every time I've heard that one, Inspector." He seemed to speak without moving his lips.

Haskins balled his fist on the table. "Let's cut to the chase here, shall we? Three strangers enter a pub in wartime and start asking questions about a nearby RAF aircraft factory. One claims to be an army driver, the second a ball bearing salesman from Sweden, the third a liaison officer, whatever that might be. What conclusions would you draw if you were in my position?"

"Please just lift the telephone. Dial that number. Ask to speak with Thomas Robertson. He will clear the whole thing up immediately."

"I've read about enemy spies in other parts of the country, I just never imagined it would happen in our town." The inspector sat back in his chair. "Let me tell you what I know. Your driver is what he says he is – probably an army deserter, driving a stolen car. The Swedish ball bearing salesman is an innocent man. His story checks out, his papers are in order, and we found a case full of ball bearings in the car. I reckon he was roped in to provide cover for you and the driver. You are the ringleader. Your mission is to gather information on the de Havilland factory to send back to the Luftwaffe in Berlin."

Kurt shook his head in disbelief. He said nothing.

"Nothing to say? I suppose you know we hang enemy spies in Great Britain."

"Just call that number..."

"You claim to be an Englishman, but what sort of name is Kevin O'Reilly? Has nobody told Adolf Hitler that Eire is no longer part of Great Britain?" He smiled at his own witticism. "Confess and I'll make sure they go easy on you. Make a short statement. The constable here will write it down."

"You have it all wrong, Inspector..."

"You're a brave man, I can see that. Only a brave man would

operate as a spy behind enemy lines. But you must see that the game is up. It's over for you now. Give me a short confession and you will spend the rest of the War with your comrades in a warm internment camp – on the Yorkshire moors, probably. If you continue to resist, I cannot be held responsible for what will happen next. God knows what the armed forces will do to you. Do you understand me?"

"Yes, I understand, but I'm telling you, you are mistaken. Call the telephone number on my card..."

The inspector picked up the file and stood. "Your boss will explain everything, right? Come on, Constable. We have work to do."

The constable's eyes opened, he struggled to his feet, and they left the room.

#

As darkness fell, the inspector and his constable returned. "You will be charged with espionage. You will spend the night in a cell. The committal papers will be prepared in the morning. Do you have anything further to say?"

"Am I not entitled to a telephone call?"

They took him to a room with a telephone. Kurt rang the office and spoke with the night duty officer. He explained what had happened.

The duty officer yawned. "I'll leave a note on the major's desk for the morning. Is there anything else I can help you with?"

Kurt exploded. "You will do nothing of the sort. Call the major right now—"

"He'll be in bed."

"I don't care where he is. If you want to keep your job, you will call him immediately. Ask him – no, *tell* him – to call this number and speak with Inspector Haskins. I have no intention of spending the night in a prison cell. Do you hear me?"

"I hear you, O'Reilly. Give me the telephone number."

Five minutes later, Major Robertson was on the telephone talking to the inspector. Kurt heard one half of the conversation.

"Yes, Major, I understand that... I hear what you're saying, but we both have our jobs to do... Three strange men in a luxury car... They seemed very interested in... The charge is espionage... yes... We caught him with his two companions asking questions... Yes, Major, but you must understand how it appears... The War effort?... Even so,

I'm going to have to proceed... I understand that, Major, but you could be anybody... No, I'm not calling you a liar, but look at it from my... Very well, I'll expect his call."

The inspector handed the telephone receiver back to Kurt.

Major Robertson's voice was as sharp and his Scots accent as pronounced as Kurt had ever heard it. "What are ye playin' at, man? What part of 'be discreet' did ye no' understand?"

"I'm sorry, sir."

The major took a deep breath that might have been a sigh of exasperation. "Why didn't you give the inspector the office number right away?"

"I did, sir."

"I'm going to make some calls to sort this out. It should take no more than thirty minutes. As soon as they release you, get Arnold back to the house without any further delay, and I want to see your draft signal on my desk first thing in the morning."

The major cut the call.

A constable led Kurt to a cell and locked him in. Twenty minutes later, the cell door opened again. Inspector Haskins stepped in. "Come with me."

The inspector took Kurt to the front desk and signed a release. "You're free to go."

In the car, Kurt drafted a signal for transmission to the Abwehr. He put it in a sealed envelope, and handed it to the driver to drop into Major Robertson's office.

Chapter 15

Thursday February 24, 1944

It was after midnight by the time he got back to the flat. Lina was sleeping. He managed to slip into bed without disturbing her.

Once again, the Luftwaffe unleashed a load of incendiaries on the hapless inhabitants of London. Lina slept right through it, and Kurt let her sleep. That night the bombers concentrated on central London. It seemed Fulham had been given a free pass, for now. He watched the fireworks through the cracked glass of the bedroom window.

In the morning, Lina demanded to know what had kept him out so late.

He gave her a sheepish smile. "A field trip. Went on a bit longer than expected."

"You could have left a note, warning me that you might be late. Your supper was ruined. I had to throw it out."

"I'm sorry, Lina."

"The next time you go on one of your field trips, don't expect a meal when you get home." She stomped out of the room.

#

On the way in through the front door at Perrymead Street, he met a middle-aged man on his way out. Stocky, with heavy jowls, the man was a head shorter than Kurt, built like a middleweight boxer going to seed. Their arms collided.

The stranger wasn't looking where he was going. The collision was his fault, but Kurt was the one who apologised. "I beg your pardon."

"Watch where you're going," was the only reply. The man continued on his way.

"That was Henk Janssen, the new cleaner," said Harry, the ancient guard. "Charming fellow."

The morning dispatch envelope contained a copy of Kurt's draft signal. One word had been changed and one word removed. Kurt encoded the altered message, summoned Arnold, and switched on the radio in time to receive any signals from Hamburg.

There was just a single incoming signal. Decoded, it read in translation:

MOST URGENT BY ALL MEANS SEEK INTEL ON OPERATION FORTITUDE

Kurt met John in the café as usual at 8:30 a.m. As soon as the handover had been completed, John continued on his rounds. Kurt hurried back to the flat in Fulham.

In the flat, Kurt threw off his clothes, and fell into bed. He had some sleep to catch up on. Without Lina under the blankets with him, it took a while to get warm, and his feet were still blocks of ice when sleep overcame him.

He dreamt he was in a cold, damp cell on an island somewhere, far removed from civilization. Someone was hammering on the cell door, louder and louder.

Chapter 16

Ðe woke. His feet still hadn't warmed up. He checked Lina's bedside clock. 11:45 a.m. He'd slept no more than two and a half hours. Someone was hammering on the door of the flat.

Bam, Bam, Bam on the door. "Open the door, Kevin." Not a voice he recognised.

He slithered out of bed, slipped on some pants, and stood by the door, the cold floor sending shivers up his legs. "Who is it?"

"Your driver from yesterday. Open up."

Kurt opened the door to let the driver in. "I have tea. Would you like some?" He shuffled into the kitchen to put a kettle on.

The driver followed him. He grabbed Kurt's upper arm. "There's no time for anything like that, Kevin. The major wants to see you."

"There's always time for a cuppa. Take a seat."

"He wants to see you immediately. Put some clothes on."

Kurt ran a hand through his hair. "I'd like to have a wash, maybe brush my teeth. Do we have time for that?"

"All right, be quick."

The sun sat low in the southern sky, low enough to interfere with the driver's vision. They made good time through light traffic to Bedford Street.

Madge Butterworth buzzed him in immediately. Major Robertson was waiting for him at the top of the stairs.

They barely made it into the major's office before the shouting started. "Have you any idea the trouble you caused? How on earth did you manage to get yourselves picked up by a country plod? Whose bright idea was it to treat yourselves to lunch? And who decided to ask a lot of damn fool questions at the bar?"

"I'm sorry, Major. The factory was fenced off. We could see very little. I would suggest setting up a proper appointment with factory management, the next time."

A voice from behind Kurt said, "Are we to take it you believe that would be a better way of approaching the problem?"

A seated figure, half-hidden behind the rubber plant, stood up and strode toward Kurt. He was in his early thirties, with a shock of dark hair and a broad nose. He held out a hand. "Kim Philby."

The man's sardonic half-smile suggested amusement at Kurt's faux pas.

Major Robertson's face was turning an interesting shade of puce. "Mr Philby is here representing the LCS committee."

Philby spoke in a silky, cultured voice that reminded Kurt of the actor Trevor Howard. "Your ill-considered actions have caused quite a stir in Whitehall."

"I'm sorry, Mr Philby. I was attempting to carry out my mission to the best of my ability."

Philby's deadpan response was cutting. "And you thought interviewing a barmaid in a country tavern was a good way of going about it?"

The word 'tavern' was a quaint touch.

Major Robertson perched his behind on the edge of his desk. With a wave of his hand, he directed Kurt and Philby to sit. Kurt took one chair. Philby took the other one, crossing his legs and placing his hands on his knee. Kurt glanced at him. The London Controlling Section man had his eyes fixed on the major.

"What did I ask you to do?" said Major Robertson.

"You asked me to take Arnold to Hatfield to investigate whether or not the de Havilland aircraft factory was being moved."

Major Robertson paced back and forth in the limited space between his desk and the two chairs, hands behind his back, like the headmaster of a school dealing with a miscreant pupil. "What I asked you to do was to take your man to the vicinity of the aircraft factory, to allow him to pick up some first-hand impressions of the place. That way, we could be confident of his ability to field any follow-up questions from Hamburg. Did you seriously think I intended for you to attempt to answer the Abwehr's questions?"

"I suppose not, no, sir."

"Anyway, that's not why I called you in. We have something much more important to worry about. The latest signal received from Hamburg by your man asked about 'Operation Fortitude'. I need to know where or how the Abwehr got hold of that name."

"I never heard of it before it came through on the signal."

"You're certain of that?"

"Yes, Major."

Major Robertson shook his head. "Could your man have transmitted a signal without your knowledge?"

"That's not possible. He doesn't have a key to the radio room, and he's under constant guard."

A buzzer sounded. The major rounded his desk, sat down, and flipped a switch on his intercom.

"Mr Masterman is here, Major," said Madge on the intercom.

"Send him in."

The door opened and a tall man in a suit entered. He was in his early fifties and looked to Kurt like a bank manager. He nodded to the major, pulled the spare chair from behind the rubber plant, and sat down.

Philby spoke quietly. "Locks can be picked, guards can sleep on duty, or they can be bribed."

Kurt looked at Philby. "Arnold would never do anything like that. Berlin must have picked up the code word from somewhere else."

Philby's only response was to brush something from his knee. The LCS man's eyes were fixed firmly on the major, as if Kurt was part of the furniture.

The major said, "So explain why your man received a signal about that operation."

"That is strange. But there's no way Arnold would risk upsetting his comfortable life. Even if he had bribed one of his guards, picked the lock, and sent a signal to Hamburg, where could he have learnt the name of the operation? He never goes anywhere on his own. No, Major, you're looking in the wrong place."

"Well, if your man didn't give it to them, I have no idea how the Abwehr could have got hold of the name," the major said. "That operation is most secret. Good God, man, the operation name was chosen by the PM only last Thursday."

"The Russians?" said Kurt. "You did say that Operation Overlord was leaked by the Russians."

"Operation Fortitude has been deliberately kept from the Russians."

Kurt shook his head. "Well, I can't imagine how Arnold could have got wind of it, sir. He never leaves the house."

"Except when he went on that field trip with you to Hatfield. Could he have picked it up then, somehow, somewhere?"

"I don't see how – or where."

"No, neither do I. I'm very much afraid we must conclude that there is an Abwehr agent in London operating beyond our control, a rogue agent, if you will." The major seemed to shrink in his seat.

Philby put a fist to his mouth and coughed. The major nodded to him and Philby said, "We have been aware for some time that there might be an Abwehr agent in London that we've missed. We picked up a mention of an unidentified call-sign in 1941, but nothing on the airwaves since then."

Finally, Masterman spoke. "Until recently, that is."

Major Robertson sat hunched over his desk. "We've got a problem, Kurt. The RDF vans in north London picked up a rogue transmission last night. The boffins haven't been able to decode it fully yet – the signal was a short one – but the call-sign is *LBK.*"

Kurt Müller said, "That's Lebkuchen – Gingerbread in English. It's not a call-sign I recognise, sir."

The major attempted a sour smile. "The timing couldn't be worse. You realise this Gingerbread could easily derail Operation Fortitude."

The major sat back heavily at his desk, hands tucked under his armpits. "Until yesterday I was confident that we had rounded up every Abwehr agent in Britain. They are all so ill-equipped and badly trained, picking them up is like shelling peas. I can't see how we could have missed one."

And yet they had.

Kurt said, "You have turned them all, Major?"

Masterman spoke again, in clipped tones. "Those that we consider suitable we turn."

"And the rest?"

Masterman and the major both remained tight-lipped. Philby said, "Anyone not suitable or any choosing not to work with us, we execute. These are enemy spies, after all."

Kurt winced internally, but maintained a bland facial expression. He continued to address his questions to Major Robertson. "Is it true that you sometimes blow an agent's cover on purpose?"

"Who have you been talking to?" the major snapped.

"Is it true?"

Philby brushed something from his knee.

The major answered the question, angrily. "Yes, it's true. Of course it's true. We are fighting a war against an evil regime. Sometimes we have to do unpleasant things. Very occasionally, it is necessary to sacrifice one agent in order to strengthen and solidify credibility in the remainder in the minds of the Nazis."

The word 'sacrifice' sent shivers running down Kurt's spine.

Masterman said, "Operation Fortitude goes to the heart of our deception plan for the invasion of mainland Europe. If it fails, the whole invasion could be at risk. Thousands of Allied servicemen will lose their lives."

Major Robertson added, "It is imperative that we find and capture this rogue agent without delay."

"How?" said Kurt.

The major responded, "I have no idea yet. I need to think about it. Until I work this out, your man's radio must be left switched off."

"Won't that be seen as suspicious in Hamburg?"

"Probably, but we'll tackle that problem when the time comes." He waved a hand. "You are dismissed."

"May I make a suggestion, Major?" said Kurt.

"Go ahead."

"Let me make contact with my friends in the Black Orchestra. They may be able to solve the puzzle for you."

"You've mentioned this Black Orchestra resistance group before. It all sounds highly improbable."

"What can I say to convince you, Major? There is a body of men – good Germans – within the Abwehr, dedicated to bringing down Hitler and the Third Reich."

Philby took up the narrative. "Admiral Canaris is the leader of this resistance movement, I think?"

"Within the Abwehr, yes. There are other leaders in other places."

"And I understand that Canaris is under house arrest."

"Yes, but—"

"And his second-in-command, Generalmajor Oster is under lock and key in some concentration camp." Philby's eyes narrowed. The half-smile had returned to his face, but it looked more menacing, now. "What makes you think that the Black Orchestra is still active?"

"The admiral and his deputy have been removed, it's true. But there are many others. I'd bet my life that they are continuing their work. Just let me talk with them. I will find this rogue agent for you."

Masterman shook his head. "I don't think so."

"It's foolhardy," said the major.

Kurt said, "Can you think of another way of uncovering this agent, sir? You said yourself you couldn't see how, and time is short."

Major Robertson gave this a few moments' thought. Then he said to Masterman, "What do you think, J.C.?"

Masterman nodded, and the major said, "Very well, I will take your suggestion upstairs in Whitehall."

Chapter 17

Bushy Park, Teddington, London
SHAEF Supreme Headquarters Allied Expeditionary Force

Responding to a phone call from his immediate superior, Lieutenant Colonel Bill Baumer presented himself at SHAEF.

"What's this I hear about the Brits' magic show?" said Colonel Faulkner, picking a cigar from his humidor.

"It's a wild ride, sir. You wouldn't believe the half of it if you read about it."

The colonel bit the end off his cigar and lit it with a lighter from his desk. "Have you brought me a copy?"

Baumer coughed. "Our friends are playing their cards close to their chests, Colonel. There are fewer than ten copies in existence, and they're all kept under lock and key."

"Okay, so give me the highlights."

Baumer outlined the main elements of the Fortitude plan. The Germans were to be persuaded that the D-Day landings would take place at the Pas-de-Calais, spearheaded by a fictional US force, called the First United States Army Group, based in Kent and led by General George S. Patton. The presence of this imaginary army would be reinforced by crisscrossing communications traffic and the activities of Tar Robertson's Double Cross agents.

"And what do you think? Will it work?"

"I believe it could, yes, sir."

"If it does work, it could save lives on the day," said Faulkner.

"Yes, sir, and the Brits are hoping it will keep the Krauts off our tails for a week after the landings."

"How is that gonna work?"

"They hope to convince the Germans that the Normandy landings are a feint, and that the real thrust will come at Calais from Patton's army."

"And will that work?"

"I believe it has a better than even chance, sir, but only if we can keep a tight lid on it."

Faulkner removed his cigar from his mouth and examined it. "I hear that could be a problem, Bill."

Baumer braced himself. He had no idea what was coming, but whatever it was, it wouldn't be good news.

Faulkner jammed the cigar back between his teeth. "Our friends in the FBI are convinced that the Russians have a mole at the highest levels of British Intelligence."

"The Russians are our allies," said Baumer.

"For the moment, yes, but theirs is a leaky ship. All it would take is a single German agent in Moscow and the whole Fortitude business could be blown sky high."

Baumer blinked. The tobacco smoke was irritating his eyes. "Do the FBI have a suspect for the London mole?"

"No, but they've been looking closely at the members of the London Controlling Section and the Twenty Committee."

"That's pretty unthinkable, sir. They are all senior military men."

"What about their sidekicks?"

"I don't know. The ones that I've met are all Oxford and Cambridge graduates. They're a pretty tight bunch from the upper classes as far as I can tell."

Faulkner placed his cigar in his ashtray. He sat forward and folded his hands on his desk. "What we have to ask ourselves is whether it's wise to continue on board a leaky vessel. It might be more sensible to let the Brits run this jamboree without us. That way none of the mud will stick to us when the balloon goes up."

Anxious to avoid any blame for a wrong decision either way, Baumer kept his counsel.

"Let's carry on as we are for a while. Keep me informed." The colonel picked up his cigar. The meeting was over.

Chapter 18

Friday February 25, 1944

The following morning, Clarence, the night guard, opened the door before Kurt reached it. "Bad news, I'm afraid, sir."

Kurt's heart leaped in his chest. "Arnold?"

Clarence shook his head. He closed the door. "Arnold's upstairs in his bed. This is much more serious. One of the major's double agents has killed his guard and his cook, and scarpered."

"Where did you hear this?"

"From another Home Facilities guard. The grapevine is humming with the news."

"Do you know where this happened?"

"No, but I knew the guard who was killed. His name was James Dennison. A good man, sir. I served with him under General Auchinleck in North Africa, and under Monty when he took over."

The guard's distress was obvious. More than ever before, he looked his age. Kurt led him into the kitchen.

Mrs Partridge, the cook, stood by the stove sipping from a cup, staring into space with unseeing eyes. Her hands were trembling. Her hair, usually tied back corralled in a neat bun, looked like a bird's nest.

"You should go home," Kurt said.

She gave no indication that she'd heard him.

"Finish your tea and go home, Mrs Partridge. You've had a shock."

She looked up. Her eyes focused on the wall behind Kurt. "I have to make a meal."

Kurt plucked her coat from where it was hanging behind the kitchen door. He helped her into it. "Arnold can feed himself for once."

"If you're sure..."

"I'm sure. Get on home."

She rinsed her cup in the sink. "Thank you, Kevin. There's cold meat in the larder and bread in the bread bin."

Kurt put a hand on her shoulder and accompanied her to the front door. "Take as long as you need, Mrs Partridge."

He opened the door to a bitter wind. A mini-whirlwind danced by, laden with grains of rubble. He watched as Mrs Partridge hurried down the road, her coat wrapped tightly around her, hands tucked into her pockets. Then he closed the door, and returned to the kitchen where Clarence sat, his shoulders hunched.

Kurt filled a fresh kettle. "How reliable is this information, Clarence?"

"You could put your house on it, sir."

"Do we have any details? When did it happen? How did the agent get his hands on a weapon?"

"Lance Corporal Dennison's throat was cut from ear to ear, so I'm told. I knew him well, sir. He was a good soldier. We served together in the Eighth Army at Tobruk and El Alamein. He was a good man."

"What about the cook?"

Clarence shook his head. Either he didn't know or he didn't want to talk about it.

Kurt gave Clarence a cup of hot tea with sugar. Clarence stirred it with a spoon, then sipped it. "You don't have anything stronger, I suppose."

Kurt patted him on the arm. "You've had a shock. Strong, sweet tea is the best thing for that." He poured a cupful for himself.

Clarence took a mouthful and winced. "Just shows you can't be too careful, sir. Let your guard down for a cock linnet and these Nazi bastards will slit your nanny goat."

"I think we're safe enough with Arnold."

Kurt went upstairs to rouse the double agent. He banged on the bedroom door.

"What is it, Clarence? What time is it?"

"Time you were up," said Kurt.

"Is that you, Kevin?" The door opened and a tousle-haired spy put his head out. "Where's Clarence?"

"He's in the kitchen. He's had a bit of a shock. Get dressed. Join us downstairs, will you?"

Kurt returned to the kitchen to find Clarence enveloped in a cloud of cigarette smoke. "I didn't think you smoked."

Clarence coughed. He waved his cigarette through the smoke. "I don't. I thought I'd give it a try to steady my nerves."

"Is there no cockney slang for nerves?" said Kurt.

"West Ham. West Ham reserves," Clarence replied with a trace of a smile.

"Have you ever heard of J. C. Masterman?" said Kurt.

"No, who's he?"

"Just someone I met. It's not important," said Kurt.

By the time Arnold arrived in the kitchen, wearing his dressing gown, the teapot was empty.

"What's happening? Clarence, are you all right?"

Clarence kept a wary eye on Arnold. He said nothing.

Kurt said, "He's had a shock. A friend of his was murdered during the night. It seems he was guarding an agent like you, when the agent killed him."

"And his cook," said Clarence.

Watching Arnold's reaction was like reading a book. First, there was shock at the news, then a smirk of satisfaction that one of his kind had struck a blow against the enemy, and finally a look of alarm at the thought of what the news might mean for him. "God in heaven, that's the end of it for me!"

Clarence banged his cup down on the table. He glared at Arnold.

"I'm sorry, Clarence, you have my sympathy, of course, but I can't imagine that this is good news for me."

Kurt frowned at Clarence while waving a hand at Arnold. "This won't affect you in any way, Arnold. Please don't worry."

Arnold ran his eyes around the kitchen in search of a dispatch envelope. "Do we have something to transmit?"

Clarence growled. "There was nothing from dispatch this morning. It seems you're not needed any more."

Kurt said, "We have been instructed to cease radio transmissions for the time being."

Arnold's face fell again. Clearly, he knew what this could mean for his continuing survival. "What about incoming traffic?"

Kurt shook his head. "The radio will remain switched off until further notice."

Instantly, Arnold's look of misery turned to one of wide-eyed panic. He wrapped his arms around his chest. "I knew it. I knew this wouldn't last, but I hoped to make it to the end of the War, and maybe see my wife one more time."

Clarence snarled at him.

Kurt tried to reassure the agent. "This is just a temporary measure. Don't worry about it, Arnold."

But was it? Kurt couldn't be sure. Perhaps the Abwehr man was right. The major might send a party of Tommies around that afternoon to frogmarch Arnold to a waiting scaffold.

Chapter 19

Arnold retired to his bedroom to await developments, perhaps to write a farewell letter to his wife.

Clarence went back to his post in the front parlour, where he checked that his rifle was loaded and primed, ready to fire.

Kurt had a last few words with the guard before leaving. "Remember what happened to your friend is nothing to do with Arnold. Your job is to make sure he doesn't leave the house, nothing more."

"He's not going to catch me bo-peepin' at my post."

"That's the spirit, Clarence. Stay alert."

Back in his flat, Kurt turned the radio on, to catch the midday news.

In a continuation of the Allied attacks on selected sites, last night's bombing raid concentrated mainly on enemy military installations in the Calais area of Occupied France. A combined force of aircraft of the Eighth Air Force, formerly RAF Bomber Command, and the United States Strategic Air Force were used. Despite bad weather, the raid was a spectacular success, with just seven aircraft lost, and 63 servicemen reported missing in action.

There are unconfirmed reports coming in of an attempted military coup in Argentina. The presidential palace in Buenos Aires is surrounded by troops.

Then this:

News is coming in about a double murder in London. A woman and a retired serviceman have been found dead in a house in Frome Road, north London. Lance Corporal James Dennison served with distinction with Field Marshal Montgomery's Eighth Army in the North Africa Campaign. The woman has been named as Doris Pettigrew. She may have been his cook. Scotland Yard are treating the incident as serious. They have appealed for witnesses, and have issued a picture of a man they believe can help with their enquiries. Using the name Henry Pollinger, the man is six foot tall. He speaks with an east European accent. The public are advised not to approach this man, but to alert a police officer if anyone spots him. He may be armed and dangerous.

Kurt popped out to his local newsagents to buy a newspaper. The missing agent's photograph filled a quarter of the front page. The headline read: *Armed and Dangerous Double Killer on the Loose.* Henry Pollinger was thickset with dark eyes under heavy grey eyebrows. His face carried the hint of a smirk, as if amused by a private joke. Overall, the impression was of a man with a high opinion of his own worth, much like Arnold, but with an undercurrent of suppressed violence.

Kurt used his map of London to locate Frome Road. It was close to Turnpike Lane Tube station on the Piccadilly line. He put on his coat and headed out.

Frome Road was a typical London street, with two parallel rows of Georgian houses facing one another. The police car parked outside number 27 identified the murder scene. Kurt joined the small group of onlookers gathered on the opposite side of the road.

"What happened here?" he asked an old man.

"There was a grisly murder in number 27. It was on the radio."

"The killer's picture is on all the front pages," said a woman.

"Two people had their throats cut," said another man, running his thumbnail across his neck. "Ear to ear. There must have been a lot of blood."

"Didn't anyone see anything?" Kurt searched their faces. They all shook their heads.

A uniformed bobby approached and took the names and addresses of everyone in the group of onlookers.

"We live in violent times," said a familiar voice.

Kurt turned his head and found Greg Ellis standing behind him. "What are you doing here?"

"The same as you, I expect." Ellis put a hand on Kurt's back and steered him away from the crowd. He stopped beside his car. "Climb aboard. We'll take her for a spin."

The tingling sensation in Kurt's scalp made it impossible to refuse. A spin in an MG Midget was every boy's dream. He opened the passenger door and got in. Ellis leapt over his door and into the driver's seat.

They drove north. As soon as they reached the outskirts of the city, Ellis opened the throttle. Kurt's hair blew in the icy wind. His scalp froze and his eyes watered, but it was worth it for the thrill of speed.

Ellis stopped the car outside a tea shop in Cheshunt.

"Come on, this is a good place. We can talk inside."

They took a table at the back of the tea room, where they could converse without being overheard. Ellis ordered a pot of tea and a platter of fancies.

Kurt was frozen to the bone. He rubbed life into his upper body and limbs.

Ellis grinned at him. "You enjoyed that, I think?"

Kurt nodded enthusiastically. "How do you get petrol for her?"

"I have a small allowance from the army. If I need more, I can get it – at a price." He touched the side of his nose.

A waitress placed two cups, a pot of tea, and a plate of iced cakes on the table. "Will there be anything else?"

"No thanks, love," said Ellis. He picked up the teapot and began to pour. "What do you know about the killings, Kurt?"

"Only what I heard on the radio and read in the paper." Kurt grabbed a newspaper from the table beside them. Henry Pollinger's picture stared up at them.

"That's one of Tar Robertson's puppets, agent A5," said Ellis. "Don't you think he looks the part?"

Kurt took another close look at the picture. "He looks every inch a Nazi, and evil enough to have murdered two people."

"Never judge a book by its cover, old boy. You do know that Pollinger's case officer, Jack Reed, has been taken in for questioning?"

Kurt stabbed a finger at the newspaper. "There was no mention of that in here, or on the radio."

"Almost certainly suppressed using a D-Notice. Hardly surprising, really."

"Is the case officer a serious suspect?"

"I doubt it. Why kill the cook? And why kill a guard? That would be like shooting yourself in the foot." Ellis selected an iced lemon sponge, conveyed it to his mouth, closed his eyes, and took a bite.

"Unless it was something personal." Kurt peered at the picture in the paper again. "So this Henry Pollinger must be the murderer?"

Ellis spoke through a mouthful of sponge and icing. "It certainly appears that way."

"But you don't believe it?"

Ellis swallowed. "It's difficult to understand why he would do it."

"Killing the golden goose, you mean?"

"Well, yes, exactly. Can you imagine a more comfortable existence than that of a double agent? Three square meals each day, everything they need handed to them on a silver platter. They don't have to risk life and limb like the average fighting man."

"Until the War ends..."

Ellis nodded at the cakes. "Help yourself, old man." He took a second bite of his cake.

"No thanks." Kurt sipped his tea and waited for his companion to eat his fill.

Ellis swallowed again and wiped his mouth. "Admittedly, their long-term future may be a bit rocky, but can you see that as a good reason to slit someone's throat?"

Kurt gave the puzzle some thought. "So, if the case officer is not guilty and the agent didn't do it, who did? The second guard maybe? Or the cleaner?"

"The second guard is not a suspect. I heard he's in his eighties. We're just going to have to wait and see what the police come up with." He popped the rest of the cake into his mouth and reached for another one. "Pollinger's real name is Schumann, by the way, Hans Schumann, call-sign *Blitzen*."

Ellis paid the bill. As they climbed into the car, Kurt asked if Ellis knew who J. C. Masterman was.

"John Cecil. He's chairman of the Twenty Committee. Tar Robertson's boss, you could say. Good solid type. Have you met him?"

"Briefly," said Kurt.

Ellis drove Kurt back into the city, dropping him off outside number 7 Radipole Road, Fulham, well after dark.

It was only while Kurt watched his companion roaring away, that he realised Ellis had called him Kurt. Apart from Major Robertson and his secretary, everyone in the programme knew him as Kevin O'Reilly. Where had Ellis picked up his real name?

Chapter 20

Lina was reading. Without a word, she put down the book and placed a plate of lasagne on the table. Kurt poked at it with a fork. It was stuck to the plate. The pasta was like rubber.

She stood beside him, her arms folded. "What did you expect? I thought we agreed you would leave a note the next time you went on one of your field trips."

"It wasn't a field trip, exactly."

"What was it then?"

He showed her the newspaper headline with the picture of the missing agent. "This man killed two of our group. I went to take a look."

She scanned the story quickly. "You went to this address, Frome Road, in north London? Why? Are you working with the police, now?"

"No, of course not. I wanted to find out what happened."

"You haven't said why."

"I don't know why."

"And did you?"

"Did I what?"

"Did you find out what happened?"

"No, not really."

She removed the plate and scraped the food into the rubbish bin. "A wasted trip so, and no supper. I hope it was worth it."

Kurt thought of continuing the discussion in order to thaw the frosty atmosphere, but he couldn't think of anything to say.

When Lina went to bed, Kurt remained in the living room for an hour, hoping she would be asleep by the time he joined her. But when he slid into the bed, he could tell from her breathing that she was awake. He lay still.

His mind turned again to the callous, arbitrary way Major Robertson and the LCS took decisions to terminate the lives of Abwehr officers. The more he thought about it, the more precarious

Arnold's position seemed. Would he call at the house in Perrymead Street one day soon to find it empty?

Then Lina turned onto her back. "I understand how you feel, Kevin, really I do. You miss Gudrun. That's only natural. You and she have a long-term commitment to each other."

"It's not that—"

"Let me finish. When we first met, you made your feelings clear. You explained your position and I accepted that we wouldn't be together forever. We both agreed that this would be a short-term thing, that when the War was over, you would return to Gudrun."

She paused. Kurt said nothing. Lina's interpretation of his mood was well wide of the mark, but he couldn't fault her logic. Gudrun was an ever-present source of nagging guilt for him. He had every intention of returning to her and her daughter in Ireland after the War, but he hadn't worked out how he would ever be able to explain Lina to Gudrun.

"Nothing to say? I can tell that you're anxious, and I fully understand why. I would be anxious in your shoes. I know that Gudrun has your heart, but she's not here. You can't live in the past, or the future, none of us can. We need to make the most of what we have here and now..."

"Lina, that's not why I'm on edge—"

"What, you don't think I can recognize anxiety when I see it? I see anxious, shell-shocked servicemen every day of the week. I'll tell you what I say to them. You've got to learn to relax, take each day as it comes, live each day to the full and don't dwell on the past or the future. It's good advice, Kevin."

"Thank you, Lina." He rolled toward her. "Now come here. Give me a kiss."

\#

Kurt woke to a rat-tat-tat on the door. He climbed out of bed. "Who's there?"

"Police. Open up."

Kurt opened the door dressed in his pyjamas. Two bulky uniformed policemen pushed past him into the flat.

The plainclothes man on the doorstep handed him a piece of paper. "I'm from Scotland Yard. I have a warrant to search these premises."

Kurt rubbed his eyes. "What for?"

"We have reason to believe that you may be harbouring a fugitive." The streetlight reflected off his bald head as he stepped into the flat.

"What fugitive?"

The detective picked up the newspaper on the table. "This man."

"He's not here. Why would you think he was?"

A screech from the bedroom told Kurt that Lina was awake.

"Are you denying that you've been harbouring him?"

"Yes, of course. I don't know him. I've never met the man."

Lina appeared in the bedroom doorway in her housecoat. "What's going on, Kevin? There's a policeman under the bed."

"It's some sort of misunderstanding, Lina. Don't worry about it."

She shook her head and shuffled into the kitchen.

The search was over in five minutes.

"Wait for me outside," said the detective to his two men.

The two policemen left the flat.

The detective said, "Where were you on Thursday night from midnight until 2 a.m.?"

"I was here, in bed."

The detective made a note in his notepad. "Your girlfriend will corroborate that?"

"Yes, of course."

"I assume she was sleeping. You could have driven to Frome Road, committed the murders and returned."

"I don't have a car, and Lina's a light sleeper."

"You could have taken a cab." The detective checked his watch.

"What made you think the suspect might be here?"

"You were seen yesterday outside the house in Frome Road where the killings happened. Perhaps you'd like to explain what you were doing there."

"I heard about it on the radio. I was curious…"

"Lots of people heard about it on the radio, and I'm sure lots of them were curious, but very few of them took a cab to the scene."

"There was quite a crowd of onlookers, as I recall. Are you planning to search the homes of everyone there?"

"Yes. If you see this man, Pollinger, or if he makes contact with you, call me at this number." He handed Kurt a card bearing the name Detective Inspector Underwood. "And we'd like you to attend an identity parade in Scotland Yard at 2 p.m. this afternoon."

"Shouldn't you be out looking for a burglar?" said Kurt. "I assumed this was a break-in that went wrong."

Underwood shook his head. "There were no signs of illegal entry. When we find him, Henry Pollinger will explain exactly what happened on Thursday night."

Inspector Underwood left the flat, banging the door on his way out.

Lina stepped out of the kitchen. "Have they gone?"

"Yes."

It was after 6 a.m., too late to go back to bed. Kurt went into the bedroom to get dressed.

Lina continued the conversation through the open door. "What was that all about? Why did they think that man might be here?"

"Apparently, visiting the scene of the crime was enough to make me a suspect."

"That makes no sense. I'd make breakfast, but we're out of food. All we have is porridge, and we've no milk. I've made tea."

Kurt joined Lina in the kitchen. He kissed her on the cheek and slipped into his leather jacket. "I'll skip the tea, Lina. There's something I must do this morning."

"But Kevin, it's Saturday. I have the day off. I thought we might try the markets again."

"Perhaps later," said Kurt, and he left.

Chapter 21

Saturday February 26, 1944

Kurt hurried to number 12 Perrymead Street.

Clarence opened the door. "Thank 'eaven you're here, sir. Arnold's in a state."

"What's the matter with him?"

"I couldn't tell you that, sir. He's in the bathroom and won't come out. We had a conversation. He seemed fine, and then he lost it."

"What was the conversation about?"

"Nothing at all, really. He told me about his childhood. I told him about the last War, how I came home shell-shocked."

"You blamed the Germans?"

Clarence shook his head. "No, no, he was proud of his country's record in the trenches. It was when we were talking about the Double Cross programme that he changed."

"What did you say?"

"I told him the programme was going to win us the War. He asked me how many double agents there were in London. I said I thought there were over a hundred."

"Where did you get that figure from?"

"I'm not sure. Chitchat amongst the guards."

Kurt climbed the stairs, and knocked on the bathroom door. "Arnold, it's Kevin. Open the door."

"Go away. Leave me alone."

"What's the matter, Arnold? Open the door and we can talk about it."

There was no response. Kurt tried the handle, but the door was locked.

"Open the door, Arnold."

"Will we be using the radio again?"

"No, the radio is still off limits. Talk to me, man."

The bathroom door opened a crack. Arnold poked his nose out.

His eyes were bloodshot. His hair had lost its usual neat Hitler look. It hung in strands over his ears, exposing a sizeable bald spot on his pate.

He wiped his nose on the back of his hand. "You said there were twenty-four Abwehr agents in the Double Cross programme."

"That's my best estimate, yes."

"Clarence says there are a hundred." He slammed the bathroom door closed and locked it again.

"Arnold?" Kurt rapped on the door. "Open the door, Arnold."

There was no answer.

"I thought you'd be pleased. Arnold, what the devil is the matter with you?"

Kurt waited a full minute before Arnold replied through the closed door. "It's too many."

Kurt scratched his head in puzzlement. "One hundred is too many?"

"Yes. Nine was too few, but one hundred is too many."

"I don't understand."

"With only nine, the programme would have been lightweight and liable to be closed down at any time. If there are a hundred, then each agent's contribution is insignificant, and any of us could be dropped without a second thought. Twenty-four was a good number."

"I'm sure your contribution is important, Arnold. You are the kingpin for information about RAF aircraft production. You've nothing to worry about."

Was that really true? Kurt had no idea. There could be dozens of agents reporting to Berlin or Hamburg about the RAF and their aircraft.

He tapped on the door. "I have to leave now, Arnold. Clarence may be wrong. He tells me his estimate is no more than a guess. It could be wildly inaccurate. I wouldn't worry about it."

There was no response. Kurt left the building and returned to the flat.

#

He found Lina trying on hats. She had only two, but she was having difficulty deciding which one to wear.

"What do you think, Kevin?"

The hat she had on was ghastly. It was made of straw, topped with red feathers. She took it off and began to put on the other one. With mind-numbingly bad timing, Kurt said, "I like that one."

"Which one? This one or the last one?"

The second hat was blue, flat on top with what might have been a blue leather belt wrapped around it. It was hideous.

Kurt scratched his chin to show he was thinking deeply about the problem. "I like them both."

"Okay, but if you had to choose one of the two, which would you pick?"

"I don't know. I could choose either."

"You're no help. What about this one?" With a flourish, she pulled a third hat from behind the sofa. It was mostly green, shaped like a British Tommy's helmet with pieces of fruit attached. She put it on. Kurt hated it more than the other two put together.

"It's lovely. It really suits you. Now can we go? You wanted to go shopping."

"Give me a minute. I'll have to change my dress to go with this hat." She disappeared into the bedroom. "I'm glad you like it. I was worried that you might not."

Kurt thought about what Clarence had said. Could there be 100 double agents in the programme? Ellis had suggested there might be 24, but his blown agent had the designation F17. If all the letters from A to F and all the numbers from 1 to 17 were assigned to enemy agents, that would make 102. Using that number as an indicative figure and allowing five support staff for each agent, meant a total of 510 support staff, not counting the MI5 operatives handling the dispatch of incoming and outgoing signals.

John, the courier, had said the designations were provided by Tin Eye Stephens in the London Cage, and not every Abwehr agent made it into the Double Cross programme, but even so, the programme was looking huge.

Fifteen minutes later, Kurt was still waiting. Lina explained that the dress that she'd picked out to go with the new hat was too tight around the waist. "It must have shrunk in the wash." She giggled.

Finally, Lina was dressed and ready to go. She had on the blue hat. Under her coat she wore a blue and green dress, and sensible flat shoes. Her recently-acquired battered handbag completed the outfit.

Kurt opened the door to find the MI5 driver standing on the doorstep.

"What do you want? We're just on our way out."

"Sorry, Kevin, but I've been told to pick you up."

"It's Saturday. Can't it wait until Monday?"

"They want you in headquarters today."

#

The driver took them both to St James's Street. They agreed to meet at 1 p.m. at Simpsons in the Strand. Lina headed for the shops, while the driver led Kurt into SIS headquarters.

Kurt waited 30 minutes on a wooden bench in a corridor on the second floor, before a clerk appeared and showed him into a plush office. Kurt marvelled at the chesterfield furniture and oak panelled walls, a lively log fire in the fireplace.

Beside the fire stood Philby. He directed Kurt to a 2-seater sofa. Kurt took a seat, and Philby moved to an armchair facing him.

Philby cast an icy smile in Kurt's direction. "Sorry for disrupting your weekend, O'Reilly. Major Robertson is away on a trip. He asked me to speak to you, to bring you up to speed, so to speak." He pulled a cigarette case from an inside jacket pocket, flipped it open, and offered them to Kurt.

Kurt returned Philby's smile with a steely one of his own. "I don't smoke, thanks."

"Me neither." He closed the cigarette case and slipped it back in his pocket. "First, I have to tell you that your offer to speak with your Abwehr colleagues has been rejected by our masters upstairs."

"Did you explain to them about the Black Orchestra?"

"I'm sure Major Robertson did. I have to tell you that the suggestion was very poorly received. The notion of delivering a German national like yourself back into the arms of the enemy was thought of as unwise in the extreme. In your case, given your knowledge of the Double Cross programme, they thought the idea bordered on lunacy. You could say they were horrified by the idea."

Kurt bit the inside of his cheek. "I think I've proved where my sympathies lie more than once in the past year."

"Your loyalty to the Allied cause is not in question, but have you considered what could happen if you fell into the hands of the Gestapo? You know too much about British Intelligence. It's that simple."

Kurt opened his mouth to protest further, but Philby raised a palm. "Forget about it, Reilly. The decision has been made. Time to

71

move on, I think." Philby paused. "You will recall that Major Robertson was concerned about a certain code word."

"Operation Fortitude."

"That's the one. He asked me to tell you that it came in on the radio of every Double Cross agent within a 24-hour period. He now assumes that your man received it first simply because his radio was first on the air that day."

"So there's nothing to worry about?"

"I didn't say that. The code word is highly secret. It should never have reached the Abwehr. The point is that your man is off the hook."

"So can we resume radio operations on Monday morning?"

Philby's smile faded. "Afraid not. The major has decided to let you have some leave. Much deserved, I'm sure. He signed this 7-day pass." He handed a piece of paper across to Kurt.

Kurt looked at the pass without taking it in. "My man, Arnold, has been extremely agitated since he was told to cease radio operations. For the sake of his mental health, he needs to resume normal radio operations as soon as possible. I appreciate the pass, but I'd prefer to get back to work."

"That won't be necessary. You are relieved of your duties, effective immediately."

Chapter 22

Kurt's stomach did a somersault. "The major's removing me from the programme? Why?"

The SIS man checked his fingernails. "Let's just say there are some in high places who are uncomfortable with your continued involvement in the programme."

"Uncomfortable? What do they think I might do?"

"As I said, some of our masters are uncomfortable. They suspect your motivation. They worry about what you might do."

"I see. What will happen to Arnold?"

"The major tells me he has an experienced case officer available to step in and take over your duties."

Ellis!

Philby held out his hand. "Please let me have your keys to the safe house in Perrymead Street."

"I have only one key. It opens the back parlour where the transmitter is kept."

"You don't have a front door key?"

"No need. There's always a guard on duty." Kurt removed the key from his key ring and handed it over. "What of the rogue spy? Are we to take it that the agent who killed his guard and his cook is the one responsible for leaking the code word – the Gingerbread spy?"

"That's highly unlikely. There's no reason to suppose that the two events are related in any way. That agent was clearly disaffected or burdened with guilt. I've seen it before."

"So Gingerbread is still at large and unidentified."

"I'm very much afraid that many of those in high places suspect that you may be the Gingerbread agent."

"That's ridiculous. No one is more loyal, more committed to the programme than me."

"Quite so, but some prejudice is unavoidable, given your background."

"Has there been any attempt to use radio direction finders to locate Gingerbread?"

"Indeed, we have RDF vans deployed all over London, but this spy is highly mobile, he transmits infrequently, and never from the same place twice. His transmissions are always short; there's never enough time to pinpoint his location. The man is a veritable will-o-the-wisp. I fear we are not going to catch him by conventional means."

Philby stood up, and steered Kurt toward the door. "As I understand it, Major Robertson hopes to prove your innocence by removing you from the programme."

Philby opened the door. They shook hands. "Goodbye, Reilly. Enjoy your leave."

Kurt left the meeting fuming, determined to prove his loyalty to the British cause and save the Allied invasion. He had to find and silence this Gingerbread spy.

#

Simpson's on the Strand was buzzing, with a line of people waiting to be seated. Lina waved at Kurt as he entered. She had secured a table close to the back of the room. He bypassed the queue at the door, pecked her on the cheek, and took his seat at the table. A waiter placed a menu in his hand right away.

Without her hat and coat, Lina looked a picture in blue and green, her eyes sparkling. "You're late," she hissed. "What kept you?"

"I got here as soon as I could."

"Look what I bought." She let him peep inside a paper bag.

"What is it?"

"It's a pleated skirt. Just above the knee. I'll put it on when we get home. You'll like it."

"Isn't it a bit cold for short skirts?"

She laughed her donkey's bray laugh. Several people turned their heads. "It's the fashion, Kevin. Haven't you noticed? You should be more observant. You must remember the dress that Kathy was wearing at Maria's wedding. You spent enough time drooling over it..."

Kurt tuned out. How could they suspect him? After all he'd gone through since he joined the Black Orchestra, the number of Nazis he'd killed, the missions he'd completed for the British Intelligence Service, the number of times he'd put his life on the line. Hadn't he proved his unwavering loyalty, time and time again? After all that, how could they think he was spying for the Nazis? And the police obviously thought he might be a double murderer! Why else would they want to put him in an identity parade? He looked at his watch. It was 12:30 already.

"Kevin!"

"What?"

The waiter was at the table, pencil poised over his pad.

"Order something."

Kurt ran his eyes over the menu. "What can we have?"

"Just a main course."

Kurt found the cheapest thing on the menu – Spam fritters for 3/6. He shuddered and handed the menu to the waiter. "I'll have the cassoulet."

The waiter made a note on his pad and scuttled away.

Lina grinned. "You do know what that is?"

"I'm not sure. Bangers and mash?"

"It's bangers and beans. You'll have to sleep on the settee tonight." She giggled.

#

The food was delivered in record time. Lina's crispy whitebait salad had no more than a couple of tiny fish hiding in a forest of greenery. Kurt's bangers were mostly breadcrumbs, but the food was hot, and in no time at all, it was all gone. Lina took a trip to the ladies' room to freshen up while Kurt paid the bill, surrendering four of their precious food ration coupons in the process. By the time Lina re-emerged, there was a new couple seated at their table, the waiter hovering over them.

Lina reclaimed her hat and coat from the cloakroom attendant, and they stepped outside. The Strand was busy with pedestrians. Horse-drawn carriages and drays clattered by, competing for space with a few cars carrying government officials or senior brass from the armed forces. A US army jeep swerved around a pile of rubble on two wheels. Using his horn, he turned down Savoy Street at speed, heading for the river.

Lina rolled her eyes. "These Americans think they own London." She grabbed her hat as a gust of wind threatened to remove it.

"Where to next?" said Kurt.

"I'd like to take a look at a few second-hand clothes shops."

"Haven't you used up your clothes ration?"

She wrinkled her nose. "Yes, but I can look, can't I? Are you coming with me?"

"I'd love to, but there's something I need to do."

She smiled a knowing smile. "I thought so. You've had ants in your pants ever since you sat down."

Kurt walked with Lina as far as Charing Cross Tube station, where they parted company. Then he made his way on foot to Great Scotland Yard, and presented himself at the reception desk.

After taking his details, the desk clerk led him to a narrow anteroom. "Wait here. You'll be called when we're ready for you."

There was no furniture in the room, apart from a long wooden bench occupied by five men. One of them stood up. "Hello, Kevin. Fancy meeting you here." It was Ellis.

Another man stood up, a tall, weedy individual with a pencil moustache. Ellis introduced him. "This is Jack Reed, Henry Pollinger's case officer."

"Not any more," said Reed, shaking Kurt's hand.

The other men shuffled along to allow the three companions to sit together. Kurt said, "I take it you're here for the same reason that I am?"

Reed grunted.

Ellis smiled toothily. "It seems one of us must be a mass murderer."

Kurt looked at his watch. "I hope this doesn't take too long."

"You and me both," said Ellis. "I have to report to the office. I've had word that I'm to be reassigned to a new case."

"Why the identity parade?" said Kurt. "I thought they knew who the killer was."

Reed said, "Pollinger's the prime suspect, but I don't believe it. And if it was him, he had an accomplice. He was seen leaving the house with another man."

That was news to Kurt. There had been no mention of a second man on the news, and no mention of a witness, either.

At 1:45 p.m. a police constable took all six men through the building to another room. There they were each given a cardboard number to hold and placed in a line with their backs to the wall. Kurt was number 3 in line, Ellis was number 5, and Reed number 6.

"Stand up straight, face that wall, eyes open, and no talking," said the constable.

A door opened, a middle-aged man came in, accompanied by the detective from the flat.

"Take your time, Mr Duckworth. If you see anyone you recognise, touch him on the shoulder."

Chapter 23

The witness walked up and down the line. He shook his head.

"Take another look," said the detective.

Mr Duckworth tried again. And again, he shook his head. "I'm sorry, I don't recognise any of these men. It was dark..."

Ten minutes later, Kurt, Reed and Ellis stood beside Ellis's car outside the police station.

"That was a waste of everyone's time," said Kurt. "Where's your new assignment, Ellis?"

"They haven't given me the address yet. I expect I'll meet my new man for the first time this evening."

"What about you, Reed?" said Ellis.

"No word from our masters yet."

Ellis jumped into his red MG Midget and drove away, revving the engine. Kurt and Reed watched it until it disappeared from view around a corner.

Reed sighed wistfully. "She's a beauty."

"Yes, he's a lucky bastard," said Kurt.

Reed strode south toward Bedford Street. Kurt made a beeline for the Tube station.

#

Perrymead Street was deserted. Nothing but a lone cat crossed his path as Kurt made his way to number 12 and knocked on the door.

He was delighted to see who opened it. "Harry, good to see you. Where's Clarence?"

The guard stood aside to let Kurt in. "I'm not sure. There was some emergency. I expect I'll hear all about it tomorrow. I thought you'd left us, sir. I was told to expect a new case officer."

"That's right. You should meet the new man this evening. They're giving me some leave."

Kurt went straight to the kitchen. Mrs Partridge had left for the day, leaving the place spotless, as usual. He took his writing pad and *Gone With the Wind* from the shelf, located the code word for the day and set about composing a message. When he'd finished encoding it, he returned to the front parlour.

Harry was engrossed in his newspaper, his rifle leaning against the wall, close at hand.

"Lend me your key, Harry. I need to transmit a signal."

Harry wasn't the brightest, but he was being asked to deviate from well-established routine. "You don't have your own key?"

"I left it at home."

The guard scratched his head. "I don't ever recall anyone using the radio at the weekend."

"This is a bit of an emergency."

"Should I get his nibs out of bed?"

Kurt shook his head. "I don't need Arnold for this one."

"I thought only Arnold could use the radio."

"Who told you that?"

"You did, sir. Remember when you explained that the Jerries could tell each operator's way of using the Morse thingumabob."

"Just let me have the key. It won't take more than a few minutes."

"Don't you have to transmit at certain times of the day?"

"Normally, yes, but as I said, this is an emergency."

By this point in the conversation, Harry's facial expression had changed from sleepy genial friend to wide-eyed suspicious Tommy. He had no idea what was happening, but he smelled a large rat.

"I'm sorry, sir. Call me stupid if you like, call me pig-headed, but I can't give you the key."

"Look here, Harry, how long have we known each other?"

"A few months."

"You trust me, don't you?"

Obviously conflicted, Harry shook his head. "I'm sorry, sir, I trust you, but you're not having my key."

"I have to send this signal. I told you, it's an emergency."

Harry's brow furrowed. "Let me call the office, sir. If they say it's all right, I'll give you my key."

"There's no time for that, Harry. If you won't give me the key, I'll have to break down the door."

Harry reached for his rifle and chambered a round. "I wouldn't try that if I were you, sir."

#

On his way back to the flat, Kurt reviewed his options. He was determined to flush this Gingerbread into the open to prove his own innocence. He would show them that he was no Nazi spy.

In order to do that, he needed to talk with someone in the Abwehr in Berlin. The thought of returning to Berlin gave him an instant headache, but if that was what the situation demanded, then he would do it. He needed to get a message through to the Abwehr first, and without access to a radio transmitter he was hamstrung.

A plan began to take shape in his mind. There was one place where he knew he could get unfettered access to a radio: a small village called Ballyruane in Ireland where he had placed an Abwehr agent two years earlier.

#

It was dark by the time Lina arrived home, excited by her shopping excursion but frustrated that she hadn't been able to buy anything.

"I found some gorgeous dresses in a market in Oxford Street."

"How long?"

"Ankle length."

"I thought you said the latest fashion was above the knee."

"I did. When I get my hands on one of those dresses, I'll shorten it. I'll be able to do something creative with the material I remove."

"Like what?"

"Oh, use your imagination, Kevin."

She went into the bedroom to put on her new pleated skirt. Kurt smiled at her when he saw it. "It's very nice."

Lina crossed her arms and glared at him. "You don't like it. I can tell."

"It's rather short."

"Above the knee. I told you, it's the fashion." She did a twirl.

"I'm sorry, love, I have something on my mind."

"What? Tell me."

"They've given me a week's leave."

"Don't you have a job to do?"

He shook his head. "They've given my job to someone else."

She laughed nervously. "You're not serious."

"I am."

"So what will you be doing when you go back?"

"I don't know."

She thought about that for a few moments. Then she said, "Maybe I could get some time off. We could go somewhere. Wales or Scotland, maybe."

"I have to go away."

"Where to?"

He cast his gaze down to his boots.

"Don't tell me, let me guess. You're going back to Ireland."

Kurt said nothing.

"Right, well I might not be here when you get back." She flounced into the bedroom and slammed the door.

Chapter 24

The darkness was so absolute, it suffocated him. He was cold, lying on a hard floor, gagged and trussed up like a parcel, his head covered by a rough sack. He was hungry, and dying of thirst. He had lost all sensation of time, slipping in and out of sleep in an infinity of blackness. He could have been there an hour, a day, or a week. Would they ever release him, would he ever see light again, or would they leave him here to die in the darkness?

There were moments when he imagined he might already be dead, but the pains in his joints gave the lie to that notion. No, he was alive – for the moment, anyway.

The murders flashed through his mind with terrifying regularity. First the guard. That was bad enough, but then the cook. Poor Mrs Pettigrew knew what was coming. She screamed before the knife severed her windpipe. There had been so much blood! He had thought his own time had come, but the man had taken him from the house, bundled him into a car and driven him to a remote location with trees. There, he met with another man, and between them they tied him up and removed him from the light.

Part 2 – Ireland

Chapter 25

Office of Strategic Services, US Military Intelligence, London

Captain Johnson sat at his desk in his office. The walls, recently redecorated in military green, reeked of lead paint, making his eyes water.

The door opened. A US marine entered and saluted. "Kevin O'Reilly's on the move again, sir."

The captain looked up from the papers on his desk. "Who?"

"O'Reilly, sir, he's working with British Intelligence. You remember he helped us with that other business."

"Oh, right. What's he up to now?"

"He's been seen boarding a ship bound for Ireland."

Johnson wiped his eyes with a handkerchief. "And that concerns us how?"

"He's well placed with British Intelligence. He could give us an inside track in Whitehall. We should make contact with him at the very least."

Captain Johnson snorted. "Who do we have over there?"

"I've asked Piper – that's the maths professor – to keep an eye out for him."

"Okay. Keep me informed. And leave the door open on your way out."

Chapter 26

Sunday February 27, 1944

The Irish Sea was choppy. Standing on deck near the prow of the ship, collar up, hands stuffed into the pockets of his leather jacket, Kurt stamped his feet and shivered. Icy spray bit his face. There were plenty of vacant seats in the passenger cabin, there was even a bar, but Kurt felt obliged to remain outside as a sort of punishment for his sins.

But what sins?

His affair with Lina for one. He was committed to Gudrun and her daughter, Anna. When the War was over, he had every intention of returning to them. The thing with Lina was no more than a short-term fling. The problem was that he couldn't guess how Gudrun would react when she found out.

If she found out.

Could he get away with saying nothing about Lina to Gudrun? Or should he tell her and risk the consequences? Surely, she would forgive him. It was wartime, after all. On the other hand, she might consider his actions a betrayal...

Saying nothing was probably not an option. How many times had Gudrun demonstrated her uncanny ability to tell when he told a lie? His discomfort sat like a rock in his stomach.

He remembered how much he loved her, how strong his passion was for her, the way his heart leapt in his chest every time he saw her. The trouble was he couldn't *feel* that passion any longer. After six months apart, all he had was the memory of his love. Even the image of Gudrun's face had faded in his mind.

The boat continued to buck in the swell. He ducked into the cabin to avoid the next icy onslaught, and found a seat at the bar. The draughty cabin was far from warm, but compared to the deck, it was paradise. He ordered a pint of Guinness and watched the bartender prepare it for him.

Ignoring a half dozen empty stools at the bar, a man took the stool beside Kurt. Immediately suspicious, Kurt looked at him. Mid-fifties, heavy set, wearing a full-length woollen overcoat and a homburg; he showed no sign of discomfort as Kurt looked him over. He ordered a pint.

Kurt slid off his stool, but before he could walk away, the man held out a hand. "Carter, MI5."

Kurt ignored the hand. "Have we met?"

Carter grinned. "We are just about to. Don't look so worried, squire. I'm on your side."

"What does that mean?"

"Major Robertson asked me to keep an eye on you."

The rock in Kurt's stomach became a boulder. They couldn't trust him to take a 7-day pass on his own!

"Why, in God's name? I'm on leave."

"In case you decided to do something stupid."

"Like what?"

Carter plastered a fake smile on his face. "I don't know, do I? My orders are to stick to you like glue until your leave is over."

"And you thought you'd introduce yourself?"

"Why not? We're on the same team, aren't we?"

Kurt took his pint to the other end of the bar. He downed it in two swallows and left the cabin. Carter remained where he was.

Kurt stayed on deck until the boat reached its halfway point. Then he returned to the cabin and joined Carter at the bar.

Carter looked at Kurt through doleful eyes. "Too chilly out there for you?"

Kurt ordered two stiff whiskeys and presented one to Carter. "No reason we can't be friends. As you said, we are on the same side."

A broad smile lit up the MI5 man's face. He lifted the glass. "Cheers, squire."

"Down the hatch."

Carter ordered the second round...

By the time the mailboat docked, Kurt was tipsy. Carter was blotto, clinging to Kurt's arm to stay upright. "I really like you, you know, Kevin." His hand slipped from Kurt's arm, and he stumbled. "Whoops! I think I've had too much to drink."

Kurt helped him onto a stool.

"Strange how you meet people you mightn't never have met in times of peace, you know?"

Carter's eyelids were drooping. Within a minute, his head had dropped onto his arms and he was snoring gently.

Kurt patted him on the shoulder. "Sleep well, my friend."

Thanks to his Irish passport, Kevin O'Reilly passed through immigration and customs without incident. He was a little unsteady on his feet, but his determination to lose his MI5 'minder' was all it took to keep him going.

Once he'd left the terminal, he took a bus into Dublin.

Alighting from the bus at the quays on the River Liffey, he set out toward the terminus for provincial buses. There he bought a ticket for Rathnew in County Wicklow, found his bus, and climbed aboard.

A quick scan of the terminus, as the bus was pulling out, assured him that he was free of his tail, and he settled back in the seat for the journey.

The bone-rattling bus carried Kurt to County Wicklow. He thanked the driver as he left the bus at Rathnew, and set off at a brisk pace down the boreen to Ballyruane.

The village hadn't changed. A post office, a public house, a few shops, a café and a church. Kurt entered the café. The place was empty. He waited five minutes before the owner appeared with a pad in one hand, a pencil in the other.

"Welcome back. What can I get you?"

"You remember me?"

"Yes, of course, you came in with Fritz. You ordered tea and cakes." She wore the same coloured apron she had the last time.

"That was two years ago."

"Was it? I expect you're right. Tea and cakes again, is it?" She wrote on her pad and went back to the kitchen.

She had used Fritz Blesset's real first name. His cover name was Rory O'Reilly.

When she returned with the tea and cakes, Kurt asked about 'his friend'.

"He's a nice lad, Fritz. Everybody likes him."

"Where can I find him?"

"He lives with Jane Jackman. In her cottage." A cocked, quivering eyebrow hinted at an unregistered union.

"Thank you. I know where that is." He stood up.

"Aren't you going to drink your tea? I can't serve those cakes to anyone else, you know. I'll have to throw them out."

Kurt took a 10-shilling note from his pocket. "How much do I owe you?"

She recoiled from the note. A garter snake would have produced a milder reaction. "I can't change that."

"Keep the change." He placed the money on the table.

Jane Jackman's cottage was the last one at the edge of the village. He knocked on the door and Fritz Blesset opened it.

Chapter 27

A broad smile lit up Blesset's face. "Kurt! What are you doing here? Come in." He spoke in English.

Blesset led him into the front room and waved at an armchair. "Sit, please. Can I get you something? Tea? I have whiskey."

"No thanks, Blesset. How have you been?"

Blesset beamed. "Wonderful. There's nothing like the love of a good woman to make a man whole." He had developed an Irish accent, coloured by a trace of his German origins. "How are you? How's your mother?"

"I'm well, thank you. I haven't been to visit Mother yet, but I believe she is well."

"That's good. I'm sorry Jane's not here to meet you. She's out visiting one of the farms in search of fresh eggs. We have food rationing. You know the War has made everything difficult to get, even here, deep in the countryside of neutral Ireland."

"How's your health?"

"Couldn't be better. Oh you mean my Tourette's? That's all gone."

"You're off the medication?"

"Completely. Jane has cured me. I owe you a great debt, Kurt. I'm out of the War, blissfully happy."

"The love of a good woman."

"*Jawohl, Herr Oberleutnant.*"

"What do you live on?"

Blesset continued to smile. "We have enough. Jane does some light secretarial work, and I still have some of the money you gave me."

"I'm happy for you, Blesset."

"Thank you. Now tell me why you've come."

"I need to use your transmitter. Where do you keep it?"

"It's in the attic. I don't... I mean I haven't used it in a while."

"Why? When was the last time you sent a signal?"

Blesset shrugged. "I'm not sure. Several months ago, maybe a year."

The front door opened and Jane Jackman came in. "A visitor!" She held out a hand to Kurt. "Introduce us, Fritz."

"This is Oberleutnant—"

"Kevin O'Reilly." Kurt held out his hand. She grasped it.

Kurt remembered her from their brief meeting two years earlier. The lines on her face and grey streaks in her hair reflected the passage of time. She might have been 40. Blesset was 28.

"Kevin is my boss from Berlin. You remember he was the one who brought me here early in 1942?"

"Yes, I remember. Has Fritz offered you anything? A drink? Some food, perhaps."

"I'm fine, Miss Jackman, thank you. I have some business to complete with Fritz, then I'll be leaving. It won't take long."

"Nonsense. You've come all this way to visit us. We have a spare room. I'll make up a bed. You must stay the night. You can borrow a pair of Blesset's pyjamas. And call me Jane."

"I only ever used to transmit at nine o'clock in the morning," said Blesset. "So you might as well spend the night."

Kurt made no objection. The long journey and the drink he'd consumed on the mailboat were taking their toll.

Jane made a meal for three. They had pork, potatoes and carrots. At the table, the conversation revolved around Jane and Fritz's life together. Kurt could contribute little. They assumed he had travelled from Germany, and carefully avoided asking any questions about Berlin or the Abwehr. They were clearly in love. Blesset had changed. No longer the gauche young man with involuntary shouts and arm movements that Kurt had taken to Ireland in January, 1942; the new Blesset was assured, confident, and happy. Nor was this Blesset still operating as an Abwehr spy. Blesset had gone native.

After the meal, Jane and Blesset tidied up. Kurt offered to help, but they waved him back to his armchair.

Blesset said, "How's the professor? Have you seen him?"

"No, I came straight here."

"How did you get here?" said Jane. "Did you come in a submarine like before, or did they drop you from an airplane?"

Kurt had no ready answer for that question. He hesitated for an awkward moment.

Blesset came to his rescue. "Why don't you make up the bed for our guest, love, while I prepare a nightcap?"

Jane left the room.

Kurt said, "I noticed you're not using your Irish alias."

"No, it's not necessary. The villagers are sympathetic, and I could never pass as an Irishman, as you know well."

Blesset was aware of his limitations as a spy. Had he worked out the wider conspiracy, the existence of the Black Orchestra within the Abwehr? There was no rancour in his tone. Whatever conclusions he had come to, Blesset was content. Kurt ignored the remark. Perhaps Jane's influence had washed his mind clean of his Nazi ideology.

Blesset boiled a kettle. He rinsed three glasses, opened a bottle of whiskey and poured a small measure into each.

"If you're making a drink for me, I've had enough already today to sink the battleship *Tirpitz*."

"I'm making hot whiskeys. You'll have to try this. It's a favourite amongst the locals here."

Kurt was well acquainted with the hot whiskey from his student days in Dublin, but he said nothing. He was too tired to object.

Jane came back, and Blesset handed round the drinks.

"What shall we drink to?" said Jane. "The end of the War, perhaps?"

"Peace," said Kurt.

"Peace!" They touched glasses.

Jane said, "I'm looking forward to when we can all get back to living normal lives again. Do you have a girlfriend, Kevin?"

"Yes, her name's Gudrun."

"A good German name. She'll be happy when you return to Berlin."

"Actually, she lives in Dublin with her daughter and my mother."

Blesset said, "You'll definitely have to pay them a visit before you return to Germany." To Jane, he said, "Kevin's mother is Irish."

Jane raised an enquiring eyebrow. "And your father?"

"My father was German. He died before the War."

"I'm sorry," said Jane. She looked at the clock on the mantelpiece. "Turn on the radio, Fritz, it's time for the news."

Blesset switched on the radio.

This is the BBC Home Service. Here is the news and this is Alvar Lidell reading it. The War Office has today announced a major Allied victory in the Far East. The Green Islands have been captured from the Imperial Japanese Army by a combined force of United States and New Zealand troops. The operation, which began on the fifteenth of February was completed yesterday, with minimal Allied losses. Admiral William Halsey of the United States Navy, commanding, had this to say about the entire operation. "A small advance party made landfall to survey the area and assess the disposition of the enemy. The local Melanesians provided vital intelligence. Armed with this information, the landings went without a hitch and the whole operation was an unqualified success. I wish to acknowledge the key role played in this action by our allies from the Army of New Zealand under the command of Major General Harold Barrowclough."

In other news, the United States General George S. Patton has arrived in Britain and was to be seen in his jeep wearing his pearl-handled pistols. Our Kent correspondent, Henry Giles, caught up with him and recorded this interview...

Kurt's eyelids closed.

"Come on, Kevin, you look all in," said Blesset. "I'll show you to your bed."

Chapter 28

Monday February 28, 1944

Lina climbed out of bed in her cold flat. Like millions of other young women in Britain, she was alone again, with no certainty that she would ever see Kevin again.

As she made her breakfast, she decided that she would throw herself into her work with renewed vigour. If she kept busy she wouldn't have time for feeling lonely.

The Luftwaffe raid of the night before had concentrated on some distant parts of the city. The Tube was running and she was able to take it to Victoria and walk the rest of the way to work in bright, early morning sunshine.

Matron had two police detectives in her office. Lina asked Dan the porter what that was all about, but Dan had no clue. She had to wait 15 minutes until the two detectives left and Matron called her in to her office.

"I have a new assignment for you," she said. "You did such a good job over the past few days, I've decided to make you our administration assistant. You will be responsible for the disposition and control of all victims of the bombing that pass through our doors."

Lina's heart leapt in her chest. This sounded more like the sort of job a nurse should be doing. "You mean I will be responsible for triage of the injured patients?"

"Not triage, no. The doctors will look after that, but you will decide where to send the more serious cases – I will explain how to do that later – and I will expect you to maintain accurate records on all the patients, their details, their injuries, where they were sent, and so on." She picked up a bundle of patient files. "Come with me and I'll show you to your new office."

Matron led Lina to the elevator. They stepped inside and Matron punched the button for the basement. Lina's heart sank to her boots. She bit her tongue and said nothing.

The basement was as cold and forbidding as ever. Its peculiar smell awakened all of Lina's latent fears. Still, she said nothing.

Matron unlocked the door to a small room equipped with a desk, a file cabinet, and a telephone. "This will be your office. You can start on these files. Take a seat and I'll show you what I want you to do..."

The next few hours passed slowly, as Lina tried her best to banish her fears by concentrating really hard on her work. By midday, she felt no better about her new quarters. She was alone. Her isolation, together with the oppressive atmosphere and peculiar smell weighed heavily on her mind. Added to that, the basement made strange, unexplained clicking, tapping, and wheezing noises. Lina couldn't shake the idea that she was inside the belly of a large beast.

She took an early lunch break. Rather than face the hostile glares of the other nurses in the canteen, she threw on her coat over her uniform and left the hospital, intending to find a quick, cheap meal in a nearby 'British restaurant'.

She was barely outside the entrance to the building when she collided with a passing stranger wearing a trench coat and a hat. He stumbled and fell to the pavement. His hat fell off and his head struck the ground.

She reached down to help him to his feet. "I'm dreadfully sorry, I wasn't looking where I was going."

He spoke in Dutch. "It wasn't your fault." He sounded out of breath.

She picked up his hat and handed it to him. "Are you all right? Maybe you should step inside the hospital, let one of the doctors take a look at you."

He placed a hand on her shoulder to steady himself. He was about as tall as Kevin, and about the same age, but with a quirky, charming smile. Kevin never wore a hat. "No, no, I'll be fine in a minute," he said. "I was looking for somewhere to grab a bite to eat. I'm not familiar with this part of the city. Could you suggest somewhere?"

She took him to the restaurant – a scout hall before the War. He had a dizzy spell as he sat down, and Lina went to the counter to get him a glass of water. He removed his hat. As he sipped the water, she said, "Are you from Holland?"

He replied in Dutch. "Yes, I'm a refugee from Utrecht."

"I'm from Eindhoven," she said. "How long have you lived in Britain?"

"I've been in London since 1940."

"What a strange coincidence that we should bump into each other."

"Not really so strange. There are thousands of refugees from the Netherlands in London. What's your name?"

"Lina Smit."

"Jan de Groot. How do you do?" They shook hands. "You are a nurse at the hospital?"

"How did you guess?"

He smiled, and she felt weak at the knees.

He said, "I expect you're very busy since the German bombers have returned to London."

"The past few days have been horrible. I heard in the news that they dropped some bombs on our queen."

The smile left his face. "I heard that, but I thought she was unhurt."

"I believe so, although some of her guards were killed."

"The Nazi bastards would love to kill her, but they'll never succeed." His smile returned. "She will rule a free Netherlands again some day."

She stretched her lunch hour as far as she dared. When it was time to go, he asked if she'd like to meet him again. Throughout the meal, Lina's mind had been working on her response to this hypothetical question. She replied without hesitation, "When and where?"

Back in her miserable basement office she reviewed her actions. Kevin was out of the country. He had returned to Gudrun, his one true love. There was no knowing if he would ever return. Lina and Kevin's affair was a loose arrangement, after all. Neither had made any long-term commitment. They were free to pursue other opportunities when, and if, they presented themselves. She had no reason to reproach herself, nothing at all to be ashamed of.

Chapter 29

Monday February 28, 1944

In the cottage in Ballyruane, Kurt slept long and deep. He awoke refreshed, surprised that he had no hangover.

Jane had already left for work by the time he was dressed.

Blesset boiled two real eggs for breakfast. "I hope you'll stay a few nights more, Kurt. I have so much to show you. The countryside around here is beautiful."

"Sorry, Blesset, I have to get on."

Blesset seemed unusually animated. "What's on your mind?" said Kurt.

"Today is February 28, and it's a leap year."

"So?"

"There's a tradition that a girl can propose to a man on February 29. I'm hoping that Jane will seize the opportunity."

Kurt laughed. "If not, you'll have to wait another four years."

After breakfast, Blesset placed a wooden A-frame ladder under the hatch, climbed up, and disappeared into the attic. When he reappeared, he lowered a suitcase down to Kurt. "Be careful, it's heavy."

Kurt manhandled the suitcase to the ground and carried it into the kitchen. It contained Blesset's Abwehr r/t radio, complete with Morse keypad and code book.

Blesset plugged in the transmitter. As it warmed up, Kurt worked out the code for the day and encoded his message.

At exactly 9 a.m., Blesset keyed in Kurt's encoded message. After keying in the *Ende* code, they waited for confirmation. Nothing happened.

"Are we on the right frequency?" said Kurt.

"Yes."

"So why have we received no confirmation code?"

Blesset shook his head. "I don't know. Perhaps they've forgotten about me. It's been such a long time."

Blesset removed the back of the set, using a rusty old screwdriver. Layers of dust wafted out from the insides. Kurt spotted a couple of spiders scuttling about in the glow of the valves. One of the valves was black inside. It had blown.

"There's the problem," said Kurt. "The set is useless."

Blesset was crestfallen. "I'm sorry, Kurt. This is my fault. If you can wait another day, I'll see if I can replace that broken valve. There's an electrical shop in Wicklow Town that I could try."

"Forget about the transmitter. I'll keep this." Kurt rolled the code book and put it in his coat pocket. "I can't stay any longer."

They shook hands briefly on the doorstep.

"Looks like you've had a wasted trip," said Blesset.

"The trip wasn't wasted, Fritz. It was good to see you and to meet Jane again. Just put the set back in the attic. You won't need it again. Thank Jane for everything. Perhaps we'll meet again when the War is over. And I hope she realises that it's a leap year."

#

The bus took him back to Dublin. He arrived at the front gate of Trinity College at lunchtime, and hunted down a sandwich before making his way to the Department of Mathematics in number 39, New Square.

He knocked on a door bearing the legend: Stephan Hirsch, Professor.

"Come in."

The professor looked much as he had the last time Kurt had seen him. A tall man with a receding hairline and an infectious smile. He held out a hand. "Kurt Müller, by all that's holy. I never thought I'd see you again. When did we last meet?"

Kurt shook his hand warmly in both of his own. "It was early last year, Professor. March, I think."

"And what have you been up to since then? How have you been getting on with the British Secret Service people?" The professor's soft American accent hadn't changed.

"You knew I was working for them?"

"I guessed they must have taken you on, since you're still upright." He waved Kurt to seat at a table. The professor sat facing him.

"I've done some work for them in London. Right at the moment, I'm on a 7-day pass."

"And you came all this way to visit me. I'm flattered."

"It's not just a social visit, Professor."

He threw his head back and laughed. "You don't think I worked that out? When did you ever pay me a social visit?"

"I'm sorry to trouble you again, Professor, but..."

"Don't worry about it, Kurt. What is it this time? An introduction to the American OSS, perhaps, or a letter of recommendation to the King's equerry?"

"I was hoping to use your transmitter. I need to contact some old friends."

"The British couldn't let you use one of theirs?"

"It's a long story, Professor."

"That's okay, shoot. I'm a good listener."

Kurt told the professor about how an Abwehr double agent had killed his guard and gone to ground. "No one has any idea where he could be hiding. He seems to have vanished into thin air."

"I suppose MI5 couldn't ask the civilian police to find him," said the professor. "What's his name – this killer spy?"

"Henry Pollinger, and Scotland Yard has been looking for him for days. His picture has been on the front page of all the newspapers."

"Any idea where he could be hiding?"

"None."

"How can I help?" The professor looked perplexed.

"We have another problem. There's a rogue spy operating in Britain somewhere, interfering with MI5's plans."

"This Pollinger?"

"Possibly, possibly not. The trouble is that the British think I could be the rogue agent."

"Haven't you proved yourself to them?"

"Many times over."

"I get it. You need to identify this rogue agent to prove your innocence?"

"Exactly."

The professor got up, opened a door in a sideboard, and removed a bottle of Scotch. "I've been saving this. It's a fine single malt. If you don't think it's too early..."

Kurt looked at his watch. It was 2:15 in the afternoon. "Never too early for a single malt. Just a small one, thank you."

Professor Hirsch found two glasses and poured a measure into each. He handed a glass to Kurt. "Cheers." He took a sip.

"*Sláinte!*" Kurt took a mouthful. It was the best Scotch he'd ever tasted, slithering down his gullet like a warm eel.

"What do you know about this rogue spy?"

"Not much. Nothing, really. He seems to be very well-informed. He's using an unknown coding system. We have his call-sign: Lebkuchen – that's Gingerbread in English."

"How do you know his call-sign if his signals can't be deciphered?"

"I'm not sure, but his call-sign is all the boffins have come up with so far. They've nothing much to work on."

"Okay, so how do they know how well-informed he is?"

"That has come from the requests for intelligence coming back from Berlin to the other agents."

"I see." The professor finished his whisky. "Another drop?"

"No thanks, Professor. Do you still have your transmitter?"

"In the house. It hasn't been switched on for months, but I still have it, yes."

"I was hoping that I could use it. I need to communicate with my old friends in the Black Orchestra."

The professor beamed. "Of course you can use it, if you can get it to work. It'll be like old times. I have a couple of lectures. Meet me back here at six o'clock."

Chapter 30

Kurt finished his drink, thanked the professor, and wandered into Trinity College's Front Square. The place was alive with students. Kurt was too old to pass as a student, but people might think he was a lecturer – a visiting lecturer from overseas, perhaps.

He was aware of a disturbance in his stomach. Perhaps the Scotch was reacting badly to the sandwich he'd had earlier. The closer he got to the front gate the worse his symptoms grew.

His mother's flat was in Wicklow Street, no more than 400 yards from where he was standing. Gudrun could be there. He had three and a half hours to spare. A large part of him wanted to spend the time with his mother and Gudrun. But another part of him was dreading the prospect of lying to Gudrun about Lina. The alternative – telling her everything – was even more terrifying.

He spun on his heel back toward the lecture halls. Picking one at random, he opened the door and slipped inside.

A lecturer in a black gown was delivering a lecture to a roomful of second year sociology students. Kurt took a seat at the back and was soon engrossed in the various degrees of positivism and empirical methods used in sociology since its inception.

Kurt's mind wandered from the lecture topic. Where was he going to spend the night, if not at his mother's flat? His cash reserves were running low. He would probably have enough for a night in a cheap hotel, but what if he had to spend more than one night in Dublin? He liked to eat!

The frustrating thing was that when Kurt, Gudrun and Anna had first escaped from Germany, he carried a briefcase stuffed with cash. The money, close to £250,000, was given to Kurt for the IRA. It was now lying in a Dublin bank account in Gudrun's name. Kurt couldn't touch it.

The lecture was over. The students were starting to leave. He checked his watch. He still had 2 hours 45 minutes to kill. Where to next?

Outside the lecture hall, he touched a young student on the arm as she passed. "Excuse me, I'm new to these lectures. Can you tell me what's next on the timetable?"

"That depends." She smiled at him. "What's your major subject?"

"I don't have one. I mean, I'm visiting from another university. I'm just playing it by ear, you know?"

"Oh, okay. Why don't you follow me? My next lecture is on societal structures."

Kurt tagged along. He found the second session more rewarding than the first. Marxism was the main topic of the day. Unfortunately, he had missed all the earlier sessions, covering Fascism in Spain and the Third Reich.

After that lecture, Kurt's young companion took him to the campus café where they shared a pot of tea. Kurt had to pay, further depleting his meagre finances.

Her name was Tammi, aged 25, a blond from America. When she asked about Kurt's background, he supplied the bare minimum, heavily edited. She was happy with those few morsels. She told him all about herself, her father, who was a teacher, her brothers, and her three flatmates. She smiled a lot, touching his arm several times as she spoke.

The third lecture was on social policy. Kurt had difficulty keeping his eyes open during that one. By the end of that lecture it was too late to call in to his mother's flat.

"Where are you staying?" she said.

"I haven't arranged anything yet. I'll find a small hotel somewhere. Could you recommend one?"

She laughed. "You could stay with us, if you don't mind sharing with four girls. The flat's not far away, and we have a spare bed you could use."

Kurt was tempted, but he declined politely. "You're very kind, but I have a lot of paperwork to do."

She shrugged. "Will I see you here again tomorrow or in the next few days?"

"Maybe, I'm not sure. If I come back I'll look out for you."

Kurt made his way back to the Mathematics department where Professor Hirsch was waiting for him. He took Kurt to his car. Kurt remembered the car, a dinky little green Riley, barely wide enough inside for two adults. The interior was freezing. They sat together like sardines in a tin for a few minutes while the professor cranked up the heater.

Kurt's mind was flooded with memories as they approached the professor's old house and barn, standing in isolation in the middle of a field. Beside the house there was a lake, complete with ducks and a rowboat tethered to a pole. Apart from the 'for sale' sign at the gate, nothing had changed in two years.

The professor smiled at the expression on Kurt's face. "You remember the old place, I see."

"Difficult to forget it, Professor. Is it as damp as it used to be?"

"It's much worse. We had a couple of really bad floods. I've had to abandon the house altogether. It's a wreck. I've been sleeping in my digs in college for well over a year."

"You're selling the house?"

"That's the general idea, but who would buy a derelict old mansion in the middle of a floodplain?"

Kurt began to feel queasy. Could the professor have forgotten about the Gestapo man's body in the lake? What if somebody bought the house and drained it?

The professor parked the car, and they entered the house.

The place reeked of mould. The walls were black with it. Mushrooms and toadstools sprouted along the skirting boards. The professor led the way up the staircase. "Watch where you place your feet, Kurt. Some of the steps are rotten. It's not really too safe anymore."

They made it to the top of the stairs and into the bedroom without mishap. The professor opened a wardrobe and pulled out his radio transmitter.

"You have electricity, I hope." Kurt tried the light switch and the light came on.

The professor plugged the transmitter into a socket. "I'm still paying the bill."

Kurt pulled Blesset's code book from his pocket. The professor provided pencil and paper, and Kurt encoded his message.

"What's your transmission schedule?" the professor asked.

"I don't have one. I'm just hoping someone will be listening."

"In Berlin?"

"Yes, or Hamburg."

Kurt keyed his signal into the ether. After he'd keyed in the *Ende* character, he was greatly relieved to receive a confirmation code back.

"Are you expecting a fast reply?" said the professor.

"That depends on where the signal was received and who decodes it. It may take some time to reach its intended target."

"They will know who sent it?"

"If it gets to the right people, yes. I used my old call-sign."

"I'll put a kettle on," said the professor.

Chapter 31

When the professor returned with two hot cups, Kurt was still huddled over the radio set.

"Any response?"

"Nothing yet. I expect it'll take a while."

"Who are you trying to contact?"

"Oberst von Neumann, ideally, or failing him, Hauptmann von Pfaffel on the Britain desk."

Professor Hirsch handed Kurt a cup. "Kaltenbrunner is the nominal head of the Abwehr since the admiral was suspended. The new man in charge in Berlin is Leopold Bürkner. Do you know him?"

Kurt shook his head. "No, I don't think he was there in my time. Who is he?"

"He was in charge of liaison between the Abwehr and the OKW. He's very well connected with senior SS figures. If it hadn't been for his deep connections and wide influence, Walter Schellenberg would be running the Abwehr by now."

Kurt remembered Schellenberg from his time in the Abwehr in Berlin. Everyone in the security services knew him as a slippery eel with an infallible instinct for survival. "I thought Kaltenbrunner took over Reinhard Heydrich's job," said Kurt.

"He did, but Schellenberg heads up the SD-Ausland, and he will not rest until he has control over the Abwehr. He has already blown every Abwehr agent in Switzerland. He handed their names to the head of Swiss security."

"That's high treason," said Kurt.

"Nevertheless, that's what he did, probably under Himmler's direct orders. He has a private line direct to Himmler's desk." The professor grinned. "For that alone, Kaltenbrunner hates him."

Kurt sipped his tea. There was no sugar. It was strong and tart, but the aroma masked the reek of mould from the walls. "I suppose there's no hope for Generalmajor Oster."

"None, or Admiral Canaris either. The SS will take their revenge on those two, as well as many other true German patriots."

Kurt said, "You're well informed for someone living outside the conflict areas."

The professor touched the side of his nose. "I still have some friends in Germany."

"How do you keep in touch with them?"

The radio transmitter burst into life. Kurt scribbled down the Morse characters as they arrived. When the incoming signal ended, he keyed in the confirmation and switched off the set. Then he set about deciphering the incoming signal. When he'd completed it, it read, in translation:

EXPECT REPLY IN TWELVE HOURS BERLIN

"What's the matter, Kurt?"

"I have to wait 12 hours for a reply to my question."

"That's okay, surely," said the professor. "You didn't expect an instant response, did you?"

"No, but I've nowhere to stay and very little money left."

"Doesn't your mother live in Dublin? And your girl?"

"Yes, they do, but I'm not ready to talk to them yet..."

The professor stared at Kurt in disbelief.

"Don't ask, Professor, it's complicated."

The professor slapped him on the back. "That's no problem. You can stay with me. I have a spare room in my digs at Trinity College. Switch off the set. We'll take it with us." Rummaging in a cupboard, the professor found a mouldy old suitcase. They stuffed the radio inside and Kurt carried it to the car.

#

The professor's digs were in building 9, Front Square. They struggled to carry the heavy suitcase up the stairs to the third floor, knocking it against the walls as they went.

The rooms were comfortable, if a little cramped. They set up the radio on the living room table, and Kurt switched it on. He was anxious to check that it was still working after its bruising journey up the stairs.

"Everything okay?" said the professor.

The radio was humming loudly. "As far as I can tell, but we won't know for definite until we receive an incoming signal."

The professor showed Kurt into the spare bedroom. Small, but functional, it had all the basics: a single bed, a wardrobe, a chair and writing desk, and on the windowsill, a 7-stem menorah. The view from the window took Kurt back to his student days. Trinity College was at its mystical best in the quiet of the evenings when the mass of students were gone, and only the residents moved about a front square bathed in weak, diffused light from the ancient lamps.

"Come on," said the professor. "I know a place where we can eat in comfort."

They climbed back down the three flights of stairs. The temperature had dropped a couple of degrees and a heavy drizzle had taken over Front Square.

The professor turned his collar up. "It's not far. Follow me."

A few blocks up Dame Street, the professor turned left into Dame Lane and ducked through a green door. Kurt could see nothing on or near the door to indicate that food was served inside.

The girl who took their coats didn't look like a waitress. She greeted the professor like an old friend, planting kisses on both of his cheeks. Then she led them through a bead curtain to a compact dining room. She showed them to a corner table, handed them menus, and left.

Kurt looked around. "What's this place called? Is it new?" Of the six tables in the room, three were unoccupied. Two skimpily dressed waitresses drifted around the room.

The professor gave him a thin smile. "It's called the Unicorn. I believe it's been here, in one guise or another, since the Stone Age. Didn't you come here as a student?"

"No, I've never been here before." He ran his eyes over the menu. "What would you recommend?"

"The jugged hare is excellent."

"Sounds good."

The professor raised a finger, and a waitress shimmied over to the table. He ordered two plates of jugged hare and a bottle of Beaujolais.

When the wine arrived, the waitress poured a little into Kurt's glass and waited for him to taste it. He took a mouthful.

"It's delicious, thank you."

The waitress topped up Kurt's glass and filled Professor Hirsch's. A few moments later, she returned with the food.

When they were alone again, Kurt asked the professor how long his house had been up for sale.

"It's been on the market for about 18 months, but I've had very few potential purchasers. I expect someone will knock it down some day and build a department store in the field."

"They'd have to drain the lake."

"Probably, but you and I will be long gone by then." The professor took a slug from his glass.

After that, they both gave their full attention to their food. Within 15 minutes, both plates were littered with small bones.

Kurt sat back in his chair with a sigh of contentment. "That was delicious."

The professor wiped his mouth with his napkin. He topped up their glasses. "Now tell me what you've been doing since we last spoke."

"Working for the British. I can't give you any specifics."

"Good man. I'm sure everything you've done has furthered the aims and traditions of the Black Orchestra. The Third Reich will soon fall."

"You really think so?"

His eyes sparkled. "I'm certain of it. How can such evil endure with good men like you working against it?"

Kurt wasn't sure if the professor was making fun of him. "Sometimes I wonder... I mean... I've seen terrible things... sights that made me question..."

The professor took another mouthful of wine, emptying his glass.

"Tell me, Professor, don't you ever have doubts?"

The professor poured himself another glassful. "About bringing down the Third Reich?"

Kurt nodded. "Sometimes I wonder if both sides are as bad as each other."

"How can you say that?"

"If you'd seen the RAF bombing of Hamburg you'd understand. The destruction was horrific. Thousands of civilians were incinerated."

The professor's eyes narrowed. "You must be aware of the Holocaust."

Kurt lowered his voice. "I've heard stories, Professor. It's difficult to believe some of them, they sound so extreme."

"They are all true, Kurt. Hundreds of thousands of Jews have been murdered by death squads in Poland and in Nazi concentration camps. Perhaps millions. We won't know the full extent of the slaughter until the War ends. You know I have Jewish blood?"

Kurt looked at him. "No, I didn't know that, but I noticed the menorah on the windowsill. Is it a family heirloom?"

"My maternal great-grandfather was a Jewish merchant in Barcelona. He and his family converted to Christianity during the pogroms of fifteenth century Spain. I picked up the menorah in a pawn shop last summer." The professor pushed his plate away from him. "There's a new word in the English language for the Nazi pogrom. They're calling it 'genocide', the elimination of an entire race." He shook his head. "You must never doubt that you are on the right side."

The waitress came over and began to clear the table.

"Thank you, Theresa," said the professor.

"Madeline would like a word with you, Professor," she replied. "She said to remind you that you have unfinished business."

The professor slapped his belly and laughed loudly. "Well we mustn't disappoint Madeline, must we? Tell her I'll be along in two shakes."

He tossed his keys to Kurt. "You go on back to college. I'll be along eventually. Don't wait up for me."

Back at the professor's rooms, Kurt used the bathroom.

He couldn't look at himself in the mirror. He'd wasted the whole afternoon, throwing away a golden opportunity to spend time with his beloved Gudrun and his mother. Instead, he'd spent the time with a charming young student. Tammi was obviously attracted to him. She'd been helpful and kind, and he'd repaid her kindness with a pack of lies.

Was he really going to avoid all contact with Gudrun while he was in Dublin? What was he afraid of? He was such a lily-livered spineless chicken!

Chapter 32

Tuesday February 29, 1944

By 6:55 a.m. the following morning, Kurt and his host had polished off a light breakfast of the professor's homemade muesli, the radio receiver was humming, and Kurt was sitting beside it ready to record any incoming signals. At 7:02 the set burst into life. Kurt wrote down the Morse characters as they arrived. After the *Ende* character, he responded with the *Confirm* and set about decoding the signal. When he'd finished, he translated it into English:

AVENIDA PALACE LISBON ELEVEN AM MARCH FIVE EVN

Kurt's heart was pounding in his chest. EVN must surely be Oberst Erwin von Neumann, the head of the Abwehr overseas espionage operations, a leading member of the Black Orchestra.

He showed the signal to the professor.

The professor handed it back. "You've certainly got their attention. But how are you going to get to Lisbon by March 5?"

"By flying boat? That was how Gudrun, Anna and I got to Dublin from Hamburg in '42."

"You travelled as diplomatic staff, didn't you? That was what made all the difference. Every seat on those planes is accounted for, Kurt. Only urgent military trips and diplomatic officials can use them."

"I have money. Can't I buy a seat on a flight?"

Kurt was broke, but Gudrun had access to that £250,000 in an Irish bank account.

"Not a hope," said the professor. "All the money in the world wouldn't buy a seat on one of those flights. You'll need a good reason to fly, or a diplomatic passport."

Kurt's heart rate increased. "I'm going to have to find a way. I have to make that meeting on March 5."

Professor Hirsch scratched his head. Then he gave Kurt a name. "There's only one man I know that might be able to help you. His name's Liam Diskin."

"Where do I find this Liam Diskin?"

"He lives in the Iveagh Flats, near the south quays. Ask anyone there, they all know him. If you do manage to get your hands on the right papers, you'll need to book your ticket in Hewitts the travel agency. Their offices are directly across the road from Front Square."

Kurt shook hands with the professor at the door.

"If you do get to Lisbon, watch your back," said the professor. "The city is a hotbed of spies – from all sides."

Kurt thanked him and set out on foot for the River Liffey.

The Iveagh Flats building in Kevin Street was looking the worse for wear, its sturdy redbrick exterior scarred with soot from domestic fires and grey dust rising from a nearby building site. A plaque on the wall said it had been erected in 1892, funded by a charitable endowment from the Guinness family.

A chaos of children surrounded Kurt as he entered the courtyard, lines of washing hung high above, and fat pigeons strutted about everywhere. Fascinated by the appearance of a tall, dark stranger in their midst, the children dogged his steps.

"I'm looking for Liam Diskin," said Kurt with a smile.

"He lives in number 38," a young boy replied.

"He's not there, but," said a girl.

"He is too," said the boy.

The girl stuck out her tongue at the boy. "Isn't. I saw him leave early this morning."

"Where did he go?" said Kurt.

The children looked at each other in silent conference.

A second boy piped up, "He's prob'ly gone to see Charlie."

"Charlie's his son," said the girl to Kurt. "He has a flat over the north side somewhere."

"No he doesn't," said the first boy, and another argument started.

Scattering the pigeons as he walked, Kurt reached one of the entrances, found a diagram of the building, and checked for flat 38. It was on the second floor. As soon as he put a foot on the staircase, the children all ran past him up the stairs, shouting to one another.

By the time Kurt reached the second floor, the children had all vanished. He knocked on the door of flat 38.

The door was opened by a woman in a linen apron, carrying a

dishcloth. "The kids tell me you're looking for Liam. Well, you're out of luck. He's not here. He's away on business. You'd best come back on Thursday morning."

Kurt thanked her and left. The children were all back at play in the courtyard. They ignored him. He was old news now.

Thursday was cutting it fine. He had to be in Lisbon by Sunday.

Exiting the courtyard, he passed a scruffy looking individual, smoking a foul-smelling pipe. "I hear you're looking for Liam Diskin. What business do you have with him?"

"I'll discuss that with him when I see him," said Kurt, walking away.

The man called after him, "Please yourself, but I reckon you won't see him before the weekend."

Kurt stopped and strode back. He couldn't wait that long. "I need to get to Lisbon in a hurry. I was told Liam could help."

"When you say 'in a hurry' what do you mean?"

"I need to get there by noon on Sunday."

"Oh, Liam would be your man, all right, if he was here," said the man. "But I know someone else who might be able to help. Tell me what you had in mind."

"I'm told the seats on the flying boats are reserved for diplomatic staff. I thought Liam might get me the right sort of passport."

"You can pay?"

"Yes. Can you help?"

"I told you, I know someone. He can do anything for a price. It'll cost you, though."

"How much?"

The man puffed on his pipe, running his eyes over Kurt. "I'd say fifty should cover it. I'll take a tenner for setting it up."

Kurt sucked in a breath for dramatic effect. "That's a hell of a lot. What guarantee do I have that your friend can deliver in time?"

The man shook spittle from the stem of his pipe. "It's up to you."

"I don't have the money with me, but I can get it. I can be back with the money in a couple of hours."

"Okay, you get the money. In the meantime, I'll have a word with my friend. Meet me at this spot at midday."

#

Kurt hurried back to the town centre. On his way to Wicklow Street, he dropped in to Hewitts, the travel agency, and enquired about the times of flights to Lisbon.

The clerk peered at him with narrow eyes. "Those flights are reserved."

Kurt gritted his teeth. "I am aware of that."

The clerk shrugged his shoulders. "The flights leave at midday on Mondays and Thursdays."

"How much does the fare cost?"

"£88 each way. But you'll need the correct paperwork to get a ticket."

Kurt thanked the clerk and left the shop. Straightening his shoulders, he strode to his mother's apartment in Wicklow Street and knocked on the door.

Someone tapped him on the shoulder. "Hello there, squire."

Kurt's heart sank. "Carter, what are you doing here?"

"I'm doing my job. Where've you been for the last couple of days?"

"I've been here with my mother."

"I don't think so. I've been watching the apartment day and night."

"Perhaps you dozed off," said Kurt. "Have you been drinking?"

Carter flushed with a look like a startled chicken. "Seriously, squire, where did you go? I need something to put in my report." He placed a hand on Kurt's shoulder.

Kurt shrugged the hand off. "Make something up, Carter."

The apartment door opened. Kurt's mother stood there. It took her two seconds to register who was on her doorstep. Then she beamed and embraced her son. "My God, son, is it really you?"

He hugged her.

She stood back, opening the door wide. "Come in, come in. Gudrun will be delighted to see you. And Anna. Come in."

Kurt glanced at Carter before stepping inside. "See you later – *squire*."

A scowling Carter adjusted his hat and jammed his hands into his overcoat pockets.

"Gudrun's at work, and Anna's at school," said Mrs O'Reilly. "You'll see them both this evening. You will stay for a few days?"

"I need to talk to Gudrun, Mother. Is she still working at the German legation?"

She went to the kitchen to fill a kettle, calling out, "Yes. You do remember where that is?"

"I have to go, Mother. I'll speak to you later."

She emerged from the kitchen with a puzzled expression on her face. "Where are you going? The kettle's not boiled yet."

"Sorry, Mother, I have to find Gudrun. It's urgent." He kissed her on the cheek. "I'll try to get back by this evening."

He opened the front door. She put a hand on his back. "Dinner's at six, Kurt. I'll expect you then."

He closed the door and ran, weaving his way around the pedestrians in the streets. Carter followed him, but found the going tough, and quickly fell behind.

Kurt circled a couple of blocks, weaving in and out of small streets and narrow laneways until he was sure he'd lost his tail. Then he jumped on a southbound bus. He climbed the stairs. The upper deck was deserted. The conductor followed him up the stairs, and Kurt paid the fare.

The bus arrived at Northumberland Road within ten minutes. The trees that lined the road were stripped of their leaves, but the two parallel rows of Georgian houses looked as affluent as ever. Kurt rang the doorbell of the German legation at number 58.

A voice answered on an intercom, "Yes, can I help you?"

Kurt couldn't tell whether the voice was male or female.

"I am a German citizen," said Kurt in German. "Please open the door."

"I'm sorry, sir," the voice replied. "The legation doesn't open to the public until 11 a.m. Do you have an appointment?"

"I'm here to see Gudrun von Sommerfeld. It's urgent."

After a long pause, the voice said, "Are you a relative of the Fräulein's?"

"I am her fiancé. She will want to speak with me."

The door opened. The voice belonged to a slim figure dressed in tweed. Kurt was still unsure if this was a man or a woman. The features were too fine for a man, but the hair was too short for a woman. The physique could have been male or female.

"Thank you, Herr..."

"This way," said the official.

Gudrun was sitting at a desk in a warm office, hunched over a document. A flood of memories washed over Kurt: the garden party where they first met, their first night together... their last night together in a hotel in London. Within seconds, the flame of his passion for her reignited, burning bright within him. And there was the shame for his betrayal, now crushing his soul. How could he have forgotten that face?

"Fräulein, there's a visitor here to see you," said the official.

Gudrun leapt to her feet, scattering her papers everywhere. "Kurt!" She ran to him and flung her arms around his neck. The official slipped away.

They embraced silently. Fleeting images of Lina taunted him. Their affair was so hollow and sordid. His shame deepened, turning into a worm of guilt stirring below his ribcage.

"I missed you, Kurt. Have you just arrived? How long can you stay? Are you still living in London? What have you been doing? Why haven't you been writing?"

"I've been very busy, working for the Allies." He rubbed a knuckle across an eyelid. "How's Anna?"

She smiled at him. "Anna's fine. She never stops talking about you, asking when we'll see you again. She'll be very happy to see you."

"I can't stay long, Gudrun. There's something I must do."

"For the British?"

"For the War. I need some money."

Gudrun reached for her purse. "How much? I have nearly £6, but I can go to the bank tomorrow..."

"I need £160, Gudrun, and I need it today."

She covered her mouth with her hand. "You want me to take £160 from that other account? We agreed never to touch that money. It's tainted."

"Yes, I know, but it's in a good cause. There's every chance that what I'm doing will help the Allies win the War."

She put her coat on. She made her excuses to the official, and they left the legation together.

They took a bus to O'Connell Street. Gudrun went into the Royal Bank of Ireland, presented her identity papers to the teller and asked for £160 in cash. The teller called the manager. The manager led her to an inner office. Twenty minutes later, she emerged with the cash in a couple of envelopes.

"What a palaver!" She handed the cash to Kurt.

He tucked the envelopes into his jacket pockets. "I have to go, but I'll try to get back to the flat this evening."

He left, hurrying toward the River Liffey, without looking back.

Chapter 33

He arrived back at the Iveagh Flats at 12:30 p.m.

The scruffy man was waiting for him, puffing on his pipe. "You're late. You have the money?"

"I have it."

"Right, so. Give me my ten."

Kurt took out one of the envelopes, removed two £5 notes, and handed them over.

The man tucked the cash into his pocket. "Follow me." He set out at a rapid pace to the north, through a part of the city Kurt had never visited before. After 15 minutes, Pipe Man dodged into an alley.

Kurt began to feel uneasy. "Where are we going?"

"Wait here," said the man, taking a couple of steps backwards. "My friends will make contact."

A tingling sensation on Kurt's scalp was sending him urgent warning signals. He turned to leave the alley and found two burly individuals blocking his path. The bigger of the two looked like a bull, with a neck as wide as the trunk of a tree, and clenched fists for hooves.

The second man held out a grubby hand. "Hand over the cash and you won't get hurt."

Kurt ducked his head and threw himself forward, aiming for the narrow space between the two men. The big guy swung a wild fist that connected with Kurt's nose. Kurt's left shoulder bounced off the big man. His right shoulder hit the second man in the midriff. Not a significant contact, but enough to knock him off balance. The bull made a grab for Kurt from behind. Kurt kicked backwards, connecting solidly with his genitals. The big man went down with a groan.

The second man squared off with raised fists. Kurt got the first blow in – a decent cross to the cheekbone – followed by a fist in the gut. The man retaliated, catching Kurt on the side of his head with a blow that knocked Kurt to his knees. The man smiled and took a step back.

Kurt got to his feet quickly. Then he caught the flash of a blade in the man's left hand. The man with the pipe joined the fray, grabbing Kurt in a bear hug from behind. "Go on, Jonjo, stick him."

The knife man – Jonjo – took a step forward, drawing his knife arm back. Kurt pivoted quickly, putting all his weight into the manoeuvre. The thrust of the knife glanced off his jacket. The pipe man screamed, lost his grip and slipped from Kurt's back. The knife man swore, looking in wide-eyed horror at his knife buried in his friend's lower back. Without another word, he took to his heels. The bull struggled to his knees with an angry roar. Kurt poleaxed him with a swift kick to the head. The pipe man lay in a growing pool of his own blood. Kurt checked for a pulse, before running from the scene.

He stopped at the first public telephone he came to, and called for an ambulance for the injured man. When the operator asked for his name, he hung up and ran back to the centre of town.

He was winded by the time he arrived at Wicklow Street. Carter was nowhere to be seen. Kurt hammered on the door of the flat. Mrs O'Reilly opened it, and he fell inside.

"What happened to you, Kurt?" His mother glared at him, hands on her hips. "Your nose is bleeding and you have the makings of a black eye. I hope you haven't been in a fight."

Kurt went into the bathroom to clean up. He locked the door. The nosebleed was nothing but a trickle, but his left eye was swollen and well on its way to a shiner. He dabbed it with cold water and cleaned the blood from his upper lip.

The knife had opened a new pocket in his jacket. There was nothing he could do about that.

When he emerged from the bathroom, his mother handed him a cup of tea and a newspaper. "We'll say no more about it, Kurt." The bewildered expression on her face stirred vague long-forgotten memories from his childhood.

He hung his jacket on the back of a chair, and sat by the fire, sipping his tea. He dozed off.

He was wakened by Anna jumping onto his lap with a screech. "Papa, you've come home!"

Kurt liked the way she called him 'Papa'. He wrapped his arms around her and held her tight. "Did you miss me?"

She nodded solemnly. "What happened to your face, Papa?"

"I was in a fight with three men."

Anna's eyes opened wide. "I bet you beat them all."

"I did. I punched them and they ran away."

Mrs O'Reilly led a complaining Anna from the room. She had homework to do. Kurt opened his newspaper and fell back to sleep almost immediately.

#

He awoke to find Anna shaking his shoulder.

Gudrun stood looking down at him with her arms crossed.

"What time is it?" he said.

"It's half-past five."

He'd slept for two and a half hours.

"What happened to you? Where did you go after you left the bank?"

"I had a business meeting."

"A business meeting. Hah! Have you looked in the mirror recently?"

Kurt touched his eye. "It got a bit rough."

"Do you still have the money?" Gudrun patted his jacket pockets.

"Yes, most of it. I have to meet someone else tomorrow morning. I'm hoping I'll have more luck then."

"You've torn your jacket! What are these meetings about, Kurt? I wish you'd tell me. I might be able to help."

Kurt shook his head. "It'll all be sorted by tomorrow."

"You'll be leaving us again after that?"

"Yes, there's something I must do."

Anna wrapped her arms around his neck.

Mrs O'Reilly put a meal on the table. During the meal and afterwards, Kurt devoted his full attention to Anna. The young girl spoke in German and English with equal fluency. She showed him her doll's house and what she'd been working on in school. She introduced him to her dolls.

After two hours, Gudrun put Anna to bed. They turned the radio on in time to catch the late news. A man had been stabbed with a knife in a laneway in north Dublin. He was in a serious condition in the Mater hospital. The police were appealing for witnesses.

"How terrible," said Mrs O'Reilly, and she retired to her bedroom.

Gudrun and Kurt were alone. She added a log to the fire and sat on the floor by Kurt's legs. "You're on leave?"

"I have a 7-day pass."

"When did you arrive in the country? You came in on the mailboat, I suppose?"

"Yes. I landed a couple of days ago."

"Your friend told me it was Sunday last."

"My friend?"

"Humphrey Carter."

"When did you meet Carter?"

"Yesterday. He introduced himself. Your mother gave him tea. Charming man."

"He's not a friend. British Intelligence sent him to keep an eye on me."

"Why would they need to do that?"

"Some of them don't trust me."

"After all you've done for them, they still don't trust you?"

Kurt shrugged. "I'm German."

The fire flared, spitting a glowing splinter onto the rug. Gudrun picked it up quickly between finger and thumb and threw it back. "What has your life been like in London?"

"Pretty dull, really. I have an unchanging routine, the same procedure every day. Sometimes I wonder if I'm making any real contribution."

"You live alone over there?"

Kurt's heart skipped a beat. Could Carter have told Gudrun about Lina? Had British Intelligence been watching him in London?

"Yes, of course." He rubbed a knuckle across his uninjured eyelid.

Gudrun stared into the fire. "I wouldn't blame you if you found someone, Kurt. I know how miserable it can be living on your own in a strange country."

Kurt said nothing.

Chapter 34

Wednesday morning March 1, 1944

In the morning, Gudrun left for work. Kurt headed out for the Iveagh Flats. Walking briskly, his feet barely touching the ground, he covered the distance in no time. A night with Gudrun had given him a new vigour, a new sense of purpose, and a renewed passion for the woman he loved.

The Iveagh Flats appeared deserted. Where were all the children? Even the pigeons had vanished. High above his head the washing still hung on the lines, and there were the pigeons, fluttering about from windowsill to windowsill in the blinding morning sunshine.

He knocked on the door of flat number 38. A man opened it.

"Liam Diskin?" said Kurt.

"Who wants to know?"

Diskin was of slight build with a shiny bald pate and a tonsure of grey hair. He held a fork in one hand.

"Sorry to disturb your meal, Mr Diskin, but I need your help."

Diskin squinted at him. "Who the divil are you?"

"My name's O'Reilly. I need to get to Lisbon in the next few days. I need paperwork to get on board the flying boat."

Diskin's face lit up. "You'll be needing a diplomatic passport and a letter of authorization. That can be arranged. You have money?"

"I have £50."

"It'll cost a hundred. Do you have that much?"

"I can get it."

Diskin slipped the fork into his breast pocket. "When do you need this by?"

"I have to get to Lisbon by next Sunday."

Diskin gave this some thought. "You need the Thursday flight, so. That's very tight, but it should be possible. You get the money. I'll set up a photo session and make the other arrangements. Wait here for a minute." He stepped away from the door. When he returned, he handed Kurt a piece of paper. "Meet me at this address at 7 o'clock this evening. Bring the money with you."

"All of it?"

"All of it." Diskin closed the door.

Kurt took a bus back to the German legation and rang the doorbell. It was 10:30 a.m., but the same androgynous official let him in and took him to Gudrun's office. Gudrun was at her desk, a tall, blond individual leaning over her, scanning a document.

She looked up, and the blond guy straightened his back.

"Kevin, this is Jürgen."

The blond guy held out a hand. Kurt shook it.

"Give us a minute, Jürgen," she said. Jürgen left the room, closing the door behind him.

When they were alone, Kurt said, "Who's he?"

Her cheeks flushed. "Jürgen's a junior attaché. Forget him. Why have you come back?"

"I need another £50."

Gudrun's eyes opened wide in alarm. "Don't tell me you lost the money I gave you."

"No, I still have it. It's not enough."

Frowning, she said, "What's the money for?"

"I can't tell you that."

"I can't take any more time off." She looked at the clock. "You'll have to wait until lunchtime."

"Don't the banks close for lunch?"

"They do. I'll take an early lunch." She showed him to a waiting room, left him there, and closed the door.

Hearing voices in the corridor, Kurt opened the door and caught a glimpse of Jürgen returning to Gudrun's office. He closed the door again, selected an armchair, and picked up a magazine.

#

Gudrun opened the door at 12:35 p.m., pulling her coat on. "I wish you'd tell me what this is all about."

Kurt made no response.

They hailed a taxi, got back to the bank in O'Connell Street, and slipped inside, just as the doors were closing.

The bank teller looked even more startled than before. He called a supervisor who led Gudrun into the manager's office again. The bureaucracy took longer than the last time, but she emerged with two more envelopes. "I hope this is the end of it, Kurt. You wouldn't believe the inquisition I've had to go through to get this money."

He took £100 from one of the envelopes and gave it back to her. "Look after this for me. I'll need it later. Keep it safe until I ask for it."

She tucked the money into her handbag.

They had lunch in a café in Marlborough Street, not far from the bank. The place was busy and they had to queue. Gudrun ordered a baked potato stuffed with cheese. Kurt wasn't quite so hungry. He asked for a plate of plain fried potato slices. The waiter took a coupon from Gudrun's ration book and two from Kurt's British ration book.

When Kurt objected, the waiter shrugged. "There's a war on."

They found a vacant table near the door.

"Tell me about this Jürgen," he said.

Gudrun kept her eyes on her food. "There's nothing to tell. He's a junior diplomat. He does all the fetching and carrying."

"Where's he from? And how old is he?"

"He's from Munich. He's a little older than you. I'd guess maybe about 35."

"You haven't asked him his age?"

"No, why should I?"

"I don't know. You work closely together."

"Not that closely." She squinted at him. "What are you implying?"

"Nothing. I'm not implying anything, Gudrun, but..."

"But what?"

"He seemed a little overfriendly for a work colleague."

They finished the meal in silence.

As they stepped into the street, Gudrun said, "You know I love you, Kurt, but it's been lonely here without you."

Was that a confession?

Kurt let it go. He wrapped his arms around her and held her close. "I'm sorry, Gudrun, I didn't mean to upset you."

She buried her face in his shoulder and sniffed.

He stroked her hair. "I love you too."

She raised her head. There were tears in her eyes. "That's the first time you've said that in a long, long time."

Kurt hailed a taxi. He dropped Gudrun off at the legation before heading back to his mother's flat in Wicklow Street.

\#

As darkness fell that evening, he left the flat, climbed into a taxi, and handed the driver the address Diskin had given him.

The taxi driver looked at the piece of paper and scratched his head. "You're sure this is the right address? This is in the docks. There'll be no one there at this time of night."

"I'm certain," said Kurt.

The taxi took him to an industrial area of hulking, darkened buildings, and drew up outside a warehouse within sight and smell of the Liffey. A vicious wind from the river sliced through Kurt's clothing, sending shivers up his legs and spine.

"Wait here for me," said Kurt.

The driver held out a hand. "Sorry, but I have another customer waiting."

Kurt paid him, and the taxi sped off in a cloud of dust. Kurt wrapped his arms around his chest. He would have to walk back to the centre of the city, but dead reckoning told him it was no more than a couple of miles.

He tried the warehouse door. It swung open, and he stepped inside.

Chapter 35

Wednesday March 1, 1944

It was day seven of the murder investigation. In his office in Scotland Yard, Inspector Underwood leafed through the file again. The first two photographs were of the murder victims. Both had been slaughtered like sheep. There was a lot of blood.

The first victim, James Dennison, Lance Corporal (ret'd), aged 62, was a married man with no children. He had served in North Africa. Invalided out of the army in 1942, he had spent nearly a year in Queen Alexandra's Military Hospital, Millbank under 'psychological rehabilitation'. He applied to return to his unit as soon as he was released from hospital, but his application was turned down. Undaunted, he had volunteered for duty as a Home Facilities guard.

The inspector shook his head. What a brave man. With serving men like that, the outcome of the War was never in doubt. As for Home Facilities, that was certainly an invention of the Secret Intelligence people to cover their home espionage activities.

The second victim, Doris Pettigrew, was a 66-year-old widow, a cook/housekeeper. She had lived with her daughter in Hammersmith. The inspector was certain that she was killed simply because she witnessed the guard's killing.

The third photograph on the file was of the prime suspect. The inspector's investigation team had uncovered absolutely nothing about Henry Pollinger: no birth record, no school history, and nothing on any armed services records for the past War or the present one. The man was obviously some sort of spy. Which probably explained how he'd managed to disappear so effectively.

The inspector pounded the top of his desk with a closed fist. His job was difficult enough without the obstruction he'd been getting from the Intelligence Services. Every question he'd asked was batted down with 'need to know', 'official secrets' or the catchall, 'the interests of national security'.

The fourth photograph in the file was a grainy picture of a shifty looking Irishman. Inspector Underwood peered at the picture. He was convinced that this Kevin O'Reilly knew more than he had admitted so far.

The next two pictures showed Gregory Ellis and Jack Reed, two more shady characters. None of the three had been picked out in the identity parade. That proved nothing, of course. As the witness had said, it was dark. All he could make out was two men leaving the scene of the crime.

The last picture on the file was of one Clarence Newton. The investigation had established a number of connections between Dennison and Newton. The two men were from the same infantry unit, and had served together in North Africa. Both had spent time in Millbank Military Hospital, and both were now Home Facilities guards. But, most important of all, Clarence Newton had returned from the fighting to find his wife was having an affair with his friend, James Dennison.

It was the one and only positive lead that he had.

#

On the morning of her first date with Jan de Groot, Lina got up early. She took a bath in four inches of water. Then she tied her hair in a double Dutch braid, something she hadn't done in six years.

The nurses at the hospital teased her mercilessly when they saw it. "Why don't you wear clogs while you're at it?" they said.

Lina ignored their taunts. She could have pointed out how practical Dutch clogs were in a busy work situation, but she said nothing.

The Luftwaffe had been busy again, and she had lots of work to do in her horrible office. Just for once, she was grateful for the isolation, although the atmosphere in the basement continued to send shivers up and down her spine. Her upcoming date with her new friend gave her all the comfort she needed to get through the day. How the other nurses would envy her if they knew!

Lina and Jan met in the evening in a quiet bistro off Fleet Street. Under her woollen overcoat, she wore her green dress and her new matching hat. Jan looked impressive in his 3-piece suit and trilby.

He gasped as she removed her coat and hat to hand them to the cloakroom attendant. "I haven't seen a hairstyle like that since I escaped from the Netherlands. It's beautiful, and it suits you."

He beamed at her, and she blushed. "I'm glad you like it."

The food choices were limited, but the meal passed in a whirl of shared enjoyment and conversation. He walked her to the door of her flat in Radipole Road, where he raised his hat, kissed her on the cheek, and said, *"Goede nacht."*

She opened the door. "Aren't you coming in for a nightcap?"

He hesitated. Then the air raid sirens started in the distance, and he stepped inside.

#

When she awoke in the morning, he was gone. She washed and dressed in a daze. Floating on a cloud, she took the Tube to the hospital, and smiling to herself, she took the elevator to her cold office in the basement.

It was an hour before her feet touched the ground. When she tried to recall their conversations, all she could remember was a few snatches – had he said he worked for the Foreign Office? She remembered everything she'd said. She must have sounded to him like a total chatterbox. She resolved to speak as little as possible, to listen to what he had to say on their next date.

Chapter 36

Thursday March 2, 1944

Kurt opened his eyes, but they refused to focus. He was lying on his back in a bed in bright sunshine. His head hurt. He blinked, but everything remained blurred.

"Hello, squire."

Carter.

"Where am I?"

"You're in hospital. How are you feeling?"

"What happened?"

"Your friends hit you over the head and gave you a black eye."

Someone held his wrist. "How are you feeling, Kevin?" A female voice.

"My head hurts." He moved his hand to touch his head and discovered a drip attached to his arm.

"Can you see me?" she said.

"Not really. Just a shape. Are you wearing blue and white?"

"Yes, that's very good."

She took his blood pressure and stuck a thermometer in his mouth.

Kurt tried to sit up and was struck by a wave of vertigo.

"Please lie still, Kevin."

"What time is it?"

"It's eight o'clock in the morning," said Carter.

"What day is it?" He tried to sit up, and was rewarded by a shaft of pain in his head.

"It's Thursday," said the nurse. "Please lie still. I've sent for the doctor."

Kurt lay back on the pillow.

"Can you remember what happened?" she said.

Kurt searched his memory, but nothing came to him beyond stepping through the warehouse door.

He shook his head carefully. "I remember nothing, Nurse. What's wrong with my eyes?"

She patted him on the arm. "The blow to your head has affected your vision. It will repair itself in time. Talk to the doctor about that. He'll be along in a moment." She left.

Carter said, "I think they meant to kill you. There was one ruffian with a switchblade. Luckily, I found you in time."

"You were there? You saved me?"

"It was nothing. They ran away when they saw me."

"I'm grateful, Carter." Kurt closed his eyes.

Carter was silent for a couple of minutes. Kurt thought he must have left. Then he spoke. "What were you doing in that warehouse anyway, Kevin?"

Kurt kept his eyes closed.

"I reckon you were trying to buy a gun. Am I right?"

Kurt said nothing.

"What were you planning to do with a gun? Whatever is going on, I wish you'd tell me. I could probably help."

Kurt replied without opening his eyes. "You've done enough already, Carter. I'm grateful, thank you."

Carter was silent for a few moments. Then he squeezed Kurt's arm. "Look after yourself, squire." And he left.

When the doctor arrived, he shone a light into Kurt's eyes. "I expect you're feeling a bit groggy. Just relax, let your body repair itself. You'll soon get your vision back."

"How soon, Doctor?"

"That's difficult to say. It could take a few days, a week, maybe. Count yourself lucky that your skull wasn't fractured."

A week! Whatever chance he had of making the rendezvous with Oberst von Neumann was now gone.

#

Kurt's mother and Anna came to visit him in the evening.

He detected a note of disapproval in his mother's voice. "I came as soon as I heard. I've spoken to the doctor. He says you're not seriously injured. You should make a full recovery."

"My eyesight is affected. I can barely see you."

"The nurse tells me you will get your vision back. You just have to rest. Is there anything I need to do? Should I contact someone in

London to tell them you'll be late reporting back?"

"I expect Carter will do that, Mother."

"Okay. Anything else?"

"I can't think of anything. A bunch of grapes, perhaps?"

His mother laughed.

Kurt spent some time talking with Anna. She was alarmed at the sight of the bandage on his head. His mother assured her that he would make a full recovery.

A short time after Anna and his mother had left, Gudrun arrived.

"God in heaven, Kurt, what happened?"

"I was hit over the head and robbed."

"They stole the money!"

"All but the £18 I gave you for safekeeping."

"Have you reported it to the police?"

"No, Gudrun. What could I say? I was trying to buy a forged diplomatic passport, but the forgers hit me on the head and took all my money."

"Is that what the money was for? Why do you need a forged diplomatic passport?"

"That's the only way I can get a seat on the flying boat to Lisbon."

Gudrun was quiet for a moment. "Why didn't you tell me?"

"I didn't want to get you involved."

"You should have told me, Kurt. Remember Jürgen Richter? One of his jobs is carrying the diplomatic bags to Lisbon and Madrid. He makes those journeys once or twice every week. He could carry whatever it is you need to send to Lisbon. "

"I need to go there myself to meet someone."

She hesitated. "That could be more difficult to arrange, but Jürgen might let you carry the bag to Lisbon. I'll ask him."

Kurt's heartbeat increased. "Wouldn't I need a diplomatic passport?"

"No. All you need is a letter of authorization signed by the ambassador."

"You could arrange that?"

"I think so, yes. Jürgen is a close friend."

His mind was racing. "What day is it?"

"Thursday, March the second."

Kurt swore. "I've missed today's flight. The next one leaves at midday on Monday. Could you get me that letter in time to catch that flight?"

"It's possible, Kurt, but only if Jürgen agrees."

Kurt thought he might still recover the situation if he could get there by Monday afternoon. But he needed to send another signal. He asked Gudrun to contact Professor Hirsch in the Department of Mathematics in Trinity and ask him to visit.

Gudrun kissed him on the forehead. "I hope you realise how foolish you've been," she said. "If you had told me what you wanted I could have saved you a lot of pain."

His sheepish smile confirmed the truth of her statement. Almost everything he'd done since his arrival in Ireland had been foolish.

After she'd left he wondered what she'd meant when she said Jürgen was a close friend.

#

Professor Hirsch came to visit late in the evening. Kurt heard him arguing with the duty nurse in the corridor before he gained entry.

"Hi Kurt. That dragon outside has given me five minutes. What can I do for you?"

"I need you to send another signal to our friends. You'll find the codebook under my bed. The set should still be on the correct frequency. Tell them to meet me on Tuesday March 7."

"Same location, same time?"

"Exactly."

"Your call-sign?"

"Robert. That's *RBT*."

The professor patted Kurt on the shoulder. "Rest. Get your strength back. I'll let you know if I get a response."

Chapter 37

Friday March 3, 1944

Kurt's mother came to visit him on Friday morning. She brought a bunch of flowers. The nurse put the flowers in a vase on the windowsill.

"Do you like them?" said his mother.

Kurt did his best to focus on the flowers. "Are they yellow?"

"Mostly yellow daffodils, yes, but there are some white ones. You still can't see them?"

"Not too well, but much better than yesterday."

Gudrun arrived at lunchtime. She kissed Kurt on the forehead. "I spoke to Jürgen. He has agreed to let you carry the diplomatic bag. He was reluctant at first, but I persuaded him."

Kurt wondered about the method of persuasion, but he let it pass. "On Monday?"

"Monday or Thursday, depending on how well you are."

"I'm sure I'll be well enough by Monday."

Gudrun sat on the side of the bed. "How's your head? And how are your eyes?"

"I still have a slight headache."

"How many fingers am I holding up?"

Kurt made a wild guess. "Three?"

"Two. What about now?"

"Three?"

"Four. Your eyesight's still not great, is it?"

"No, but it's getting better."

"I have to get back to work." She got up to leave. "I've asked Jürgen to pay you a visit this evening. He'll explain what to do with the bag when you get to Lisbon." She bent down and kissed him again. "I think you should aim for Thursday, Kurt."

He shook his head. "I have to go on Monday. I'm hoping to meet someone in Lisbon on Tuesday."

"Well, let's hope you're well enough by then."

#

Jürgen arrived as Kurt was finishing his evening meal. Kurt heard him arguing with a nurse before he made an appearance.

Speaking in German, he introduced himself. "Jürgen Richter, from the legation. Gudrun asked me to let you carry the diplomatic bag to Lisbon, and I've agreed."

"Thank you," said Kurt.

"You must understand that I'm taking a big risk in allowing you to do this. If, for any reason, the bag fails to arrive in the embassy, I will be in deep trouble."

"I understand," said Kurt. "You can trust me."

"I would almost certainly lose my job, my career." Jürgen sat by the bed. "First, you must tell me why you need to get to Lisbon so urgently."

Kurt's brain went into overdrive. What could he say? Jürgen was a member of the diplomatic staff of the Third Reich.

"Is the door closed?"

"Yes."

Kurt lowered his voice. "You know I'm a member of the Abwehr?"

"Gudrun mentioned something about that, but I thought you'd left."

"That's the official story. In fact, I'm still an active Abwehr agent, working within the British Intelligence Service, deep undercover, in London."

"You have proof of this?"

"Of course not. What sort of undercover spy would carry such proof around with him?"

Jürgen nodded. "I understand. What can you tell me of your need to fly to Lisbon?"

"I can tell you nothing, Jürgen. All I can say is that my mission is vital to the outcome of the War."

Frowning, Jürgen bit his lip. "Very well. You must deliver the diplomatic bag to the embassy as soon as you arrive in the city."

"Will they be suspicious when they see me?"

"I'm sure they'll be surprised, but it's not that unusual. Other people have delivered the bag on occasions in the past. As long as you show them your authorization and speak German they shouldn't be too concerned. Mention my name. You can tell them I've been ill."

"That sounds pretty simple," said Kurt. "When should I collect the bag?"

"You'll have to be at the legation at 8:30 a.m. at the latest to pick up the bag. The train to Limerick departs at 9. It gets into Limerick Junction a few minutes before 10:30. You change there for Foynes."

Kurt had not forgotten that the Irish seaplane terminal was in the Shannon estuary. He said, "What about the tickets? Will you buy them?"

"The legation will look after the tickets, and Gudrun will type up your letter of authorization. Have you ever been to Portugal? Do you speak Portuguese?"

"No."

"All you need is the word *Obrigado*. It means thank you. If you're talking to a woman, it's *Obrigada*."

"Got it," said Kurt.

#

His headache eased and his eyesight improved steadily. By Sunday evening he could see the daffodils in the vase on the windowsill. His near sight was still blurred.

Anna, Gudrun and his mother came to visit each day and stayed for the whole of visiting hours.

Mrs O'Reilly apologised for bringing him nothing to eat. To make up for this, Anna gave him a drawing she'd made of a bunch of grapes and a banana.

On Saturday morning, one of the day nurses removed the bandage from his head. A doctor examined his eyes and said, with a smile, "You're mending well. We should be able to let you go in a few days."

Carter popped in a couple of times each day, too. Kurt reckoned Carter was checking that he hadn't discharged himself from the hospital.

Professor Hirsch arrived on Sunday to say that he had transmitted Kurt's signal, but there had been no response.

"Are you certain they received it?" said Kurt.

"Yes, they acknowledged the signal. I left the set on for several hours, but there was no reply. I'm sorry, Kurt."

Gudrun paid him her last visit on Sunday evening. "Everything is ready," she said. "I've typed up your authorization letter and left it on the ambassador's desk to be signed. What should I do with the money?"

"I'll need £20. You can return the rest to the bank."

They embraced. "I'll leave £20 and your passport with Jürgen for the morning."

Chapter 38

Monday March 6, 1944

At 8 a.m. Monday morning, Kurt climbed out of his bed, removed his clothes from the bedside locker, and got dressed.

A nurse stopped him in the corridor. "Where do you think you're going, young man?"

"I'm leaving," said Kurt. "I have an urgent meeting that I cannot afford to miss."

"You're going nowhere until the doctor sees you."

"When will the doctor be here?"

"Around nine o'clock. Now please return to your room." She placed a hand firmly on his upper arm.

"I have to catch a train to Limerick at nine," said Kurt.

The nurse tightened her grip on his arm. "You can't leave the hospital until you have been properly discharged."

"Can't you discharge me?"

"Only in an emergency."

"Consider this an emergency, Nurse. Whatever happens, I'm leaving the hospital in the next ten minutes."

She released his arm, scuttled off, and returned with his chart. "How are you feeling? How's your head?"

"It's fine. Headache's all gone."

"And your vision?"

"Greatly improved."

"How many fingers can you see?"

"Three."

"All right," said the nurse. "Sign this release."

She handed him a document. Kurt could make out the heading: 'Discharge Authorization' and the name of the hospital. The rest was a blur.

"Where do I sign?"

She pointed to the bottom of the page. Kurt signed it.

"Do you have an envelope?" he said.

The nurse found him one. He wrote his London address on it, put a piece of paper inside and sealed it.

"Can you put a stamp on this and post it for me?" he said.

"No problem," said the nurse.

#

He took a taxi to the German legation in Northumberland Road, where Jürgen Richter was waiting for him. He handed Kurt his passport and letter of authorization, and gave him instructions about how to find the German embassy in Lisbon. Finally, he handed Kurt his money, his train and flight tickets, and a bulging leather case.

Kurt examined the tickets, holding them at arm's length. They allowed for an overnight stay in Lisbon. "What if I need to stay in Lisbon longer than a single day?"

Jürgen shrugged his shoulders. "In that case, I suppose you'll have to negotiate with the airline to change your ticket."

The telephone on Jürgen's desk rang. He picked it up, and put it down again. "Your taxi's here, Kevin."

Kurt thanked the young attaché for his help.

"Don't mention it." They shook hands. "Just be sure to deliver the bag to the embassy unopened."

Wearing her winter coat, Gudrun was waiting for him by the open door of the taxi. "I packed a few things for you in a suitcase." She pecked him on the cheek and they climbed into the car.

She put her head on his shoulder, holding his arm. "I couldn't let you go to Portugal with no spare underwear, and without saying goodbye."

They left the taxi at Kingsbridge station. Kurt showed his rail ticket at the barrier, and Gudrun sweet-talked her way onto the platform. They held one another until the last moment. Then they kissed one last time, Kurt lifted the diplomatic bag and his suitcase onto the train, the conductor waved his green flag and blew his whistle, and the train began to move.

Kurt stuck his head out of an open window. Gudrun waved.

"Tell Anna I love her," he shouted, but his words were drowned out by a release of steam from the engine.

#

The express train from Dublin to Limerick consisted of seven battered carriages, one first class, four second class and two third class. Kurt checked his ticket and took a seat in a second class compartment occupied by a family of five. After hauling his bags onto the overhead rack, he settled down for the journey.

The children looked him over. "What happened to your eye, Mister?" said the younger of the two boys.

Kurt put on a sombre face. "I was in a boxing match."

"Did you win?" said the older boy.

Kurt grinned. "Does it look like it?"

All the children laughed.

"Leave the man alone," said their mother. "Read your comics."

Then the compartment door slid open. "Hello, squire," said a voice.

Kurt groaned. "I thought I'd lost you, Carter."

The MI5 man stepped into the compartment and sat down heavily beside Kurt. "Is that any way to greet an old friend? Where are we off to today?"

Kurt made no reply. He closed his eyes, praying for a miracle that would spirit Carter away. When he opened them again, Carter was still there, his head buried in a copy of *The London Times*. Kurt closed his eyes again and feigned sleep. Anything to avoid conversation with Carter. The rocking of the carriage and the rhythmical clackety-clack of the wheels on the tracks soon worked their magic. Feigned sleep became real sleep.

A loud blast from the whistle woke him. Carter was playing 'I spy' with the children in the compartment. Kurt checked his watch. They were 20 minutes from Limerick Junction. He left the compartment and went in search of a toilet, taking the diplomatic bag with him. When he emerged, he found Carter leaning against a carriage window.

"What's in the bag?" said Carter.

"I've no idea," Kurt replied. "I'm transporting it for a friend."

Carter's eyebrows did the fandango. "Shouldn't you check to see what's inside, Kevin? I mean you could be carrying guns or large amounts of cash."

Kurt ignored him. He returned to his seat. Carter remained in the corridor.

A light drizzle greeted them when they got off the train at Limerick Junction. A public announcement told Kurt that the Foynes shuttle train was standing at platform 2. Making his way there, Kurt mingled with the crowd, hoping to lose his tail, but Carter stayed with him.

Just three old carriages and a locomotive made up the shuttle train to Foynes. Compared to this, the express from Dublin had been the height of luxury. Kurt and his MI5 tail boarded together.

Carter looked puzzled. "What's in Foynes?"

"It's a beauty spot on the Shannon estuary. You'll like it, I'm sure."

Carter's puzzlement gave way to a look of suspicion.

Limerick Junction to Foynes station took an hour. In Foynes, the drizzle was thicker than ever. As he left the station, Kurt caught sight of a seaplane bobbing on the water at a pier, the legend BOAC painted in tall, white letters on its fuselage.

When Carter spotted it, he realised what was going on. He stood in Kurt's way, wagging a finger in his face. "I can't let you leave Ireland."

"You have no power to stop me."

Kurt, his luggage and Carter were causing an obstruction to other passengers.

"I outrank you, Kevin. I order you in His Majesty's name, not to board that airplane." Carter hopped from foot to foot, doing his impression of a headless chicken.

"I think you're forgetting where we are," said Kurt. "This is the Irish Free State. His Majesty has no jurisdiction here."

The other passengers pushed forward then, and Carter was forced to step aside. Kurt strode to the end of the pier, where an official checked his paperwork before waving him to proceed. Kurt hoisted his luggage through the door, and climbed aboard the seaplane.

Once all the passengers were on board and the door closed, the flying boat taxied to the centre of the estuary, the 'fasten seat belts' and 'no smoking' signs were lit, the engines wound up, the airplane skipped along the crests of the waves and took off. The view from Kurt's window as it banked to the left took in a long stretch of the Atlantic coast bathed in bright sunshine. Kurt caught sight of Carter standing on the pier.

Once the plane had broken through the cloud cover it levelled off. The 'fasten seat belts' and 'no smoking' signs were switched off.

The air steward made an announcement over the address system. "Refreshments will now be served. You may smoke, but not while moving about the cabin. Thank you for flying with British Overseas

Airways Corporation, and enjoy your flight."

A young woman took the empty seat beside him.

Tammi!

Kurt was immediately suspicious. Was she another British Intelligence tail? "What are you doing on this flight? Are you following me?"

She laughed. "Of course I am."

"You're with British Intelligence? With Carter?"

She shook her head. "Who's Carter? I'm with the Americans, the OSS."

The steward offered drinks. Tammi ordered a coffee.

Kurt waved the steward away. "What possible interest could the OSS have in me?"

She sipped her coffee. "I don't know. I just follow orders."

"They told you to follow me?"

"I'm to stick to you like a limpet."

"How did you get on this flight?"

"That wasn't easy. I missed the train. I had to take a taxi from Dublin. My boss in London arranged everything."

"Well, I hope it's all worth it." Kurt was baffled, but he was impressed by what the OSS could do at short notice. He rearranged his thoughts. "So you've been keeping tabs on me the whole time?"

"Since you arrived in Trinity College."

Chapter 39

Monday March 6, 1944

Carter waved a fist at the airplane as it took off. He watched as it turned left and headed south, climbing steadily. When it had disappeared from view above the clouds, he hurried to the BOAC office at the head of the pier and demanded to know the plane's estimated time of arrival at its destination.

"It's heading to Lisbon, Portugal," a young airline clerk answered sweetly.

"I know where Lisbon is," Carter growled. "How long does it take to get there?"

"Anywhere from seven to nine hours, depending on weather conditions," was the reply.

Carter turned away from the clerk. He checked his watch. It was 30 minutes past midday. The seaplane would arrive in Lisbon at 7:30 at the earliest. That gave him plenty of time to get back to the British embassy in Dublin and report to his superiors in London. He turned to the BOAC clerk again. "What time's the next train to Dublin?"

The clerk sniffed at him. "You'll need to ask them at the railway station, but I think you've missed it."

Foynes railway station was deserted. He headed for the ticket office, where he found a railway worker with a kettle poised over a teapot.

"When's the next train to Dublin?" Carter said.

The railwayman filled the teapot with hot water. "It left five minutes ago. You've missed it."

Carter clenched his fists. "When's the next one?"

"Well, let's see," said the man. "What day is it today?"

"Monday."

"In that case, the next train will be about this time tomorrow."

"You mean to tell me there are no trains out of here until tomorrow?"

"That's right. There are no more flights until tomorrow, so there are no more trains. Stands to reason, if you think about it."

Carter blew a gasket. He knew it would only make a bad situation worse, but he couldn't help himself. "You mean I'm stuck in this godforsaken dump for 24 hours? What sort of backward country is this?"

The clerk stirred the teapot slowly. "If this was a Tuesday you'd have more luck. There are two flights to Poole on Tuesdays, two in and two out. There's just the one flight in and out to Lisbon on Mondays. So, there's only one train."

Carter thought he detected a tone of insubordination in the man's voice. He could be telling him a pack of lies. "I want to speak to the stationmaster."

"That would be me," said the railwayman.

Carter dialled back his anger. He attempted a conciliatory smile. "I need to get back to Dublin today. What would you suggest?"

The clerk shrugged. "You could catch a train from Limerick."

"And how do you suggest I get to Limerick? How far is that?"

"From here to Limerick is about 24 miles as the crow flies. You could walk it in six hours. A fit man like you could probably do it in five."

"Could I hire a taxi?"

"You could if there was any..."

"Aren't there any taxis in Foynes?"

"Afraid not."

Carter left the station and wandered the streets of Foynes. He asked the owner of a grocery-shop-cum-pub that doubled as an undertaker if anyone might be heading toward Limerick in a car. He had no luck. By two o'clock, he'd run out of ideas. Then he spotted a child on a bicycle and he remembered that the grocery-pub-cum-undertakers shop sold bicycles.

By three o'clock, Carter was halfway to Limerick on a bicycle that groaned like an arthritic old man. Mercifully, the drizzle had lifted, but his tweed suit was wet through. By 3:30 p.m. his rear tyre had developed a slow puncture. The rest of the journey to Limerick was painfully slow, punctuated by frequent stops to pump up his tyre.

By 5:20 p.m. he was sitting in a first class carriage on the Limerick to Dublin express, sweating like a prize fighter after ten rounds, his clothes steaming gently. He had abandoned the bicycle in disgust outside the station, its rear tyre completely flat.

A quick mental calculation told him he still had plenty of time on hand. He would arrive in Dublin at 6:30. A taxi would take him to the embassy by 7 at the latest, at least a half-hour before Kevin's flight arrived in Lisbon.

At 5:40 the train drew in to Ballybrophy station, and ten minutes after leaving that station, it came to a shuddering halt. It sat there for five minutes, before Carter leapt to his feet and stuck his head out through a window. All he could see was flat green countryside, the engine blowing steam at a herd of cows in a field. Clicking his tongue with impatience, he headed back through the train to the guard's van at the rear.

The guard's van door was wide open, but the guard was nowhere to be seen. Carter stuck his head out through the open door, and caught sight of the guard standing by the engine, talking to the train driver.

After a few minutes, the guard climbed into the first carriage. The Limerick to Dublin express remained immobile. All but one of the cows had ambled to the far end of the field. The maverick cow seemed to enjoy having her hide steam cleaned. She moved closer to the locomotive.

Carter headed back toward the engine. He met the guard as he made his way through the train explaining the problem to the passengers.

"What's the delay?" said Carter.

"There's an obstruction on the line, sir," said the guard. "We've sent word to the stationmaster at Ballybrophy. Hopefully, it shouldn't take too long to clear the line. I apologise for any inconvenience."

#

The train pulled in to Kingsbridge station in Dublin at 7:15 p.m., 45 minutes behind schedule. The station loudspeakers blared an apology for the unavoidable delay as the weary, crumpled passengers tumbled from the carriages.

Carter muscled his way to the head of the queue at the taxi rank. Climbing into a taxi, he told the driver to take him to the British embassy. "There's an extra shilling in it for you if you can get me there in ten minutes."

The driver laughed. "That's very generous of you, sir, but I don't think it's possible. Not at this time of the night."

"Do your best, squire," said Carter.

He arrived at the embassy at 7:35, to find it closed for the night. He hammered on the door. It took five more minutes to gain entry, and another five to get through to the London duty officer on the telephone.

At 7:50 he replaced the telephone on its receiver, ending the call. He had done all he could. He could only hope that it wasn't too late and that London would act on his information.

#

In Berlin, a young SS man stood at an array of pigeonholes, sorting a pile of decoded signals, when an even younger interoffice runner arrived and added more to the pile in his in-tray.

The SS man checked his watch. "*Vielen Dank,*" he said, his tone heavy with sarcasm.

The runner grinned and moved on.

The young SS man began to work his way through the new signals. He had stuffed 12 into the pigeonholes before he came to a signal that sent the blood racing through his veins. It was from the legation in Dublin, Ireland.

SUSPECTED SUBVERSIVE KURT MULLER ALIAS KEVIN OREILLY EN ROUTE TO LISBON ETA EIGHT PM MARCH SIX

The time stamp on the signal showed that it had been received nearly 12 hours earlier. He looked at his watch: 9:27 p.m. The local time in Lisbon was 8:27. He jumped from his chair and took the stairs to an upper floor as fast as his legs would take him.

Chapter 40

They removed the bag from his head, untied him, and took him to a toilet in an adjoining room. They gave him water and food – reconstituted egg powder and some sort of meat – and then the interrogations started.

Name? Hans Schumann

Age? 43

Born where? Leipzig

Abwehr call-sign? Blitzen *BZN*

British designation? A5

British alias? Henry Pollinger

Case officer's name? Jack Reed

How long since he'd been turned? Since 1940

Those were the easy questions. The rest were harder.

What could he tell them about the Allied invasion plans? "Nothing."

How many other Abwehr agents had been turned by the British? "I don't know."

What do you know of Operation Overlord? "Nothing."

What misinformation have you been sending to the Abwehr in Berlin?

The answer to this question was that he simply keyed the coded signals. He didn't know what they contained. But these men clearly had no understanding of how the British Double Cross system worked. It dawned on him that they would lose interest in him if there was nothing he could tell them. They would slit his throat without a second's thought.

He said, "A lot of the signals were weather reports. Some concerned the movement of troops to Scotland."

"What about Operation Fortitude?" they asked.

He'd never heard of Operation Fortitude. He made a wild guess that it must have something to do with the Allied invasion plans.

"I have picked up a few snippets about that," he said. "There have been mass movements of US and British troops all along the south coast."

"Is that all you have?"

"No, there's more, but I need time to piece it all together."

One of the men slapped him across the face. "Stop stalling. Tell us what you know."

He tasted blood. "I have heard that General Montgomery is to be the supreme commander in charge of the operation."

"You mean General Bernard Montgomery?"

"Yes."

While the questioning continued, he cast his eyes around. He was in a room with a low ceiling and no windows, under artificial light, probably a cellar. The only furniture was a wooden chair that they sat him on. Overhead there were pipes.

Judging by the number of meals they gave him, the interrogation continued for days. They let him use a toilet in an adjoining room at the end of each session, but then they tied him up again. He pleaded with them not to, but they left him on the chair, trussed up in darkness.

Alone with his thoughts, he concocted a version of the invasion plan and snippets of information to back this up. It occurred to him that they had spoken to him in English, never in German.

Who are these men?

Part 3 – Lisbon

Chapter 41

Monday March 6, 1944

Kurt stepped from the seaplane and helped Tammi down. Flying all the way into a south-westerly wind, the journey had taken 8 hours 15 minutes. The air steward passed Kurt's bags out through the door. Kurt took them and followed the other passengers to the currency exchange kiosk at the end of the pier. Tammi walked by his side, carrying a small, overnight bag.

They both exchanged sterling for Portuguese escudos at the kiosk. Then Kurt went in search of a taxi. Tammi tagged along.

The air temperature was at least ten degrees higher in Lisbon than in Dublin, but there were heavy dark clouds on the horizon to the south.

If his eyesight had been better, Kurt might have noticed that the taxi at the head of the queue was separated and parked at a slight angle from the others. And if he hadn't been exhausted from the journey he might have been surprised that the driver spoke to him in English.

"Where to, guv?"

"Hotel Avenida Palace."

The driver stowed their three bags in the boot and got behind the wheel. Kurt and Tammi climbed aboard. The journey lasted no more than 20 minutes.

When the taxi came to a halt, Kurt peered through the window. All he could see was a row of suburban houses on a darkened street. "Where's the hotel?"

"Hop out and I'll show you," said the driver.

Kurt opened the door and climbed out. Two men appeared from nowhere, grabbed Kurt by the arms, and marched him into a house. They dropped him onto a dusty old armchair. "Wait here," said one of the men in English, and they left, closing and locking the door.

Concerned about what might have happened to Tammi, Kurt listened at the door. He heard nothing. He looked around the room. There wasn't much to see: a second armchair, a threadbare carpet, a light bulb hanging from the ceiling, his own face reflected in a window. He shivered. Could he be in the hands of the Gestapo again?

Two men in plain clothes came in and searched him. They removed his papers and left. A few minutes later, the door opened again, and a third man entered. Tall, with a rigid backbone, an officer's baton tucked under his arm, he wore civilian clothes, topped with an officer's cap. Kurt knew immediately that he was in the hands of the British; only the British would dress like that.

"Sit," said the officer.

Kurt crossed his arms. He glared at the officer. "What have you done with the young woman I was with?"

"Nothing. She left in the taxi. Please sit."

Kurt took a seat and the officer sat facing him. Leaning forward, leafing through Kurt's passport, he said, "Kevin O'Reilly, Irish national. What are you doing in Lisbon?"

"I'm here to deliver a diplomatic bag to the German embassy."

"Why would an Irish national do that?"

"My girlfriend works in the German legation in Dublin. She asked me to deputize for the usual courier, who's unwell. You'll find a letter of authorization inside my passport, signed by the German ambassador in Ireland."

The officer unfolded the letter and scanned it quickly. Then he tucked it back inside the passport and stared wide-eyed at Kurt for a full ten seconds. "That's your story, is it? You have no other reason for flying to Lisbon?"

"That's it. I've never been to Portugal. I was happy to volunteer. I like to travel."

The officer straightened his back. "Here's what we know about you, O'Reilly. You are a member of His Majesty's armed forces. You report to a unit in London called 'Overseas Logistics'."

Carter must have alerted MI5.

"We have been informed that you are on a 7-day pass that runs out at midnight tonight. That makes you a deserter, since there's no way you could get back to England tonight. I could throw you in jail for that alone."

Kurt thought: he's fishing.

"You're right, Major," he said. "Unfortunately I was delayed in Ireland."

"That's Captain," said the officer. "Go on."

"There was an accident. I had to spend two days in a hospital in Dublin. If you're in touch with my unit, please let them know I'll get home as soon as I can."

The captain flexed his baton between his hands, like a headmaster about to deliver six of the best. "I don't believe Kevin O'Reilly is your real name. What is the function of this 'Overseas Logistics' unit of yours?"

"I'm with Intelligence, Captain. That's all I can say, I'm sure you understand."

The captain stormed out of the room.

Kurt assessed his position. He might be AWOL, but he was too hot to handle. This captain couldn't hold him, and he knew it, not if he had plans to continue in the British army and he cared about his career.

Kurt was left alone in the room for a couple of hours. He tried the door, but it was locked. He banged on it and shouted, "Hey out there, I need food."

No one answered.

The captain returned shortly after that. "I've decided to let you go. I haven't been able to contact your unit. If you take my advice you'll catch the next flight back to England." He handed Kurt his papers.

A Tommy returned his suitcase and the diplomatic bag and led him to the front door. "Go left. You'll come to a main road. You should find a cab there." He slammed the door.

Kurt examined the diplomatic bag. It had been opened and resealed crudely. He wasn't surprised. He picked up the two bags and turned left as the Tommy had suggested. Trudging wearily to the end of the road, he hailed a passing taxi.

"Take me to the German embassy," he said.

The embassy was closed; all the lights were off. "Wait here," said Kurt to the driver. He hammered on the door. There was no response. He tried again and waited a few moments before a light came on. The door opened to reveal an old man in slippers and dressing gown. He waved an angry hand and said something in Portuguese.

"I have a diplomatic bag from Dublin," said Kurt, in German.

The old man took the bag. A glance told him that the seal had been broken. He curled his lip. "Who are you?"

Kurt handed over his letter of authorization. "Jürgen Richter was ill. He asked me to carry the bag."

The man examined the letter. "That seems to be in order, but the bag has been interfered with. What possessed you to open it?"

"I didn't. I was picked up by the British as soon as my plane landed. They opened it."

"That is most irregular. You should have told them the bag was protected under international law."

"Take it up with the British embassy," said Kurt, and he returned to his taxi.

The taxi took him to the Hotel Avenida Palace.

Situated on Lisbon's main thoroughfare, the hotel was a blaze of lights. A porter wearing a morning coat offered to help Kurt with his suitcase. Kurt accepted gratefully. He checked in. A bellboy carried his suitcase to the lift and showed Kurt to room 410 on the fourth floor.

Kurt thanked the bellboy, handing him five escudos. The bellboy stood like a statue, a frozen smile on his face until Kurt placed ten escudos more on his outstretched hand. Then he left.

Kurt collapsed onto the bed and fell asleep almost immediately.

Chapter 42

A knock on the door woke Kurt. He checked his watch. It was 11:30 p.m. He struggled to his feet and went to the door. "Who's there?"

"A friend."

Kurt recognised the gruff voice of Oberst Erwin von Neumann, the man who had been his head of section in the Abwehr in Berlin. He opened the door.

Von Neumann greeted him with a broad smile. "Kurt Müller! How the devil are you?"

"Herr Oberst, I'm glad to see you. Come in." Kurt stood aside.

Von Neumann hadn't changed. His broad smile was undiminished. Underneath a leather flying jacket he was wearing his usual bottle green woollen jumper. He stepped into the room and shook Kurt's hand with a firm grip.

The Oberst reeked of pipe smoke.

Kurt's stomach growled, and von Neumann laughed. "You sound hungry. Have you missed a meal?"

"I had something to eat on the plane, but that was over five hours ago. I expect I won't get anything more before breakfast."

"Why don't you call the kitchen? I'm sure they'll be happy to prepare something for you."

Kurt thought that unlikely. "At this hour?"

"Yes, of course. This is a top-flight hotel. I'm sure it must cater for its guests at all hours of the day and night."

Kurt lifted the telephone. Reception answered immediately. He asked for the kitchen and ordered a chicken salad.

"Ask for a bottle of wine," said the Oberst, and Kurt did so.

The Oberst removed his jacket. The familiar sight of leather patches on his elbows brought a smile to Kurt's lips.

"You don't mind?" said the Abwehr spymaster, pulling his pipe from his trouser pocket.

"Of course not, Herr Oberst, there's an ashtray on the table."

"Thank you, Oberleutnant, and it's not Oberst any more, by the way. These days they call me Generalmajor."

"Congratulations, Herr General."

The general waved a dismissive hand. "I have no great interest in honorifics bestowed by the Nazis. Call me Erwin."

Kurt nodded, but he had too much respect for the man to address him by his Christian name.

The general lit his pipe with great care. Soon, the room was full of sweet-smelling smoke. "When you didn't appear yesterday, I thought you might be in trouble."

"I'm sorry, Herr General, there was nothing I could do about that. I got here as soon as I could. Did you receive a second signal from Ireland, suggesting a meeting for today?"

He squinted at Kurt through the smoke. "We received a second message. Is that what it said? It was somewhat garbled, I'm afraid."

"I asked Professor Hirsch to send that signal. His coding and keying skills may be a bit rusty."

"You couldn't send the signal yourself?"

"I spent the weekend in hospital. I was attacked and hit over the head." The general's eyes narrowed. Kurt held up a hand. "Nothing to do with the Nazis."

"That explains the black eye, I suppose. Well, I couldn't wait any longer. I'm needed back in Berlin tomorrow. Tell me what you need."

"I'm working with a British Intelligence team in what they call the XX programme."

General von Neumann nodded. "The London Controlling Section's Double Cross. I know all about that programme."

Kurt was aware that his mouth was hanging open in undisguised amazement. "You know about the Double Cross programme?"

Von Neumann waved the stem of his pipe in a gesture that said *move on*. "It's the principal means by which the British send us their misinformation. We've known about it for some time."

Kurt was taken aback by this revelation. "You know that some of your agents have been turned by the British?"

"Yes, of course. We take every scrap of misinformation fed to us and pass it on to the OKW."

"Without altering it and without comment?"

"We sometimes add comments on how reliable the source is, how it has been corroborated by more than one agent, or how urgent it is, that sort of thing. We never add or remove anything of substance."

Kurt took a deep breath. "The British are convinced that the Abwehr believes everything they transmit."

"That is the nature of espionage, Kurt. Each side believes they are in control. Have you forgotten the aims of the Black Orchestra?"

Before Kurt could answer, there was a knock on the door. A porter came in with a generous plate of food and a bottle of wine. When he saw that Kurt had a guest, he apologised. "I thought the meal was for one, sir. There's cutlery for only one, and only one wine glass."

Kurt thanked the porter, "*Obrigado*," tipping him 20 escudos. The porter left.

The general eyed the feast on the table.

"Help yourself, sir," said Kurt. "There's more than enough here for two." He pulled up a chair, and transferred half the food onto a side plate for the general. The general opened the wine, while Kurt began to eat the salad with his fingers, leaving the cutlery for his guest.

The wine was a Portuguese white, slightly chilled. Kurt fetched a tumbler from the bathroom, and poured two glasses.

They touched glasses. "*Prost.*"

Kurt spoke with a mouth full of salad. "When I heard that the admiral and Generalmajor Oster were arrested, I thought..."

"You thought the Black Orchestra was finished? Nothing could be further from the truth. Since the admiral was suspended, Kaltenbrunner has been in nominal charge, but he's a dolt. He has no idea what's really going on. The Resistance thrives. We have more members than ever. Our work continues, and it will not cease until the leaders of the Nazis are all in hell, or locked up behind bars."

They finished the food in silence, Kurt basking in the warm glow of the general's words and the tingle from the delicious wine.

When he'd cleared his plate, Kurt loosened his trouser belt, sliding back as much as he could in his chair. "So tell me, General, how many agents do you have in Britain?"

"We stopped sending over new agents when we reached a sufficiently high number a couple of years ago. I can't give you an exact number, but there are certainly over 100 active agents in London."

Chapter 43

The general's figure agreed with Kurt's last estimate, but still he was shocked. Running over 100 double agents was a massive undertaking. He said, "Do you know how many of those have been turned by the British?"

"You'd have to ask British Intelligence that question, but I'm hoping they have turned them all. That was the plan, after all."

"The plan?"

"Yes, you have seen how poorly these men are trained. It was our intention from the start that the British would capture them all and put them out of commission. Turning them into double agents was a masterstroke that exceeded Generalmajor Oster's wildest ambitions."

"Some of them were executed," said Kurt.

The smile fell from the general's face. "Some of the early ones were hanged. That was unfortunate, and one man committed suicide. The Double Cross programme was a godsend. It kept our men alive and, at the same time, put them to work in the fight against Hitler."

Kurt topped up the two glasses with the last of the wine. "What will be the fate of those men when the War ends?"

"I hope the British will send them home. They will be treated as heroes in Germany."

Kurt's eyebrows expressed his doubts. "Heroes who betrayed their country?"

"Heroes who helped to bring down the Nazi regime, men who served their country well. Is this what you wanted to ask me?"

Kurt shook his head. He took another deep breath. "Until very recently, the British believed they had turned every Abwehr agent in Britain. But they have discovered a rogue agent passing uncontrolled high-level intelligence to Berlin. My mission is to identify this agent so that British Intelligence can track him down."

"How can I help?"

"I was hoping you could identify him from his call-sign, *LBK*."

General von Neumann shook his head. "That's *Lebkuchen*. It

doesn't ring a bell, but then I'm not familiar with every one of our agents' call-signs." He gave the request a few moments' thought. "What you need is a complete list of all the Abwehr agents in Britain with their call-signs and aliases. That list is the only way your friends in MI5 will be able to find this Gingerbread agent. I don't have such a list, but I can get it for you. But have you considered the other possibility?"

"What other possibility?"

"Your Gingerbread spy might not be one of ours. He could be a *Sicherheitsdienst* agent."

This suggestion was a shock to Kurt. "I thought only the Abwehr was permitted to operate agents overseas."

"That is strictly true, but we suspect that the SD has a small number of their own. The head of the SD-Ausland, Walter Schellenberg, is something of a loose cannon. He only obeys the rules that suit him, and he has the ear of Heinrich Himmler."

Kurt was aware of Schellenberg. He'd seen him come and go at Abwehr headquarters in the early days of the War. Even then he was a rising star in the ranks of the SS in Berlin, destined to fill the intellectual gap left behind after the assassination of Reinhard Heydrich.

"When Reinhard Heydrich was assassinated, and Ernst Kaltenbrunner was appointed to take over his job, Schellenberg kicked up an almighty storm. He insisted that the job should have been his. He pointed out that Kaltenbrunner was nothing but a minor lawyer from Austria who lacked any experience of espionage or counterespionage. Himmler must have agreed with him."

"But he didn't move Schellenberg into the top job?"

General von Neumann shook his head. "I assume Kaltenbrunner's appointment was sanctioned by Hitler. The chicken farmer did what he could to compensate Schellenberg financially, and set up a direct line for him to his desk. You can be sure that Schellenberg is scheming to take over the Abwehr. All he needs is proof of incompetence or organised treachery within the Abwehr and he will pounce."

"What can you tell me about Hans Schumann?"

"I remember him. He was one of our earliest recruits, a fanatical Nazi, call-sign *Blitzen*. What's he been doing?"

"He's disappeared from his safe house, and the police haven't been able to find him."

General von Neumann laughed. "That's surprising. I seem to recall he spoke English with a terrible accent. How long has he been on the run?"

Kurt did a quick calculation. "Ten days. He left two dead bodies behind in the house – a guard and a cook."

The general's smile vanished. "Good God, he killed two people?"

"We're not sure, but it seems likely."

The general pondered the problem for a few moments. "You think he might be this Gingerbread spy?"

"He's the number one suspect."

"That's unlikely. Schumann was deployed in the early years. Schellenberg was nothing but a junior official in those days. You should look elsewhere for your Gingerbread. You'll only find him when you've eliminated all of our Abwehr agents. I'll get you that list by the close of business tomorrow." The general looked at his watch. Kurt checked his. It was 1:45 a.m. "Close of business today, I mean. I would invite you to share a glass of schnapps, but I'm out of time and I expect you're exhausted. I'll arrange for someone to give you that list. You'll need a recognition exchange. How about 'The River Tagus looks beautiful this time of year'?"

"Okay, and the reply 'If only it wasn't full of rubbish'."

"Agreed."

"I have one last question, Herr General: How did the Abwehr learn the name of the British deception plan?"

The General tamped his pipe until the fire died. "You mean Operation Fortitude? We got that from the SD. They picked it up from a source they have in the Russian embassy in Madrid."

"How did the Russians in Madrid get hold of it?"

"From their NKVD man in London, I assume."

"There's an NKVD man in London?"

"Rumour has it that the NKVD are well placed in the inner circle of Intelligence in London."

Again, Kurt's mouth hung open in shocked disbelief.

"Close your mouth, Kurt. That's common knowledge in some diplomatic circles."

"Do you have a name?"

"No, but it's probably someone who worked in Madrid before the War." He slipped his coat on. "By the way, if you tell the British we're on to their Double Cross programme, they probably wouldn't believe you."

Kurt thanked him for his help.

"It was nothing, Kurt. Please convey my best wishes to Major Robertson and his Twenty Committee. Tell him he's doing an outstanding job. And if you want to tell the British something that might help, tell them to make their misinformation less confusing. No one in the OKW believes Operation Fortitude North."

Kurt frowned. "I've heard of Fortitude. What's Fortitude North?"

"That's a supposed invasion from Scotland through Norway. And nobody in the Wehrmacht is stupid enough to believe that the main thrust of the invasion will come at the Bay of Biscay. Tell them to concentrate their efforts on the Pas-de-Calais. Hitler is convinced about that plan."

Chapter 44

Tuesday March 7, 1944

On the top floor of RSHA headquarters at Prinz-Albrecht Strasse 8, Berlin, the head of SD-Ausland, Walter Schellenberg, was leafing through the morning's urgent dispatches. The dispatch that caused him to leap from his chair was a copy of a signal from a Gestapo agent in Lisbon to the Gestapo office on the third floor. The Lisbon agent had received a radio signal from the German legation in Dublin alerting him that a suspected British agent was flying from Ireland to Lisbon. When the British agent disembarked, he had been identified as Kurt Müller, the notorious subversive and Black Orchestra member. The Lisbon agent had requested instructions.

The dispatch was 18 hours old.

Schellenberg lifted his telephone and barked an order. "Get me Heinrich Müller."

"Herr Müller's office. How may I help you?" The voice of Müller's personal secretary.

"This is Walter Schellenberg. Put me through to Herr Müller."

"I do apologise, Herr Schellenberg, but SS-Gruppenführer Müller is in conference. He has given strict instructions not to be disturbed."

"Interrupt him. He will thank you later."

"If you're sure..."

"I'm certain." Schellenberg waited, drumming his fingers on his desk. It took 60 seconds for Müller to come to the telephone.

"Walter? I'm tied up at the moment. Can't this wait?"

"No, Heinrich, it can't. I have a dispatch in front of me. One of your agents in Lisbon has spotted the subversive, Kurt Müller. I need to know how you intend to deal with the matter."

There was a pause at the other end of the line. "I shouldn't have to remind you, Walter, that the defence of the Fatherland against subversives is my responsibility."

Schellenberg ground his teeth. He kept his voice low and even. "This man is not just a subversive, Heinrich, he is a spy working directly with British Intelligence. The knowledge he carries is critical to our counterespionage effort, both now and in the future. He must not be harmed."

"We have no intention of harming him as you put it," Müller replied. "I have sent a team to take him into protective custody. He will be transported back to Berlin. Once we have him here, you will be given every opportunity—"

Schellenberg interrupted him, "You must not attempt to move him. It is imperative that I speak with him in Lisbon."

"What difference does it make whether you interrogate him here or there?"

"Listen to me, Heinrich. I will catch the first available flight to Lisbon. Tell your men to keep him under surveillance until I get there."

Schellenberg disconnected. That 'listen to me, Heinrich' hinted at a direct threat to bring SS-Reichsführer Himmler into the conversation. That was a battleground where Müller could never win against Schellenberg.

#

In London that evening, Lina arrived home after a busy day in her basement office. Since the last big attack on the night of March 2/3, the Luftwaffe's raids had become less intense, and keeping on top of her workload was easier with each passing night. Matron had praised the effort of all the nurses, picking out Lina for special mention. The other nurses had reacted with typical disdain to this, but nothing they said could dent Lina's newfound self-confidence. They may feel superior to her, but she had a second date with Jan, her dishy Dutchman, to look forward to.

Chapter 45

Tuesday March 7, 1944

In spite of his extreme exhaustion, Kurt slept poorly. Two hours of deep sleep were followed by five hours of disturbed writhing. His fatigue finally overcame his brain and he slept soundly until 11 a.m., when the hotel housekeeping staff came knocking on his door.

He hurried down to the reception desk. Had there been anyone looking for him? No, but there had been a telephone call. The receptionist apologised for her failure to rouse him, but the caller had left a message. She removed a note from the pigeonholes and handed it across the desk.

Kurt tore it open. 'Hope to see you at 6 p.m. for Gingerbread. S.B.'

He racked his brain, but the initials meant nothing to him.

He returned to his room. Housekeeping finished their work and left. He filled the bath, and spent 30 minutes soaking his bones. By 12:45 p.m., he was sitting in the dining room staring in disbelief at the sumptuous meal on the plate in front of him: roast beef with a variety of vegetables. He hadn't seen anything like it since 1938. He ordered a glass of the house red wine before tucking a napkin into his collar and picking up his knife and fork.

The room filled rapidly. Looking around, he identified senior officers from several armies, the Wehrmacht, the British, Poles, Russians, Americans and others. There were civilians, too, well-heeled individuals in tailored Italian suits accompanied by bejewelled women in fur coats, and there were businessmen in pairs engaged in earnest discussions. He began to feel like the ugly duckling in the room, conspicuous by his clothing and because he was the only one dining alone.

He finished his meal quickly, and headed into the city. A taxi dropped him off at the BOAC ticket office, where he quickly established that he could exchange his Lisbon-Foynes return ticket for a ticket to Poole in Dorset. The only conditions were that an empty seat could be found on the Poole flight, and that he pay a supplemental charge of 200 escudos.

He took a taxi back to the hotel and returned to his room. Best to remain out of sight until the Abwehr made contact again in the evening.

He opened the door to find the room in chaos. The contents of his suitcase were scattered over the floor. He swore quietly, closed the door, and began to gather up his scattered clothes.

A sound alerted him that someone was in the bathroom, but before he could gather his thoughts, two stocky men, dressed in dark clothing, emerged. Grabbing Kurt by the elbows, they marched him from the room and down the staircase to the street. Kurt said nothing, and neither did the two men. They bundled him into a black car.

Kurt's heartbeat raced. He was in the hands of the Gestapo!

As the car sped through the streets of Lisbon, Kurt composed a cover story. It would have to be a variation of the story he had told Jürgen Richter at the German legation in Dublin. Could he make it plausible enough? He would know soon enough.

Chapter 46

Once more, Kurt was frogmarched into a suburban house and placed in an empty room. This one had bare floorboards, two plain wooden chairs and a naked light bulb hanging from the ceiling. A strong flash of déjà vu took him back to his interrogation in Berlin in 1940. The Gestapo had taken his clothes on that occasion. Would they do the same again?

Two plainclothes men searched him while a third man watched. They removed his passport and plane ticket, handed them to the third man, and left the room. Kurt sat on one of the wooden chairs. His head was pounding.

The third man towered over him, flipping through his passport. "This passport is false." He spoke in German with a thick accent. "We know who you are, Müller. There is rather a large price on your head in Berlin."

The directness of the man's attack rocked Kurt to his core. These men acted like police. Maybe they were Portuguese police. They were certainly agents of the Gestapo. He shook his head to gain time.

"You deny your identity? You are not Kurt Müller?"

"My name is O'Reilly, Kevin O'Reilly. I'm an Irish citizen. Ireland is a neutral country, like Portugal. You have no right to hold me."

"We have alerted the police in Berlin. They have dispatched someone to talk to you. I expect they will arrive in the next six hours or so. In the meantime, you must be patient."

Kurt assumed this was an attempt at humour. He said nothing. The man left, locking the door.

#

Three hours later, Kurt was allowed a toilet break. They served him a light meal of anchovies and olives with dry bread. Four more hours passed. They gave him water to quench a raging thirst and another toilet break. It was now 8:30 p.m. Kurt had missed his meeting with the Abwehr contact. Assuming he could talk his way out of his current predicament, would S.B. wait for him? If he failed to meet him, he wouldn't get his hands on the list of Abwehr agents in Britain, and his whole trip would be a waste of time. Ruefully, he thought that he would have much more to worry about than a missed meeting when the Gestapo arrived.

He passed the time honing his cover story. His life would depend on it.

#

The Gestapo arrived at 10 o'clock the next morning. Kurt felt like a homeless man. He had slept in his clothes on the bare boards using his jacket as a pillow. His back was stiff and he was in need of another bath. He was allowed a further toilet break before two men carried a coffin into the room.

These two were Gestapo. The swagger was unmistakable.

Kurt panicked. "You can't do this. I'm an Irish citizen." He spoke in English, his voice, thin and high-pitched.

The Gestapo men placed the coffin behind the door. They seemed in high spirits. Perhaps they were happy to have captured such a notorious enemy of the Reich, or maybe they were looking forward to the reward.

"My name is Hermann, and this is Heini," said one man with a grin. He spoke in German. "Our friends tell me that you deny your identity." He took a photograph from a pocket, unfolded it, and showed it to his companion. "What do you think, Heini, do we have the wrong man?"

Heini shook his head. "This is Kurt Müller, no question about it, Hermann."

Hermann waved the picture in front of Kurt's face. "What do you think, Kurt? Are you who we think you are, or is this all some sort of dreadful mistake?"

Kurt stuck to English. "My name is Kevin O'Reilly. Take a look at my passport."

Heini pulled Kurt's passport from a pocket. "Look, Hermann, he's telling the truth. It says here that this is a man from Ireland by the name of Kevin O'Reilly. How could we have made such a terrible blunder?"

"And yet his face matches the picture of Kurt Müller, and look here, his date of birth is exactly the same as Müller's. Could his passport be a forgery, do you think?"

"I think it might be," said Heini, tossing Kurt's passport across the room.

Kurt switched to German. "This is neutral Portugal. German police have no jurisdiction here."

"His German is excellent for an Irishman," said Hermann.

"But he has a good point, Hermann. We have no jurisdiction in Portugal. What can we do?" said his companion.

"We'll just have to transport our friend here to Berlin and conclude this interview there."

Kurt fought a rising sense of hopelessness. They intended to ship him back to Berlin. *In the coffin.* "You have no right to take me to Germany against my will."

"I think we can make an exception for a hardened criminal like yourself, Kurt. What do you say, Heini?"

"I think so, Hermann."

"I am no criminal," said Kurt.

Hermann laughed. "And yet your file in Berlin is as thick as two encyclopaedia volumes. Your many acts of treason against the Führer are the stuff of legend. Your photograph is to be found on police noticeboards everywhere in Greater Germany."

Heini said, "Parents threaten their mischievous children with your image."

"I am Kurt Müller, I don't deny it. But I deny the acts of treason."

The Gestapo men smiled like Siamese twins. Heini said, "That is amusing. Your evil is known the length and breadth of Germany. God in heaven, some of your escapades are spoken about by the older children."

"Those stories are false," said Kurt. "You cannot believe everything you read about me. I am not the traitor you think I am. What if I told you I am still secretly working for the Abwehr?"

"This is a fairy tale," said Hermann. "Soon, you will be shipped back to the Fatherland where you will face a judge of the Third Reich. You will hang for your heinous acts of treason, make no mistake about it."

The Gestapo men left the room.

Kurt held his breath. He had planted the seed of his elaborate cover story in their minds. His only hope was that he would be given the opportunity to expand on it. He was gambling on their natural curiosity and the power of suggestion.

They left him on his own with the coffin for an hour.

When they returned there were three of them. Kurt's heart rate increased at the sight of the third man. He wore a white coat and carried a doctor's bag.

Hermann and Heini held him in the chair while the doctor rummaged through his bag, pulled something out and held it up to the light. It was barely in Kurt's line of sight, but the way he was holding it suggested a syringe and a vial of liquid. Kurt squirmed in the seat in a vain attempt to break free.

"Remove his jacket and roll up his sleeve," said the doctor, moving closer.

The Gestapo men struggled to remove Kurt's jacket. Then one of them let go and tugged at Kurt's sleeve. He shook himself violently and managed to break free. But only for a moment. The two men pounced on him, knocking him to the ground on his face.

"Turn him over," said the doctor.

They turned him onto his back. One of the men sat on his chest while the other one rolled up his sleeve.

"Let me go!" Kurt yelled. "You have no right to stick needles in me."

Someone put a hand over his mouth. Someone else pressed his arm to the floor. It took a moment for the doctor to find a vein. Kurt panicked when the needle went in, warm liquid surging into his arm.

"How long does it take?" said one of the men.

"Not long," the doctor replied.

Had he been injected with a truth drug? Would he answer all their questions and betray everyone in the Black Orchestra? Would he compromise the British deception programme and undermine all their efforts at confusing the Reich about D-Day? Warmth flooded his body. The men were talking, their voices faint, distant, drifting away...

#

Kurt opened his eyes in total darkness. He had a raging thirst, and his head was throbbing. It took a few moments to recall his own name, and a few more to remember where he was. The Gestapo had drugged him and put him in the coffin. He was on his back, his mouth stuffed with something woollen. An old sock, maybe, judging by the smell. He tried to call out, but all he managed was a weak moan. His arms were jammed tight by his sides, his hands and fingers numb. He was alive, but tied up tight, gagged, and lying in a coffin, he might as well be dead. How long had he been asleep? Had they taken him to Berlin?

Chapter 47

Wednesday March 8, 1944

Walter Schellenberg stepped off the plane. He hurried to the end of the pier and climbed into a taxi, pushing another traveller aside.

He gave the address to the driver and sat back in his seat to put his thoughts in order for the confrontation to come.

Heinrich Müller of the Gestapo was an incompetent fool, interested in nothing but the advancement of his own miserable career and how he appeared in the eyes of Heinrich Himmler and the Führer. He was more than a fool, capable of the grossest of misjudgements. The man could quite easily cause havoc by his blundering actions. And what did he know of international espionage? Nothing. Meddling in matters outside his expertise could lose us the War.

What business did he have running agents beyond the borders of the Fatherland, anyway? This was a serious matter. The disposition of agents on foreign soil was the exclusive purview of the Abwehr. Could Reichsführer-SS Himmler be aware of this breach of protocol? Of course he could. Himmler was the master of equivocation, the prevaricator-in-chief, with all the cunning of a supreme manipulator.

The capture of Kurt Müller was a prize to be envied, an achievement on a par with winning a gold medal at the 1936 Olympic Games. Whatever happened from today onward, there was no way that prize could be wrestled from the hands of the Gestapo man. This was an inescapable fact, but Schellenberg knew that he could trump that by concentrating on the bigger picture and salvaging the espionage situation.

If he wasn't too late...

He leapt from the taxi, offering reichsmarks to the driver. The driver held up his palms, demanding payment in Portuguese escudos. It was a trivial amount, equivalent to less than five reichsmarks. Schellenberg tossed ten through the window and strode away from the car.

He hammered on the door with his fist, ignoring the ornate knocker. Best to make a strong impression. The door was opened by a giant of a man in a suit. Schellenberg pushed past him impatiently. The man closed the door and followed Schellenberg down the hall.

"Where is he?" Schellenberg demanded. "Where are you keeping the subversive, Müller?"

"He's not here," said the man. "There's no one here but me."

"Where have they taken him?"

"He's been transported to Berlin in a coffin."

Schellenberg squared off to the giant, peering up at him in the dim light of the hall. "What do you mean? Is he dead? Have you killed him already?"

The giant's face cracked into a smile. "He's asleep. He's not dead."

"Asleep, in a coffin?"

"We drilled holes in it to allow him to breathe. Small holes."

Schellenberg stamped his foot. "Take me to where they are holding him."

"I can't. They're gone."

"Tell me how I can make contact with them, or you will hang, as God is my witness." A bit over the top, admittedly, but this idiot needed to be shaken from his slumber.

"You might catch them at the undertakers if you hurry," said the giant.

"Where is that?" Schellenberg was aware that he was spraying the giant's chest with spittle. He didn't care.

"I'm not sure..."

"Come on, man, think. How can I catch them before it's too late?"

"I have the undertaker's address here somewhere..."

Schellenberg arrived at the undertaker's just in time to stop the hearse from leaving. The driver and his sidekick looked like Gestapo thugs, although both wore dark, sombre suits. They knew who he was, of course. A display of bluster and a few well-chosen threats were enough to get the two men to remove the coffin from the hearse and return it to the undertaker's.

"Open it," said Schellenberg.

"I don't think that's a good idea," said one of the men.

"What's your name?" said Schellenberg.

He clicked his heels. "SS-Unterscharführer Hermann Klein, sir. This is SS-Schütze Heini Schwann." He saluted. "*Heil Hitler.*"

"Right, Hermann, open the coffin. I won't ask you again."

They unscrewed the coffin lid and removed it. Kurt Müller lay inside the coffin, wearing a gag, blinking rapidly.

"Untie him. Help him out."

Heini and Hermann exchanged a glance. Hermann said, "I'm sorry, sir, we have orders to keep him in the coffin until we reach Berlin."

Schellenberg pulled the gag from Kurt's mouth. "I'm countermanding those orders. Get him out of there. And step lively."

#

In London, Lina paced up and down outside the picture-house in Leicester Square. She had been waiting 30 minutes, and the film was due to start in another five. Where was Jan?

She couldn't believe that he would stand her up after spending just a single night with her. Her mind raced through several possibilities. Had she said or done something to upset him? Could he have been killed in the Luftwaffe's latest raid? Or perhaps there was some kind of flap on in the Foreign Office.

She had no way of contacting him. Unless he came looking for her in the hospital or at the flat, she would never see him again. She waited another 15 minutes before giving up on him and making her way home. People on the Tube stared at her, all dressed up with her hair in braids and nowhere to go. It must have looked obvious to everyone that she'd been stood up. She blushed, and tried to avoid their eyes.

By the time she arrived home, she was feeling foolish. Jan de Groot was some kind of playboy. He probably used his charms to have his way with women all over London. Perhaps she'd had a lucky escape.

From the moment she opened the door of the flat, she sensed that something was wrong. To a casual observer, everything looked as it should be, but Lina was immediately aware that her things had been disturbed. Nothing in the flat was located exactly where she had left it that morning.

A glance around the kitchen confirmed her suspicions. Things were out of place, and there were traces of food on the floor. Someone had searched the flat while she was out. But how had they got in? She found the answer to that question in the bathroom, where a small window had been forced open.

She spoke to the occupants of the other two flats. None of them had been burgled, and nobody had noticed anything unusual.

What on earth could they have been looking for? She had no money in the flat, and nothing worth stealing.

Before going to bed, she combed the braids from her hair.

#

She was on the morning shift the next day. She took the Tube to Victoria, and arrived at the hospital feeling lightheaded. She had put the missed date with Jan from her mind. If he showed up again she would have a few words to say to him, but she really couldn't care if she never set eyes on the man again.

The overnight Luftwaffe raid had been a small-scale affair. The East End had taken the brunt of it, and there were no new casualties in Millbank. Lina was relieved; there was no reason for her to return to the dreadful office in the basement.

As she emerged from the changing room, she was met by Kathy Benson and Julie Parker.

"Oh look who it is," said Kathy. "It's the trainee from the Low Countries. What was her name again?"

Lina erupted. "I've had enough of your taunts, your cruelty. Find someone else to annoy."

As she stormed off, one of the nurses said, "Listen to those clogs go!"

"Bécassine. Run away."

Lina almost laughed. She was fond of the French cartoon character and her sabots, having followed her from childhood. Mentally, she patted herself on the back. She had stood up for herself at last, and it felt good.

Chapter 48

They untied Kurt's hands.

"Where am I? Am I in Germany?"

A voice he didn't recognise said, "You're in Lisbon."

They lifted him into a sitting position and then helped him out of the coffin. Gingerly, he got to his feet. He shook his arms to regain control of his hands. Pins and needles raced up his arms to his shoulders.

His eyes began to focus. Three faces peered at him. Two of them could have been the Gestapo men, Hermann and Heini. He didn't recognise the third man.

They led him to a chair.

"How are you feeling?" said the new voice.

"Thirsty. And my eyes aren't focusing properly."

A blurred face appeared in front of him. "My name is Schämmel, Hauptmann Schämmel. I have some questions for you. Can you hear me, Kurt?"

"Yes," said Kurt. "I hear you, and I'll be happy to answer your questions. But could I have some water first?"

Someone pressed a glass into his hand. He drank. The water was cool, a gift from heaven.

Kurt said, "Are we alone?"

Schämmel's face vanished. When it came back, he moved close to Kurt. "We are now. You may speak freely to me. Tell me why you came to Lisbon."

Kurt's heart leapt in his chest. He recognised the man. This was Walter Schellenberg, the head of SD-Ausland!

Kurt inhaled slowly to calm his heartbeat. "You know that I came to Lisbon from Ireland."

"Yes."

"And do you know that I have been working with British Intelligence in London?"

"I know that too. Tell me why they sent you to Lisbon."

"Herr Hauptmann, first, you must understand that I remain a loyal member of the Abwehr."

"You'll have to explain that."

"I've been working for the Abwehr undercover ever since I left Berlin."

"That is hard to believe." Schellenberg snorted. "Every report I've seen says you're a member of the Black Orchestra."

Kurt nodded. "Over many years, the Abwehr has built up my reputation as a subversive, a disenchanted anti-Nazi, hell-bent on destroying the Third Reich."

"You're saying this is all an illusion?"

"Precisely. None of it is true. It is an elaborate fiction designed to give me credibility as an enemy of the Reich, to fool British Intelligence into accepting me within their ranks."

"You operate as a double agent?"

"Yes. My long-term mission has been to infiltrate British Intelligence and report back to the Abwehr in Berlin. In my current position within MI5 I have access to the highest levels of secret information."

"That is quite a story," said Schellenberg. "You know about the programme that the British call the Double Cross?"

"I do. That programme is the reason why I have come to Lisbon."

"You explained all this to the Gestapo?"

"I tried, but they were too stupid to listen."

"I see," said Schellenberg. "Go on with your story. You came to Lisbon on a mission..."

Kurt shivered. He could see Schellenberg's piercing steel-blue eyes clearly now. He was sitting uncomfortably close. "We know that some of our Abwehr agents in Britain have been sending misinformation to Berlin. These turncoats are cowards, committing high treason against the Reich to save their worthless necks. What we don't know is how many there are, or who they are."

"How many do you think there are?" Schellenberg whispered as if someone might overhear him.

"We estimate there may be as many as twenty." Schellenberg's eyes seemed to light up. Kurt pressed on, "This is the reason why I have come to Lisbon. If we cannot weed out the bad intelligence from the good, the work of the Wehrmacht is made immeasurably more difficult. My mission is to make contact with the Abwehr to obtain a complete list of all our agents in Britain so that I can work out which ones are still operating free of British interference and which ones have been turned."

"There are twenty double agents, you say?"

"Yes, Herr Hauptmann. There may be more."

"How will this list help?"

"I have a small network of agents loyal to the Reich working in minor roles in the Double Cross programme – cleaners and cooks. With their help we will be able to narrow the search and uncover any Abwehr agents that have been turned."

Schellenberg said, "If what you say is true, this is important work."

"What could be more important?" Kurt nodded. "In view of the Allied plans for the upcoming invasion of continental Europe, the outcome of the War could be at stake."

Schellenberg scratched his head. "How can I know that you are telling me the truth?"

"I don't know how I can convince you, Herr Hauptmann. I can give you the names of the two double agents that I have identified so far. Their names are Hoffmeister and Schumann."

"How have you uncovered those names?"

"I am the case officer for Hoffmeister. I uncovered Schumann by following one of the guards."

Schellenberg sat back in his chair. "Is that all you can tell me?"

Kurt hesitated. Then he lowered his voice. "There is just one more piece of the puzzle that I have uncovered, but it's highly sensitive."

Schellenberg leant forward again. "Go on."

"The British suspect an Abwehr agent with call-sign *LBK*, but so far they have been unable to trace him. They sent me to Lisbon to see if I could identify him."

"Why Lisbon, and why did you travel to Ireland first?"

"Lisbon is a hotbed of spies. The British were sure I could pick up some information here. And I have family in Ireland. I imagine they were hoping that travelling there first would throw the Abwehr off my scent."

That was all Kurt could do. He had played his last card. His fate would be decided in the next 60 seconds. He watched Schellenberg's face and waited for his response.

Schellenberg said, "If I contact Generalmajor von Neumann will he back up your story?"

"He might, but my position is so delicate, and the stakes are so high he may well deny the whole thing."

Schellenberg got up from his chair and paced around the room for over five minutes. When he returned to his chair, he said, "What can you tell me of this *Lebkuchen*?"

"The call-sign is all I have. The British are searching for him with radio direction finders, but he moves around a lot, and they haven't been able to locate him."

Schellenberg paused for a few moments. Then he said, "You say you are case officer for Arnold Hoffmeister?"

Kurt almost corrected Schellenberg's mistake. The agent's real name was Paul Hoffmeister. Arnold was his alias. "I am, yes."

"Who has taken over from you while you're on this mission?"

"His name's Greg. I've met him, but I can't recall if I ever picked up his family name."

Once more, Schellenberg paced the room. Kurt set his mind to the task of controlling his galloping heartbeat.

"I believe you," said Schellenberg at last. "You will be released on my authority. You will continue with your mission."

"Thank you, Herr Hauptmann."

"There are conditions, however. You must send the list of Abwehr agents to me as soon as you get it, and when you have completed your mission you will report your findings to me. I will give you a unique radio frequency to use."

Kurt said, "Generalmajor von Neumann will be expecting my report."

"You may report your findings to the Generalmajor, but only 24 hours after you've reported to me. Do you understand?"

"Yes, Herr Hauptmann." Kurt had no access to a transmitter in London, but Schellenberg didn't know that. He asked the obvious next question. "What code book and call-sign should I use?"

"Where are you staying?"

"The Hotel Avenida Palace, room 410."

"I'll arrange for a code book to be sent to your room. How about the call-sign *KPS* for *Klapperschlange*?"

Rattlesnake! How appropriate, thought Kurt.

Chapter 49

Kurt took a taxi to the hotel. The clock in the reception area read 4:05 p.m. He had missed his meeting with S.B. by 22 hours. He could only hope that the meeting with the Abwehr man would still go ahead one day late.

He hung around the bar and lounge areas for a couple of hours, dipping into the newspapers, fending off offers of drinks from the barman. Everywhere he looked there were swarthy characters in dark clothing, some in pairs or small groups, conversing in a variety of languages, Spanish, German, Russian, English, French and others he couldn't identify. The professor was right; Lisbon was a hotbed of spies.

No one seemed remotely interested in him.

Six o'clock came and went. Kurt was hungry. He took a copy of *The London Times* from the lounge with him to the dining room on the second floor. He waited to be shown to a table in a corner of the room, ordered a steak, rare, and a bottle of Portuguese red. He opened the paper. It was three days old, but full of interest. The progress of the Americans in Italy featured on several pages. They still hadn't succeeded in seizing the monastery at Monte Cassino.

His steak arrived. He pierced it with a fork and was pleased with the result. He picked up his knife and sliced off a generous mouthful.

A woman approached his table. "You don't mind, do you?" she said in English, pulling out a chair. She wore a tailored grey tunic over a woollen skirt and stout walking shoes.

Kurt's mouth was too full to reply. He waved his fork. The woman sat down, and the waiter handed her a menu. She ordered a tuna salad and a glass of white wine.

She was in her late forties or early fifties, with salt and pepper hair. Probably a lonely tourist, he thought. He concentrated on his food.

"Are you staying in this hotel?" she said.

Kurt nodded.

"I arrived yesterday. The hotel I stayed in last night was pretty poor. Would you recommend this place?"

Is she making a pass at me?

He swallowed and wiped his mouth. "Yes."

"I hope you didn't mind my sitting here. I noticed you were reading *The Times*. There aren't too many British people here, are there? I expect the War makes it difficult for them to travel. Have you been here long? Where are you from?"

"I'm Irish," he said.

"That's close enough." She smiled. "Do you speak Portuguese?"

Kurt's mouth was full again. He shook his head.

"I worked in Madrid for a number of years and picked up a bit of Spanish, but never could get my head around Portuguese. The Muslim influence seems stronger, don't you agree? The river looks beautiful, don't you think?"

Kurt looked up sharply. He swallowed his food. "What did you say?"

"The Tagus, it looks beautiful at this time of the year."

"Yes, but it's a pity it's full of rubbish."

"That's close enough." She reached across the table, and they shook hands. "I'm Sofia Beckman."

The waiter arrived with her food.

Kurt took a closer look at his table guest while she ate. Her hair, tied in a bun, more grey than brown, reminded him of his mother. Her deep blue eyes and fine facial features echoed the faded beauty of her youth. He racked his memories but couldn't recall a single woman anywhere in Abwehr headquarters in Tirpitzufer, Berlin.

Was she German? Everything about her looked English. She sounded English. If this was a disguise it was masterful.

"Where are you from?" he said.

"A small village in the south."

That told him nothing. The south of England, presumably.

They finished their food in silence. When the bill arrived, Kurt put his on his room tab; she paid hers in cash.

She recovered a light overcoat from the porter at reception, and they left the hotel together. She led him to the nearby Rossio Square that featured two elaborate fountains on either side of a tall column, supporting a statue. Terraces of apartment buildings over shops surrounded the square on all sides.

"We can talk here. No one but Pedro will overhear us."

"Pedro?"

She pointed to the statue. "Pedro IV, king of Portugal and first emperor of Brazil."

"You have something for me?"

She frowned at him. "You must answer a few questions first. We can walk."

They strode out together, sharing the space with a few tourists, wealthy people for whom the War was nothing but a distant, vague inconvenience limiting their choices of holiday locations.

"What is your name?"

"Kevin O'Reilly."

"I meant your real name."

"If you are who you say you are, you'll know my real name," Kurt replied, testily.

"Very well, Herr Müller. You are 24 hours late for our meeting."

"Sorry about that. I was unavoidably detained yesterday. Who sent you?"

She clicked her tongue like a schoolmistress. "Where do you think I came from?"

"From Tirpitzufer, Berlin. Who sent you? And do you have the list?"

She smiled. "That's two questions. Our mutual friend Erwin sent me. And I have the list back at my hotel. I can fetch it in ten minutes."

"Are you really British?"

"My mother was English, my father is German."

"And did you really work in Madrid?"

"In the British embassy before the War, yes. Why?"

"Could you let me have a list of the British people you knew that worked in Madrid at that time?"

"In the embassy, you mean?"

"In the embassy or anywhere else in Madrid."

She gave that a moment's thought. "I can think of a few, but I'm not sure I can remember all the names. Why do you need it?"

"I'm working on a theory that may involve someone on that list."

"What theory?"

"I can't tell you that, but it is important."

She hesitated. "Very well. I'll need to make a couple of telephone calls to compile that second list, and I'll have to get clearance from Berlin, but it shouldn't take long. Meet me here in one hour."

"How many names are on the Abwehr list?"

"One hundred and twenty-two," she said, and she walked away.

Kurt remained where he was, walking briskly in circles around the square. His body tingled with anticipation. That number was higher than he expected. Allowing five support staff for each agent, 122 agents would require an army of 610 support workers.

He couldn't wait to get his hands on the Abwehr list. The Madrid list was a bonus that could uncover the Russian mole within British Intelligence. He'd been through a lot since he'd left Britain. He'd survived a couple of killers in Dublin and a Gestapo attempt to ship him back to Berlin from Lisbon. The promise he'd made to Schellenberg was a niggling complication, but once he was safely back in London, he would be beyond his reach.

Sofia returned in less than an hour. She hooked her hand into his arm, and they strolled together toward the column at the centre of the square.

"I've picked up a tail," she said, chewing her lower lip.

He peered over her shoulder. There was no one within 100 metres behind them. "Are you sure? I can't see anyone."

"Trust me, I'm sure."

"You have the two lists?"

"They're in my coat pocket," she said.

In that instant, her head exploded, spraying him with her blood and brain matter.

Chapter 50

A shot rang out. Sofia fell, pulling him down with her. The sound of a second shot was followed by a scream. Twenty metres behind them, an elderly woman bent over the body of her husband.

They're shooting at me!

Kurt jumped to his feet and ran. The tourists scattered.

He saw the flash of a third shot in a window high in one of the terraces on the eastern side of the square. Using the column for cover, he made it to the safety of an alley to the west before the sniper could fire another shot.

He looked back across the square. It had emptied of tourists. Only the elderly dead man and Sofia's body remained, lying on the decorative cobblestones. Sofia had the two lists in her pocket. Could he risk running back to retrieve them? In answer to his question, a fourth shot rang out, taking a chip of masonry from the wall near his head. He ran. The alley was a cul de sac, the only way out a metal staircase mounting a wall 20-metres high at the far end.

Kurt took the stairs two at a time, passing a beggar woman at the midpoint. As he reached the top, a bullet pinged off the metal bannister. Keeping his head down, he continued uphill, over a set of cobbled steps. Rounding a bend, he was out of the line of fire, and safe for the moment.

He stopped to gather his breath and an image from the moment of Sofia's death surfaced in his mind, his stomach churned, and he lost his evening meal at his feet.

Someone wanted him dead. Police sirens sounded in the square below. Panicked, he ran, turning left and right at random, seeking smaller streets, looking for a hiding place. After 15 minutes, he stopped in a laneway to catch his breath. He looked at his hands. They were shaking and covered in blood. A noise alerted him that someone was coming. Retreating deeper into the laneway, he came to a dead end. He turned to face his pursuers, his fists balled, and Tammi appeared in front of him, her blond hair in disarray.

She clutched her side. "For God sakes slow down."

He said, "You saw what happened back there?"

She sat against a wall. "Give me a minute, Kevin."

"You shouldn't have followed me. It's not safe. They're trying to kill me."

"I saw a sniper shoot your contact. What makes you think they want you dead, too? And who are 'they' anyhow?"

"I don't know who they are, but they fired three shots at me. You saw what happened to Sofia!" Tammi seemed to be taking it all too calmly.

She nodded and her expression darkened. "Not a pretty sight. Look at you, you're covered in blood."

Kurt removed his jacket and threw it from him. He rubbed his hands together in an effort to clean them, the wail of distant police sirens accompanying the chattering of his teeth.

"You're shaking. I think you're suffering from shock." She led him to a window ledge.

Kurt sat down. He rubbed his hands some more. She tore a strip of material from the lining of his jacket, spat on it and cleaned the blood from his face.

She inspected his hands and face when she'd finished. "You'll do." She scrubbed the blood from his jacket and handed it to him, but he refused to put it on. "It's not perfect, but you need to keep warm until we can get you to safety."

"It's not safe for you here with me," said Kurt. "You go back to the hotel. I'll join you after dark."

"Do you know the way back?"

Kurt shook his head. He was totally disoriented.

"When you think it's safe, head south, downhill to the river. Turn left and follow the river to the giant arch. Go through the arch and follow the roads straight north to Rossio Square."

He threw her a questioning look.

"The one with the statue of King Pedro, where your friend was shot. You should be able to find the hotel from there. If you get lost, look for a taxi. I'll wait for you in my room. It's on the fifth floor, room 512." She stood up. "Can you remember that? Are you going to be all right?"

"I'll be fine. Room 512. I'll try to get to you after dark."

"You should wear the jacket," she said, and she left.

When Tammi had gone, the shaking grew more intense. He was

warm, but somehow chilled to the bone. The image of Sofia's last moment haunted him. He picked up the jacket and put it on. Overcome by exhaustion, he closed his eyes.

#

A strong breeze woke him, a foul taste in his mouth. Overhead, a big moon played hide and seek behind thick clouds. He was still sitting in the alley on the ground near the window ledge, shivering from the cold, but the severe shakes had gone.

It was 3:30 a.m. Instinct told him that the killers were still out there, searching for him. He needed to move on. He had already spent too long in one place, but it was too early to return to the hotel. Emerging from the alleyway, he again followed a random pattern uphill and in a general direction away from where he thought the hotel was.

Two police cars approached at speed, sirens blaring, blue lights flashing. Kurt melted into a doorway and watched them fly past. He couldn't imagine where they might be going.

Turning a corner, he startled a courting couple in a church doorway. He walked on for 20 minutes, before settling in a small archway leading to a car park in another dark alley. The clouds had darkened overhead, hiding the moon. He froze, fully alert, his ears tuned to every sound. The distant drone of the city, more police sirens far away, somewhere close by, a car engine receding, a couple of cats mewling at each other, and a dog's eager bark, coming closer.

They have a dog! It must have picked up my scent from the other alleyway.

He got to his feet and set out at a canter, moving at right angles to the direction of the sound. His plan was to complete a wide half-circle that would take him down to the banks of the river. If he could make it there, he might have a chance. There could be tourists enjoying the nightlife of the city. Up here in the deserted suburban streets and laneways, it would be easy for the killers to finish him off and make their escape.

After a few minutes running mostly downhill toward the river, the skies opened. Within 60 seconds, his jacket and pants were soaking wet. He paused to listen for the dog. It was gaining on him. He increased his speed.

He came to a short flight of steps running upward to his right.

Hoping to find a hiding place, and with no notion whether it was a good choice or not, he ran up the steps. He passed a craggy black-trunked tree, and found himself in a small courtyard consisting of six or eight garage lock-ups.

One of the garage doors swung open, and a young man stepped out. He gestured to Kurt to enter. Kurt ducked inside, and the man closed the garage door.

Chapter 51

Thursday March 9, 1944

A candle lit a corner of the garage. A wooden ladder led to a makeshift structure under the roof.

The man said something to Kurt in Portuguese.

"I don't speak your language," said Kurt.

"English?"

"Yes."

"Why they chase you?" said the man.

"I don't know," said Kurt. "They have a dog. They will find me here."

The man held out a hand. "Give your coat to me."

Kurt took off his jacket and handed it over.

"You wait," said the man, pointing to the ladder.

Kurt climbed the ladder onto a wooden platform equipped with a crude bed.

"Take the ladder," said the man.

Kurt pulled the ladder up.

"No sound," said the man, and he put an ear to the garage door.

"They have guns," said Kurt. "They will shoot you."

"Stay. Hide. No sound," said the man. He blew out the candle and splashed something from a can on the floor. The acrid smell of kerosene filled Kurt's nostrils.

Kurt strained to listen. Then he heard them. His pursuers and their dog were on the other side of the door. They banged on the door. The man stepped outside and closed the door behind him.

Kurt understood nothing of the conversation that followed. The killers sounded angry, the young man responded with laughter. There were long pauses and scratching sounds. The dog whined.

The door flew open and two men came into the garage. The dog barked, running around the garage in confused circles.

Kurt froze. If the men looked up they would see his hiding place.

Then the killers were shouting to each other.

In Russian.

The Russians left.

After what felt like an eon, the young man returned and closed the garage door. He lit the candle. "Safe now. Come down."

"Wait," said Kurt. "They may come back."

They waited, Kurt in the rickety wooden structure, the man below. Five minutes later, the Russians returned. They hammered on the door. The man opened it, the Russians came in and the dog repeated his confused search.

Outside, the rain teemed down, noisily.

The Russians left, arguing amongst themselves.

Kurt waited another couple of minutes before lowering the ladder and climbing down.

His jacket was gone, and with it, his passport.

"What did you say to them?" said Kurt.

"I say I found your coat."

A mixture of confused feelings flooded Kurt's mind. There was the lingering shock of the narrow escape, admiration for this man's ingenuity, his audacity and his courage in facing down armed men. Most of all Kurt felt a surge of gratitude. This stranger had saved his life, for sure.

"Why Russians want to kill you?" said the man.

"I don't know, but thanks for helping me. You saved my life."

"*Nada.*" The man held out a hand. "Flavio. This my house."

Kurt shook his hand warmly. "I'm Kurt. It's a fine house. Why did you help me?"

Flavio shrugged. "I see you earlier, running. I know you need help, so I help."

"I'm grateful. *Obrigado*," said Kurt.

"*Nada.* You stay here tonight. I have room."

Kurt shook his head. "I must get back to my hotel."

"What hotel?"

"The Avenida Palace. Can you tell me the best way to get there?"

Flavio gave that some thought. "I show you. But first, we wait."

Flavio arranged two boxes around a foldable card table. He opened a bottle of red wine, and handed it to Kurt. They drank from the bottle in turns. Flavio had no glasses.

Flavio pointed a finger at Kurt. "*Alemanha?* You are German, I think."

"Yes."

"*Fascista?*"

Kurt shook his head. "I'm not a Nazi."

Flavio became agitated. He spoke rapidly in Portuguese, using his hands. Kurt understood nothing. When his rant had run its course, he said, "There are many *Fascistas* in my country."

Kurt was aware of Portugal's ambiguous position in the War. The country had declared itself neutral, but it had strong leanings toward the Third Reich. There were persistent rumours of secret German submarine docks in the Algarve. "The Nazis will lose the War," he said.

"Yes. Soon the Americans and the British will arrive with their army, and France will be free."

Kurt nodded. "Soon, yes."

The conversation turned to more domestic matters. Flavio revealed that he'd been living in the garage for three years, since his wife left him for another man.

When Kurt expressed sympathy, Flavio grinned. "First, I had a girl, *uma amante*, you understand?"

"You had a girlfriend, a mistress? How long were you married?"

"*Dez anos.* Ten years." Flavio was older than he looked.

"Children? Bambinos?"

Flavio smiled. "That's Italian. No children. You are married?"

"No, but I have a girlfriend. Two girlfriends."

Flavio grinned salaciously.

Kurt said, "Can a man love two women, Flavio?"

"Of course, why not?"

"Is it possible to love two women at the same time?"

Flavio rubbed his chin. Then he grinned. "To love two women is not a problem, to make two houses, that is a problem." He rubbed his fingers together.

Kurt wondered if there might be a Portuguese expression for having your cake and eating it. Did he really love two women? His love for Gudrun was beyond question, but what about Lina? He couldn't live without Gudrun, could he live without Lina?

When the bottle was empty, Flavio checked outside. The rain had eased. "We go now."

They set off, uphill.

"Why uphill?" said Kurt. "We need to get to the river."

"I have a better way," said Flavio.

They pressed on. Then the rain came again. Without his jacket, Kurt was immediately wet to the skin.

Just short of 6 a.m. they reached a park with a panoramic view across the valley, where lightning flashes lit up the ancient castle of São Jorge. Below them, a sea of terracotta roofs glistened in the rain. Kurt took a moment to absorb the breath-taking view before Flavio led him on to the top of a steep slope. Here a rickety tram sat on ancient tracks, leading downward.

Flavio said, "You take the tramcar. The hotel is 200 metres to the right at the bottom."

Kurt shook Flavio's hand and thanked him again. Then he boarded the tram, paid the driver the five escudos fare, and joined 15 sleepy early morning workers on the wooden bench.

Rainwater dripping from his clothing pooled at his feet, attracting some curious glances from the other passengers.

The ancient tram set off down the slope, the cab moaning, the wheels singing at the bends in the tracks.

The cab emptied at the terminal. Eight of the passengers turned right, and Kurt joined them, keeping close to the buildings, leaving a trail of water behind him, like a snail. The hotel lay directly ahead. A quick check confirmed that the entrance was clear before he ducked inside and asked for his key at reception.

The receptionist looked shocked by his appearance, but she handed Kurt his key. "Two men have been looking for you. I believe one of them may be waiting for you on the fourth floor." The way she said "men" and her dancing eyebrows suggested deep disapproval.

"*Obrigada*," said Kurt.

He jumped into the lift and pressed the button for the sixth floor. At the sixth floor, he jumped out, ran to the stairs and descended to the second floor. From there he took the lift back up to the sixth floor, before descending the staircase back to the fifth. Finally, he ran to Tammi's room and knocked on her door. She let him in.

"What happened? Where did you go? You're all wet."

He stripped off in her bathroom, leaving the door ajar so that he could relate his overnight adventures. Finally, he emerged wrapped in a towel. He explained his comings and goings in the lift and the staircase to confuse his pursuers and their dog.

"Who was this Flavio? Why did he help you?" she said.

"I can't answer those questions. He was a Good Samaritan, I suppose."

"Okay, so what's your next move?"

"I've lost my passport. I need to get to the British embassy, to get a new one."

"You'll be lucky to get out of the hotel in one piece," she said. "And what are you going to wear?"

"If I can stay here for an hour or two, I'm hoping my clothes will dry."

"I have a better idea." She went to the wardrobe and pulled out a floral dress. "Try this on."

Chapter 52

Kevin slipped the dress over his head. It wasn't a great fit, but it was the only spare outfit she had. He was a vision! She covered her mouth for a moment to smother a laugh.

He looked in the mirror. "I don't think it's my style."

"It's the only way you're going to get out of here alive. Take it off."

He struggled to get the dress off, and she stepped forward. "Hold still. You're going to tear it." She helped him out of the dress.

"You should get some sleep," she said, pointing at the bed. "Use that side."

Kevin thanked her and lay down. He wasn't such a bad looking guy, but he looked shattered from lack of sleep.

"How old are you?" she said.

She got no answer. He was out cold. She tried to guess his age. Early thirties, maybe. Not so much older than me, she thought.

She dozed on the bed beside Kevin until the shops opened at 8 a.m. Then she got dressed and put on her light overcoat.

She woke him. "I'm going out. I won't be long."

He said, "Take a look at the fourth floor on your way down. See if there's anyone watching room 410."

She took the stairs. One floor down, she checked the corridor, and sure enough, there was a thug hanging around outside Kevin's room. She left the hotel, walked a half block to a pharmacy and bought some supplies there. Next, she paid a visit to a beauty parlour she'd spotted the day before.

She returned to her room carrying two bags and dropped them on the bed.

He was dressed in his shorts and pants. She handed him her spare brassiere. It just about stretched around his chest and she managed to fasten it at the back.

He wriggled about, running his fingers under the elastic. "It's uncomfortable."

"It is a tight fit. Leave it alone."

She stuffed the cups with a scarf and a pair of woollen socks, and did the best she could to eliminate the bumps and bulges.

He looked at himself in the mirror and grinned. His 2-day stubble added to the surreal effect. "What a sight!"

"You're a big girl. Now, let's see what we can do with that face." She emptied the pharmacy bag onto the bed and handed him a shaving kit. He took it into the bathroom. When he emerged, he was clean shaven.

"Do your legs as well."

"What do you mean? You want me to shave my legs?"

"Yes. They look like a monkey's. I can do it for you if you prefer."

He went back into the bathroom. He came out ten minutes later, dressed in his shorts. She examined his legs. He'd done a passable job.

She sat him on the bed and applied some make-up. His black eye required special attention, but she managed to hide it under a generous layer of face powder.

After 15 minutes, he had deep red lips, highlighted eyes and rouge cheeks.

She offered to pluck his eyebrows.

"No thanks," he said.

"They're quite bushy. I can use this afterwards to finish the job." She showed him her eyebrow pencil.

"No," he said. "Leave my eyebrows alone."

"How about those eyelashes? I have some mascara here." She rummaged in her handbag.

"No thanks."

"Please yourself." She'd anticipated his reaction to that idea.

She helped him into the dress. Apart from the top button, there was no way she could close any of the buttons at the back. Kevin checked himself in the mirror again. He shook his head. "I look a mess. This is not going to work."

He still looked like a man in women's clothing, but Tammi had one more trick up her sleeve. "Sit," she said.

He sat on the bed.

"Close your eyes."

He closed his eyes. She pulled a blond wig from the beauty parlour bag and put it on his head. A few adjustments to get it straight, and she helped him to his feet. "Keep them closed." She positioned him in front of the mirror. "Now you can open them."

He opened his eyes and gasped. "That's amazing. I look… alluring… I'm even quite attractive, in a way. What do you think?"

"I wouldn't go that far, but you do look female. You're a bit tall for a woman, the wig's not great, and it's a pity about the square chin, but I think it'll do the job."

His blond locks draped over his shoulders. Turning from side to side, he twirled them in his fingers, pouting into the mirror.

"Don't tug on it, Kevin," she said.

"I'm going to need a new name," he said. "What would you suggest?"

He reminded her of a butch individual from her high school. "Colleen. You look like a Colleen to me."

Kurt blew a kiss at the mirror. "Well hello there, Colleen."

"Sit," she said. "Give me your hand."

He held out a hand. She applied nail polish to his fingernails. She did both hands, and he blew on them to dry them.

Next, she sprayed him all over with her perfume.

He coughed, and when he objected she explained that the smell would confuse the dog.

"Right, I want you on the bed," she said.

"Cheeky," said Colleen.

"On your stomach. Now lie perfectly still."

She hitched the dress up, and used her eyebrow pencil to run a line down the middle of each leg.

"That tickles," said Kevin.

"Don't move."

When she was finished, he got to his feet. She put her hat on his head, ran her eyes over her creation, and adjusted the bra one last time.

It doesn't work. The hips are okay, but the dress is too tight at the shoulders and too loose on top.

"Is that it?" he said.

"Those buttons at the back are a problem. Turn around." She made one more attempt to fasten the buttons, but it was hopeless. She removed a light blanket from the wardrobe, folded it across the diagonal and draped it over Colleen's shoulders.

"You'll do. Let's go."

Kevin put on his shoes, and she was presented with another problem.

"Give me a minute," she said.

A quick search of the corridors and she picked up a pair of open-toed sandals outside one of the guest rooms. She hurried back and handed them to Kurt.

He put them on. "They're a bit tight."

"They'll have to do." She handed him her gloves and handbag. "Let's go, Colleen."

Chapter 53

Friday March 10, 1944

The disguise worked like a charm. Clinging together, giggling like schoolgirls, they passed two policemen in the lobby and waltzed past the Russians at the hotel entrance. The dog checked them out and recoiled from Colleen's perfume.

A taxi took them to the British embassy, but when they arrived they saw strange men in flat caps hanging about all around the entrance to the building.

She tapped the driver on the shoulder. "Take us to the American legation."

"What can the Americans do?" said Kurt.

"I'm sure they'll help, but we need to get our stories straight."

"What would you suggest?"

"I'll pull OSS rank and ask for their help to get you back to England. I'll tell them you're working for MI5. The rest is up to you."

Kurt's appearance caused a few raised eyebrows at the US legation. They stowed him in a study while Tammi explained their situation.

The study door opened, and a legation official came in. He was a young man – certainly younger than Kurt – wearing a seriously furrowed brow above a pince-nez.

"Tammi tells me that you are an Irish citizen, working with British Intelligence in London, and that you've lost your passport." He stood by the fireplace. Kurt remained seated, still wearing his disguise, his bare knees crossed, feeling more foolish with every passing minute.

"I was chased by a group of Russian assassins, last night. I had help from a local guy who used my jacket to confuse their dog. I lost the jacket. Unfortunately, my passport was in a pocket."

The official suddenly seemed to grasp the comedy of Kurt's appearance. He tried, unsuccessfully, to smother a smile. "Right, tell me why the Soviets want you dead."

"I can't answer that question. You'd have to ask them. They murdered my friend and took several shots at me before I escaped."

"Give me your best guess."

"Whitehall is convinced that British Intelligence has been infiltrated by a Russian agent. I believe my friend was about to give me his name when the Russian sniper shot her. In the head." Kurt's voice shook.

The official lost his smile. "I've seen the reports in the newspapers. Two people were shot. One was an old guy from Brazil, the woman who was shot – your friend – was German. There's speculation that she might have been an agent working for German Military Intelligence, the Abwehr. What do you have to say about that?"

Kurt looked shocked. "No, that can't be right. I couldn't imagine Sofia having anything to do with German Intelligence."

"And yet she had information about a Soviet mole in London?"

"She worked in Spain before the War. I understand that's where she met the British mole."

"Okay, so what's your next move?"

"I need to get back to London as fast as possible to tell them what has happened here."

"Right, what do you need from us?"

Kurt removed the wig. "A passport, a plane ticket to London, and safe passage to the plane. Oh, and a change of clothing."

#

The Americans were happy to arrange a plane ticket to London for Kurt. They couldn't or wouldn't give him a US passport, though. They gave him a temporary US identity card. He would have to make do with that. He was fully resigned to spending the weekend in the US legation, and was delighted when the official told him his plane would leave early the next day.

A good scrub with toilet soap removed the make-up from his face, and Tammi used a bottle of acetone to remove the red paint from his fingernails. The legation staff rustled up a spare set of pants, a shirt and an old jacket for him. He was left with the tight-fitting, open-toed sandals. No one at the legation wore size 12 shoes.

They spent the night in separate rooms in the guest quarters of the legation.

Kurt slept soundly in the knowledge that he was under the protection of the United States and safe from the Russian assassins. He had a lot to be thankful for, not least the help he'd had from Tammi and a Portuguese stranger called Flavio.

Kurt and Tammi met up again for breakfast in the legation canteen.

He asked her if she would be travelling to London with him. "You did say your orders were to stick to me like a limpet."

She blushed. "I've grown quite fond of you, Kurt, but I need to return to my studies in Ireland."

"You really are a student, then?"

"Yes, of course I am."

After breakfast, an official driver appeared to take Kurt to the plane. Tammi and Kurt embraced. She treated him to one long final kiss on the lips.

"What was that for?" said Kurt.

She grinned. "Just to show you what you'll be missing."

Kurt touched her face. "Look after yourself. Don't go back to the hotel. The Russians will have figured out by now how you helped me, and you can be sure they'll be lying in wait for you back there."

They embraced one last time.

The driver took him to the embarkation pier in the minister's 1926 6-cylinder, maroon-coloured Chrysler. When Kurt admired the car, the driver responded that it was "the best darn thing on four wheels" and spent the whole of the short journey itemizing its outstanding features.

Chapter 54

Saturday March 11, 1944

Kurt boarded the seaplane and sat at the back of the cabin, deep in thought. Another traumatic episode in his life had drawn to a close. He had met two new women, one of whom had been killed. His involvement with the other could have blossomed into a full-blown relationship, and he was sure it would have if he had accepted Tammi's initial invitation of accommodation back in Ireland.

The graphic images from Sofia's death would haunt his dreams for a long time to come, and returned in flashes every time he closed his eyes. The Russians were cold-blooded; they played for keeps. They had used a snub-nosed bullet, what the Americans called a dum-dum, to make sure that one bullet did the job.

He regretted asking Sofia for that second list. He was sure that was what got her killed. The calls she'd made from her hotel room must have alerted the Russians, and it had taken them no more than 15 or 20 minutes to get their sniper in position to neutralise the threat. Whoever the mole in London was, his NKVD handlers were prepared to go to any lengths to protect his identity.

He chewed his lip. Could he have retrieved the two lists from Sofia's coat pocket before running from the sniper? Probably not. The sniper had hit his target with a single shot at a distance of 100 yards. He was a crack shot. If Sofia hadn't pulled Kurt down when she fell, the second shot that killed that elderly tourist would have taken him out. He was lucky to be alive.

Did he have enough information to help identify the Russian mole? The Madrid connection would narrow the search, but would it be enough? And without the list of Abwehr agents in London, he had nothing to help identify Schellenberg's spy. Or had he? Schellenberg had let slip that he knew Arnold's alias. What did that reveal about the rogue spy? Maybe – just maybe – his trip to Lisbon had not been a total washout, and maybe poor Sofia hadn't died for nothing.

#

The seaplane landed at Poole. The passengers disembarked, went through customs and immigration checks, and were steered toward a train for London.

Kurt was held back by the immigration staff. His temporary US identity card was seen as a poor substitute for his missing Irish passport. Revealing that he was a member of His Majesty's armed forces on a 7-day pass caused additional difficulties, since he couldn't produce the pass, but a telephone call to his unit in London answered all outstanding objections. He made a solemn promise to the immigration staff that he would write to the appropriate government department in Ireland for a replacement passport as soon as he arrived at his home in London, and they let him continue his journey.

The train journey to central London was painfully slow. Stopping at every station along the way, and between stations here and there for no discernible reason, it took four hours.

The general mood amongst the passengers was upbeat. The sun shone, and the end of the War was within sight. Laughing children played in the carriages and corridors. People were smiling and joking, seemingly unfazed by the pace of the train. Kurt found their optimism at odds with his own feelings. His trip to Lisbon had promised so much, but he had gained so little. How was he ever going to uncover the Gingerbread spy? If he failed, Operation Overlord would be a disaster. The War might easily drag on for another five or ten years.

#

A half-hour beyond Winchester, 30 minutes from Waterloo, Kurt made his way to the toilet at the end of the carriage. He edged sideways past one of the ticket inspectors, standing in the corridor. He was a man of considerable bulk, dressed in a woollen serge overcoat.

When he emerged from the toilet, the ticket inspector stood in his path. "Mr O'Reilly?"

Kurt was immediately alarmed. "How do you know my name?"

"I have a small parcel for you in the guard's van." Something in the man's accent niggled at Kurt's mind.

"How is that possible?" said Kurt.

"It was left for you at the BOAC office in Lisbon by a Frau Beckman. Frau Sofia Beckman."

Sofia! She found a way to get the two lists to me, after all.

"It's that way, sir..." He pointed.

Kurt headed toward the tail of the train. The ticket inspector followed.

The guard's van was a chaotic jumble of crates, parcels, mailbags and packages, a slider door rattled on its rails on one side.

"You'll find it on my desk, at the back," said the ticket inspector, pointing behind a pile of crates.

This direction alerted Kurt to danger. He braced for action, turning to face the man. The evil glint in the man's eyes confirmed his suspicions, that and the snub-nosed gun in his hand.

Kurt was trapped. There was nowhere to go behind him, and the man with the gun barred his route back to the carriage. He grabbed the nearest parcel from the pile to his right and held it in front of him as a shield.

The man fired. The parcel was torn from Kurt's hands, but it deflected the bullet. Before the man could fire a second time, Kurt seized a heavy crate from the pile and pulled it down onto the gunman. The gunman fell, the second bullet whistling over Kurt's head into the ceiling.

Kurt lunged forward and kicked the gun from the man's hand. The man shook the crate off and bounced back to his feet quickly. He swore long and loud in Russian, pulling a long blade from his clothing.

The first sideways swipe missed Kurt's stomach by millimetres. Kurt immediately shoulder-charged the man, hoping to knock him off balance, but the man fell against the crates and packages and they held him upright. Levelling the point of the knife at Kurt, he thrust forward.

There was no room to avoid the thrust. Instinct took over. Kurt used a technique he'd learnt years earlier in his Wehrmacht training to divert the knife and take control of the arm that held it. Now, the blade was in the air, pointing at the ceiling, while Kurt and the heavy man wrestled for control, face to face. Both of Kurt's hands were busy holding the knife arm, but his adversary had an arm free, and he used it to pile-drive his fist into Kurt's midriff. Kurt crumpled under the blow, losing all the air in his lungs and slipping to his knees.

The Russian shouted in triumph. He raised his blade above his head. "You fought well, English," he said. "Say good day to Sofia from me."

Kurt grabbed the man's ankles, pulled with all his strength, and brought him crashing down on his back. The knife clattered away across the floor. Kurt jumped on the prostate Russian, pinning him to the floor with an arm on his throat. But the Russian was too strong. He shrugged Kurt off like a rag doll, picked up the knife, and got to his feet.

Kurt's head clattered into the sliding door. He fell to the floor on his back, spots in front of his eyes. The Russian stepped up in front of him, blade raised to deliver the *coup de grâce*.

Out of the corner of his eye, Kurt saw the gun. He reached out, grabbed it, pointed, and fired.

The heavy Russian fell backwards, landing on the floor with a thump, raising a cloud of dust. Kurt got to his feet. He felt for a pulse. The man was dead, a small hole in his forehead. He opened the sliding door and tossed the knife and the gun out. It took all his strength to drag the body of the Russian to the opening and heave him from the train. Then he closed the door.

Before returning to the seat in his carriage, Kurt checked the guard's desk. Finding nothing there was no great surprise.

Chapter 55

The two men removed the bag from his head and undid his bonds. His mind had adjusted to the darkness enough to allow a crude measurement of time. He knew it had been several hours since the last interrogation.

The lights blazed overhead, blinding him.

They gave him water. He drank eagerly.

They took him to the adjoining room and let him use the toilet. Then they sat him in the chair and retied his hands tightly behind his back.

"I'm hungry," he said. His eyes adjusted to the light, and he looked at the faces of his torturers.

Who are these men?

"We'll feed you later," said one man.

The other one pulled a fob watch from his waistcoat pocket. He held the watch up, swinging it back and forth on the end of its chain. "Listen to my voice. You're feeling sleepy. Your eyelids are growing heavy..."

He panicked. He tried to get out of the chair, but the second man held him down with hands on his shoulders.

"Listen to me. Hear my voice. You are falling asleep..."

The drone of the man's voice filled his mind. He couldn't tear his eyes from the swinging watch, no matter how hard he tried. Back and forth it swung, back and forth, left to right to left, back and forth...

"Now you can hear nothing but my voice. Your eyes are closing, slowly, slowly. You are slipping into a deep sleep."

When he awoke, he felt lightheaded, his mind clouded. He was alone and in darkness again, strapped securely to the chair, the bag over his head, the gag in his mouth. What had he told them?

Who are these men?

#

Lina was on duty in the hospital on Saturday morning. Following a busy night, all but three of the nurses had been sent home, and the rest of the hospital was reduced to a skeleton staff.

Lina was in the canteen, having a quick break, when the air raid sirens started.

In broad daylight!

Surely this was a mistake, or maybe they were testing the sirens. They would stop in a minute or two.

But the sirens continued. And soon she could hear the distant drone of heavy planes.

The catering staff disappeared. Lina ran back to the wards. She was close to St Dymphna's, the psych ward, when she heard the roar of a bomber heading their way. She ran outside. Dan, the porter, Colonel Victor Macintyre, and four of the walking wounded were there in bright sunlight, looking to the sky.

Dan pointed to the east, shielding his eyes. "Here she comes."

And there it was, a dark shape against a clear blue sky, heading straight toward the hospital, black smoke pouring from its port engine.

"Shouldn't we get inside?" Lina shouted. "It's going to crash."

"It's too high. It won't hit us," said Dan. "But get everyone indoors."

The colonel refused to move. He waved a fist and shouted something at the plane.

Lina herded the other patients back into the hospital as the plane passed over their heads, its damaged engine coughing, clearly doomed to crash somewhere close to the west of them.

Then she heard the whistle of a bomb.

"Get down everybody!" she shouted. She threw herself to the floor as the bomb exploded with an ear-shattering bang and the wall to her right disintegrated, showering everyone with plaster and rubble. She got to her feet, shrugged off the debris, and checked the patients in the lobby. There were no new injuries that she could see.

She ran outside. Dan and the colonel were half-buried under a pile of blocks. It was a hopeless task, but she tore at the rubble to free them, breaking her fingernails.

Within seconds, she had help. People rallied around her and began to work at the rubble. They got Dan and Victor out and onto stretchers. The colonel was covered in dust. He was unhurt.

Dan was conscious, but his head was bleeding. A young doctor assessed his injuries. He had a gash in the skull that would require careful monitoring and a broken tibia.

The bomb had shaken Lina to her core, and her ears were ringing, but she steeled herself and got to work. As the most experienced nurse on duty, it fell to her to take charge. She marshalled the other nurses to clean up and settle the patients in their wards, while she took the wounded porter to X-ray. When the doctors had set his leg, she put it in plaster. And then she sat with him, monitoring his vital signs every half-hour for most of the day.

She waited until he had fallen asleep and she was sure she could leave her patient for a short while, then she went to the canteen. The evening shift had started, and Kathy and Julie were sitting at a table with two other nurses. Lina ignored them. She collected her food and headed for a table by herself.

Kathy waved at her. "Hey, Lina. Come sit with us."

Lina sat at her chosen table. She was not going to give them any opportunity to be nasty to her. Not ever again. A sprinkle of plaster dust fell from her hair. She brushed it from her food.

Julie and Kathy picked up their plates and cups, came over to Lina's table, and sat down on either side of her.

"Before you say anything, I want to apologise," said Kathy. "Julie and I have been rude to you for too long. We would like to be your friends."

Lina said nothing. It was an obvious trick to get her to say something that would give them ammunition to make more fun of her.

"Honestly," said Julie. "We are very sorry. We've seen how you've been looking after Dan. You are a fine nurse, and we are honoured to work with you."

Lina looked into Julie's eyes. Could she be sincere, or was this another cruel trick?

Part 4 – London

Chapter 56

Saturday March 11, 1944

Two plainclothes policemen were waiting for Kurt at Waterloo station. Could the police have found the body of the Russian already?

They took him to Scotland Yard and put him in an interview room, where he was joined by Detective Inspector Underwood.

"Where have you been?" said Underwood. "I thought I told you not to leave the country."

"I don't remember that," said Kurt. "My unit gave me a 7-day pass. I took the mailboat to Ireland to visit my mother."

"And returned on a flight from Lisbon. What were you doing in Portugal?" He fixed Kurt with piercing eyes.

Kurt stared back. "Am I to understand that you still haven't located the double murderer, Henry Pollinger?"

"Alleged double murderer," said the inspector. "What was your business in Portugal?"

"I was on a sightseeing tour. It's particularly beautiful this time of the year."

Inspector Underwood hesitated. Then he changed tack. "Tell me what you know about Clarence Newton."

"Never heard of him."

"He says otherwise. He says he has been guarding a house in Fulham that you visit regularly. He says you can vouch for him for the night of the two murders in Frome Road."

"I know Clarence the guard. I didn't know his surname."

"Can you vouch for him on the night in question?"

Kurt thought back to the night of the murders. "Clarence was the one who broke the news about the killings to me when I arrived in the morning. He was on guard duty from midnight that night."

"So, you cannot actually vouch for him?"

"Well, no, but he seemed genuinely shocked by the news. He served with the murdered guard in North Africa. What was his name?"

"Lance Corporal James Dennison. Were you aware that Dennison and Newton were patients in Queen Alexandra's Military Hospital at the same time?"

"I had no idea. Is that significant?" Kurt knew the hospital. It was where Lina worked as a nurse.

"Dennison was invalided out of the army in 1942, Newton in 1943. When Newton arrived in the hospital, they renewed their acquaintance."

"Are you suggesting that Clarence Newton may be a suspect for the murders?"

"We have information that the two men had a falling out when they met again in the hospital. Newton held a serious grudge against his old friend."

"And murdered him?" Kurt laughed. "What about the cook? Why would he have killed her?"

"She may have witnessed the murder. We're working on the assumption that he killed her to keep her quiet."

"And Pollinger and the second man?"

"We're still working on that. Now tell me where you got that black eye, and why you went to Portugal."

"I got the black eye in Dublin. You know what Irish pubs are like. And I volunteered to transport a diplomatic bag from the German embassy in Dublin for the regular courier, who was ill."

Underwood frowned. "Why on earth would you do such a thing?"

Kurt shrugged. "I was doing the man a favour. In exchange I got a free plane ride, a night in a fancy hotel, and a chance to visit a country I hadn't seen before."

The inspector blinked. "One more question. Who or what was Clarence Newton guarding in the house at Perrymead Street, and what was your reason for visiting there regularly?"

"I'd love to answer those questions, Inspector, but I'm prohibited from doing so under the Official Secrets Act."

Inspector Underwood grunted. He terminated the interview and left Kurt alone with his thoughts.

Pollinger was still at large, after 14 days! Kurt had first-hand experience of the abysmal training that the Abwehr gave to its agents. Left to his own devices, Pollinger would have been captured within hours. He must have had help, and a place to hide.

Thirty minutes later, they released him, and he took the Tube to Walham Green in Fulham, knowing that Lina's debriefing would be much more thorough than any Scotland Yard could come up with.

Chapter 57

Saturday March 11 – Sunday March 12, 1944

Kurt used the time on the Tube to work on his story. He planned to give Lina an edited version of his adventures, but experience had taught him that he needed to stick as close to the truth as possible in order to avoid tripping himself up later.

He arrived at their flat at 11:45 p.m. Lina was working late. Seizing his opportunity, he undressed and got into bed. Within minutes, he was sound asleep.

#

She woke him in the morning with a peck on the cheek. She made breakfast. And soon, they were sitting face to face tucking in to streaky bacon and scrambled egg made from powder.

"How did you get the black eye?" was her first question.

He gave her the same answer he'd given the police. "I got involved in a pub brawl in Dublin."

She rolled her eyes. "Why am I not surprised? How was your mother?"

"She's well."

"And Anna?"

"As lively as ever. She tired me out."

"And Gudrun?"

"Gudrun was fine. She's working as a translator in the German legation in Dublin."

"Why did your trip take so long? I expected you back a week ago."

"I was delayed. It's a long story."

"You spent the time with Gudrun?"

"Just one night."

"Just one night? Why? Where else did you sleep?"

"I stayed with Professor Hirsch in his college rooms."

"Oh, why?"

Kurt struggled to answer that question. "I had some business to attend to. I didn't want to get her involved."

She seemed unconvinced by that reply, but she pressed on. "Was your 'business' successful?"

"Yes, but I had to travel to Lisbon to get what I needed."

"You flew to Portugal? When?"

"On Monday last."

"So, how many days were you in Ireland?"

"About a week."

"And you spent only one night with Gudrun?"

"I was in hospital for three days after the pub fight."

"Okay, so what happened in Lisbon?"

"Nothing much. I went to a couple of meetings, met a couple of contacts. It was pretty dull."

She pulled his US identity card from the pocket of her apron and waved it in his face. "What is this? Where's your passport, where did you get those sandals, and what did you do with your jacket and your other clothes?"

Kurt backtracked rapidly. "I ran into some bother with the Russians. They seemed intent on killing me."

"Why would the Russians want to kill you?"

"I never got close enough to ask."

"So how did you lose your clothes?"

"I had to wear a disguise to get away from them. The staff at the US legation gave me some new clothes."

"The British embassy was closed, I suppose?"

"The Russians had put a watch on the British embassy. A friend suggested trying the US legation."

"A female friend?"

"Yes, an American woman called Tammi. She gave me the disguise that enabled me to escape from the hotel. She took me to her embassy."

Kurt could feel the hole he'd dug for himself getting deeper and deeper.

Lina stood up, facing him. "What a dull, boring time you had in Lisbon! Tell me more about this disguise and your American friend, Tammi."

The conversation continued in that vein for 30 minutes. It was like dodging bullets, but he was pretty sure she hadn't caught him in an actual lie. She laughed at the thought of him dressed as a woman, wearing a wig.

She told him about the break-in.

Kurt examined the damaged window. "Did they steal anything?"

"Nothing."

Kurt filed the information away for later consideration. He was sure the break-in was somehow related to the Gingerbread affair.

When he asked how she'd been getting on at the hospital, she told him about the bomb and how she'd had to nurse the porter on her own for a morning.

"Are the other nurses still freezing you out?" he asked.

"Well, no. I think they're starting to thaw," she replied, and she told him about the episode in the canteen. "They seemed to be trying to make peace with me, but I'm not entirely convinced."

"That sounds good. We should celebrate."

"How about a meal in a restaurant tomorrow evening? You must have some spare coupons in your ration book. We could celebrate your successful return."

"Good idea," he said. "Where and what time?"

"Chez Phillipe's at 6 p.m., and don't be late this time."

Chapter 58

Sunday March 12, 1944

Kurt took the Tube to Charing Cross and walked to Bedford Street. He pressed the intercom on the door of Overseas Logistics Limited, and was buzzed inside straight away.

The building was like an icebox. The heating was off for the weekend. He climbed the stairs.

A tight-lipped Madge Butterworth sat at her desk wearing a houndstooth check overcoat. She blew on her hands. "Go straight in. He's expecting you."

He threw her a smile, but she wasn't looking in his direction.

"In here," from the open door of Major Robertson's office.

Tar Robertson, wearing a greatcoat, was seated behind his desk, his chair swivelled 90 degrees to the right so that he could watch the street outside. Kim Philby sat facing the desk, dressed in a suit, and looking thoroughly miserable.

"Pull up a chair, Kevin," said the major. "You will remember Philby from the London Controlling Section."

Kurt nodded to Philby, who ignored him.

He took a seat, and the major turned away from the window. "I try to keep Sundays free, but I couldn't wait to hear your explanation for recent events, and why you disobeyed a direct order."

There was no rancour in the major's voice, but Kurt was instantly on his guard. "Mr Philby gave me a 7-day pass. I didn't think there were any conditions attached. I went to Ireland to visit my mother and my girlfriend."

Kurt glanced at a tight-lipped Philby, who continued to stare straight ahead at the major.

"Before you left, you attempted to send an unauthorized signal from your man's radio transmitter. I received a short report from one of the guards at Perrymead Street."

"I tried to make contact with the Abwehr."

"In defiance of a direct order not to do so. You do realise I could have you court-martialled for that?"

Kurt adjusted his seating. "Yes, I apologise for that, Major."

"And while you were in Ireland, what did you do?"

Kurt reckoned it was a rhetorical question. "I made contact with my friends in the Black Orchestra."

"Didn't I leave strict instructions forbidding any such contact? Perhaps Philby wasn't clear in his instructions?" The major's eyes blazed.

Again, Kurt glanced at Philby, who remained impassive.

"He was, but I thought as long as I was on a pass, I could do what I wanted." Kurt's voice hardened. "Put yourself in my shoes, Major. If you were wrongfully accused of working for the enemy, wouldn't you do whatever you could to clear your name?"

The major said, "You have a lot to learn about the army and following orders, soldier."

Finally, Philby spoke. "Was it worth it?"

"I think so. I arranged to meet Generalmajor von Neumann in Lisbon. He was most helpful. He sent a courier, a member of his staff with the complete list of Abwehr agents in London."

Robertson leaned forward across his desk. "You have the list?"

"No, Major. She gave me the number of agents: 122, but unfortunately, she was shot before she could hand over the list."

The major wrote the number on his desk pad. "Who was this woman?"

"Her name was Sofia Beckman. I had never met her before."

"And yet you were satisfied that she was from the Abwehr?" said Philby.

"We used a recognition sequence."

The major said, "She was shot, you say. Who shot her?"

"A Russian sniper. It was a messy business. He used a dum-dum bullet. I was lucky to escape with my own life."

"That explains the shiner," said Philby.

"No, I picked that up earlier, in Dublin."

Philby snorted.

The major picked up a paperweight from his desk and hefted it in his hand. "What has all this to do with the Russians?"

"Generalmajor von Neumann told me that the Abwehr first learned about Operation Fortitude from a German spy in the Russian embassy in Madrid. He reckoned the information originated here, in London."

Philby raised an eyebrow. "How does that make any sense?"

"His theory is that the NKVD have a source within the Intelligence Services in London."

"That's ridiculous," said the major. "When it first got out, the code word Fortitude was known only to a handful of people in our innermost Intelligence circles, and if there was a mole in London, why would he send the information to Madrid?"

"General von Neumann reckons the mole must have worked in Madrid before the War."

"I see, but that doesn't explain why the Russians had to shoot this Abwehr woman? What was her name again?"

"Sofia Beckman. That was my fault, I'm afraid, Major. She mentioned that she'd worked in the British embassy in Madrid before the War. I asked her to compile a list of British who worked in Madrid while she was there. She agreed to make some telephone calls and provide such a list."

Philby said, "You never got that list either, I suppose."

Kurt directed his reply to Major Robertson. "No, I'm afraid not, but I thought knowledge of the Madrid connection might help you to identify the mole."

The major gave this some thought. Then he said, "I'll let you handle the Russian connection, Philby. You spent some time in Madrid, writing for *The Times*, if I'm not mistaken."

Philby looked at his watch and stood up. "If you'll excuse me, Major, I have a luncheon appointment at the War Office."

Major Robertson nodded curtly. "Thanks for coming in. Keep me posted."

Chapter 59

Major Robertson waited until Philby had left the room before continuing. "We've had a report from our American friends about your exploits in Lisbon. It makes astonishing reading. They say you turned up at their legation dressed as a woman and with no passport. You claimed to be under lethal attack from the Russians."

"That's all true, Major. It was pretty hairy. They used a dog to track me through the streets above Lisbon. That's when I lost my passport."

"And yet you survived."

"I had help."

"From one of their OSS operatives. They mentioned the name Tammi."

Kurt nodded. "She helped with the disguise, but I also owe a great debt to a local man, called Flavio, who got me through the night."

"Let's hope the Russians have lost interest in you, now that you're safely home in London."

Kurt considered telling the major about the attack on the train from Poole. He decided to keep that to himself. He said, "Inspector Underwood of Scotland Yard tells me they have a new suspect for the double murder."

The major snorted. "Clarence Newton. Yes, I heard that, but I don't believe it for a moment. Could you imagine Clarence slitting someone's throat?"

"Why do they suspect him?" said Kurt.

"Apparently the first murder victim, James Dennison, was invalided out of the army. Clarence's wife was a nurse at the hospital. She and Dennison had an affair while Clarence was still fighting in Africa. The two men met up again in the hospital last year."

"Why wait until now to kill him?"

"I suppose he didn't find out about the affair until recently," said the major. "But I find the whole theory very thin."

"Is he under arrest?"

"For the moment, yes. They're holding him under the emergency legislation."

"Generalmajor von Neumann gave me a message for you. He said to tell you you're doing a fine job."

The major recoiled in his seat. "I don't think I'm interested in any messages from the enemy. Does he know who I am?"

"Oh yes, sir. He said you should concentrate on Fortitude South. He says no one in Berlin believes Fortitude North or the plan to invade the Bay of Biscay or the other one, through the south of France."

"The impertinence of the man!"

"He made it clear that the Abwehr – or rather the Black Orchestra, within the Abwehr – is well aware of the Double Cross programme."

"He mentioned it by name?"

"Yes, sir. He mentioned your name, the London Controlling Section, and the Twenty Committee. He said they are fully aware that you are feeding them misinformation. He and his team pass on every scrap that they receive to the OKW. He also said that he hoped and expected that you have turned every single agent they have placed in Britain over the years."

Major Robertson slammed his paperweight onto his desk, making Kurt nearly jump from his skin. "I don't understand. Why would he act like that? And why would he hope for such a thing?"

"I've told you, Major, the Black Orchestra is committed to the downfall of the Third Reich. They are not our enemies. They are allies, working secretly behind enemy lines to ensure the outcome of the War."

Major Robertson got up from his desk. He stood at the window looking out at the Sunday shoppers moving past the rubble of what was once their homes, shops and department stores. "If what you say is true, we will have to come to grips with the fact that not all Germans are Nazis, an unpalatable notion for many in Whitehall."

Kurt said nothing.

The major returned to his seat. "The Double Cross programme will continue until the War is won and the Nazis are removed from the face of the earth. No one in Britain must ever suspect that the Abwehr knows what we are doing. We must continue to transmit false information until the day of the invasion – and beyond. That means that you must keep this knowledge to yourself. Do you understand?"

"Yes, sir.

"It may be necessary to keep this secret for many years even long after the War has been won. Can I rely on you to do that?"

"Yes, Major."

Major Robertson placed his elbows on his desk and clasped his hands together. "The PM is aware of our difficulty with this business. His personal secretary has been hounding me every second day for news about our search for Gingerbread. I was hoping you would return with something more definitive to report."

"I have something that may help," said Kurt. "Generalmajor von Neumann suggested that the rogue spy may not be a member of the Abwehr. He could be an agent of the SD. And there was something else, something Walter Schellenberg said."

The major straightened his back. "You spoke with Walter Schellenberg in Lisbon? How is that possible?"

"He called himself Hauptmann Schämmel, but I knew who he was. I recognised him."

"That was Schellenberg, no question about it. In 1939, two of MI6's finest men were lured to a trap in Venlo, Holland. Schellenberg posed as a disaffected German officer looking to negotiate a peace with Britain. He called himself Hauptmann Schämmel. What did he say?"

"He asked me what I was doing in Portugal. I convinced him that I am still working for the Abwehr, and that I needed the list in order to identify all the Abwehr agents in London who have been turned."

"He swallowed that story?"

"Yes, sir. He released me on condition that I transmit my findings to him 24 hours before reporting to the Abwehr. I think he's desperate for that information. It will give him the ammunition he needs to discredit the Abwehr."

"Did he give you any clue to the identity of the Gingerbread spy?"

"I think he did. He referred to Paul Hoffmeister as Arnold Hoffmeister."

"And the significance of that?" said the major.

"Arnold is a name used only in the safe house at Perrymead Street. Letting that name slip suggests to me that his spy must be someone from the house. I recommend that you check out everyone in the house: Arnold, the two guards, the cook, the cleaner. We should check on Greg Ellis too."

"Nonsense," said the major. "Greg Ellis was not involved in the programme at the critical period."

Kurt didn't agree, but he said nothing. When he'd met Ellis outside the murder house, he had let slip Kurt's real name. Kurt had no explanation for that.

Chapter 60

Monday March 13, 1944
Overseas Logistics Limited, London

On Monday morning, Kurt was back in Major Robertson's office. Carter was there too.

Madge Butterworth was ordered to brew up a pot of tea, and Major Robertson opened proceedings. "I have asked Carter here to help us with the next phase of our investigation. On Kevin's recent unauthorised foray to Lisbon, he identified the number of agents that the Abwehr has planted in our midst, and I can tell you now, that the headcount we have intercepted, executed or turned equates exactly to that number."

Kurt was pleased that the major hadn't used his real name. Carter knew him as Kevin O'Reilly and Kurt wanted it to stay that way.

Carter held up a hand. He had a question. "Do we have the real names and call-signs of these agents?"

"No, just a headcount," said the major. "However, it follows that the Gingerbread spy is not with the Abwehr. The balance of probability is that he is working for the SD."

"I thought the placement of agents overseas was the sole responsibility of the Abwehr," said Carter.

"Apparently not, Carter. Walter Schellenberg, the head of SD-Ausland has his own unique way of doing things. It seems this agent is one of his men. On his unauthorised trip, Kevin identified a line of enquiry that might lead us to this agent. Suffice it to say that he has established a link between the occupants of the house at Perrymead Street and the rogue spy. I've initiated a process that I'm hoping will lead to his identity."

The major paused for questions.

"Who are the suspects?" said Carter.

"The two guards, Harry Locke and Clarence Newton, and Janssen the cleaner."

"We should include Pieter Hendriks, the previous cleaner," said Kurt. "Do we know where he went?"

The major said, "I assume he picked up a better job somewhere. He was overqualified for the cleaning job. He's not in the frame. He was gone before any of this started."

"What about the cook?" said Carter, deadpan.

Major Robertson ignored him. "I've asked our colleagues in Scotland Yard to set up surveillance on Locke and Newton. Henk Janssen is the reason I have called you both here today. We haven't seen him since Thursday. He has gone to ground. I've asked Scotland Yard to trace him, but they've had no luck so far. I want you two to track him down for me." He handed a file across his desk to Carter. "As you'll see from the file, he's a refugee from the Netherlands."

Kurt looked over Carter's shoulder. There was just a single page in the file.

Carter said, "Don't we have a picture of him?"

"Apparently not, but Kurt knows what he looks like." He stood up. "Get back to me as soon as you have anything. Dismissed."

Kurt opened the door and barely avoided a collision with Madge Butterworth, carrying a tray laden with tea, cups and saucers.

Thinking on his feet, he said, "Our meeting is over, Madge, but we need a few minutes to gather our thoughts. Could we have our tea in the waiting room?"

She placed the tray on the table in the waiting room, poured a cup for the major and took it in to him.

Kurt and Carter sat side by side at the table.

"Shall I be mother?" said Carter, and he poured two cups.

Kurt opened Janssen's file. Henk Janssen, a refugee from Rotterdam, had arrived in England in August 1941, and was recruited to the Home Facilities team in June 1943. He had an address at 22 Hobbes Walk, Putney.

"We should start there," said Kurt.

Chapter 61

The terrace of houses that used to be 19 - 25 Hobbes Walk, Putney was a mound of rubble.

They knocked on the door of number 26. No one answered. They tried number 27, with the same result. They tried several houses across the street, and eventually managed to rouse an old lady.

"Excuse us," said Carter. "We're trying to contact one of your neighbours."

The old lady peered at them through her cataracts, clutching the door. She said nothing.

"We're looking for Henk Janssen. He lived on the opposite side of the road in number 22. Do you know him?"

"No." She stepped back into the house.

Kurt said, "Can you tell us when the houses across the street were bombed?"

"Most of them were hit in the early years, during the Blitz. Number 24 and 25 were bombed last week." She closed the door.

Carter said, "He must have moved to a different address when his house was bombed."

Kurt shook his head. "He arrived in London in August 1941. The Blitz was over by then. He must have given the service a false address."

"I'm sure they check that sort of thing," said Carter.

"Maybe not for cleaners."

Their next stop was at the post office. Kurt asked at the counter if they had a forwarding address for Henk Janssen, lately of 22 Hobbes Walk.

"We're not permitted to hand out that sort of information," said the desk clerk. "Are you a relative of his?"

"A friend," said Kurt. "His house is a pile of rubble. I need to know whether he's still alive and where he might be living."

"I'm sorry, sir, I can't give out that sort of information. You could ask at the morgue."

Carter stepped forward, pushing Kurt aside, and waving some sort of official card. "This is a security enquiry. Do you have a forwarding address for Henk Janssen of 22 Hobbes Walk?"

The clerk barely glanced at Carter's card, but he left the desk with a frown on his face and returned after a few minutes with a piece of paper in his hand. "No one of that name lived at 22 Hobbes Walk." He handed the sheet to Carter.

Outside the post office, Carter showed the piece of paper to Kurt. It read: 'Mavis and Daisy Kemp, 22 Hobbes Walk, Putney. RIP December 12, 1940.'

"Are you sure this Henk Janssen exists?" said Carter.

"Yes, of course he exists. He was the cleaner in my safe house. He replaced an earlier cleaner about two weeks ago."

"Are you sure he was Dutch?"

"With a name like that, of course I'm sure."

"The name could be false. He could have been masquerading as a Dutch refugee."

"He spoke Dutch."

"*Goedemiddag*," said Carter. "That proves nothing."

#

The London Association for Dutch people in exile, VNL, was located in a disused church in Stockwell. A Dutch tricolour adorned the entrance, and a framed picture of Queen Wilhelmina hung on the wall over the reception desk.

"*Goede dag*," said the girl on reception.

"Good afternoon," replied Carter. "We are trying to locate an old friend, and we're hoping you can help us. He's from Holland."

"I'll do what I can," she replied, smiling at Kurt. "What is your friend's name?"

"Henk Janssen," said Kurt. "He arrived in London in August 1941."

The receptionist laughed. "I hope you realise, that is the most common name in the Netherlands. It's like John Smith in England, or Daffy Jones in Wales." She pulled a large register from a cabinet, opened it, and ran a finger down a list of names. Her lips moved as she counted, turning page after page. "At least 50 of that name have registered with us in the past three years. Do you have an address?"

"22 Hobbes Walk, Putney," said Carter.

She checked her register again. "I'm sorry, I don't have anyone registered at that address."

"Could we step inside and talk to some of your members?" said Kurt.

She fluttered her eyelashes at him. "You could, but not today, I'm afraid. The members are all at a rally in Trafalgar Square to protest at the recent attempted assassination of our beloved queen, Wilhelmina. On the night of February 20, the Luftwaffe dropped bombs on the queen's residence in a targeted attack. Several of her staff were killed, and the queen herself had a miraculous escape. Our members were furious about it."

"I heard about it on the news," said Kurt. "Flares were fired from the ground to pinpoint the house for the bombers."

"Who would do such a thing?" said Carter.

The receptionist answered, tight-lipped, "Obviously someone who hates the Dutch royal family. Perhaps a member of the Nazi Party of Holland, the NSB."

"Where else could we look?" said Kurt.

The receptionist closed the register. "It is entirely possible that your friend hasn't registered here. Not all Dutch people in exile join our association. You could contact someone from the Netherlands Executive Committee. They were in charge of processing the earliest arrivals."

"Where are they based?" said Carter.

She shook her head. "The NEC was wound up in 1942, and its powers were transferred to the Red Cross. Freddie Knottenbelt was the original Executive Secretary."

"Do you have his address?" said Kurt.

"He had rooms in the Bonnington Hotel in Southampton Row. You might find him there."

They thanked the receptionist and left the association.

Carter waited until they were outside to ask his next question. "How could there be Dutch Nazi sympathisers now, after the death and destruction Hitler brought to the Dutch people and their cities in 1940?"

Kurt made no attempt to answer that question.

#

The receptionist at the Bonnington Hotel looked at them blankly, when they asked to speak with Mr Knottenbelt.

"He's a guest," said Kurt.

"We have no one of that name staying here." She moved along the reception desk to deal with a guest.

Carter called after her, "He was here in 1941. Perhaps you could check your records and tell us when he left."

"And if he left a forwarding address," said Kurt.

She clicked her tongue impatiently.

Carter flashed his official card at her. "We're from the Foreign Office."

"I wouldn't be able to help you, even if you were the prime minister himself. You'll have to put your request in writing to the manager."

An old man, waiting to speak with the receptionist, tapped Carter on the shoulder. "I couldn't help overhearing," he said. "I knew Freddie Knottenbelt. He was in charge of the NEC in the early years."

"You are Dutch?" said Kurt.

"Yes. My wife and I escaped to Britain from the Netherlands when the Germans invaded, in May 1940."

"Did you know a Dutch refugee called Henk Janssen?" said Carter.

The old man nodded his head. "I remember a young man of that name on the boat. He could be anywhere by now."

Another dead end.

Kurt thanked the old man for his help. He signalled to Carter that they should leave, but Carter wasn't finished with the receptionist. "Obstructing our enquiries is a serious matter punishable by a term of imprisonment."

The receptionist showed no sign that she'd heard him.

The old man said, "I have a photograph from the boat in my room. It might include Henk Janssen."

Kurt thanked the man. They waited in the lobby while he fetched the picture.

The photograph was well worn, but it showed a large group of people disembarking from a sailing vessel at Tilbury docks. Kurt scanned the faces in the picture and picked out Henk Janssen, middle-aged, short and stocky. He pointed him out to Carter. "This is our man."

He asked if he could borrow the picture for a few days.

"Keep it," said the old man.

#

They hurried to Holborn underground station, where they parted. Kurt bought a copy of the *Daily Mirror*, took it into a pub and ordered a pint of bitter.

He ran his eyes over the headlines, without taking them in. The old man's photograph had proved that Henk really was a refugee from the Netherlands, but where could he be? Was it possible for a Dutchman to disappear in Britain? Things must have been chaotic when the first refugees arrived, but they would all have been issued with National Identity cards.

Chapter 62

Kurt finished his pint and hurried back to the VNL, the Dutch association, in Stockwell. The wind was rising, storm clouds gathering overhead, and flashes of forked lightning lit up the sky to the east. By the time he reached the office of the VNL, rain was falling in big, ominous drops.

The girl on reception was closing up for the night, but she seemed pleased to see him. "Back again?"

He showed her the photograph and pointed out Henk Janssen. "Does his face ring any bells?"

"No, I'm sorry," she said.

"I'd like to take a look at your register," said Kurt.

"What are you looking for this time?"

"An old friend."

She invited him to sit at her desk. "I have to leave in a few minutes, but you can look through it while I lock up."

It took no more than two minutes for Kurt to find what he was looking for. He thanked the girl, and ran through a full-blown thunderstorm to catch a bus back to Whitehall.

#

Darkness had fallen by the time Kurt knocked on the door of Overseas Logistics. The lightning had moved farther west, but the driving rain continued to fall in torrents. Madge Butterworth let him in.

He shook the water from his hair and greeted her with a broad grin. "Looking more beautiful every time I see you."

She suppressed a smile. "You look like a drowned rat."

"Is he in?"

"Yes, go ahead. He's expecting you."

Kurt stepped inside Major Robertson's office.

The major directed him to a chair. "What have you got for me?"

Kurt sat. "Not a lot, Major. Actually, more questions than answers. We could find no trace of Henk Janssen at his home address, and according to the neighbours, his house was destroyed early on in the Blitz."

"How early?"

"Well before he arrived in the country. We must conclude that he gave a false address, and perhaps a false name as well. Apparently, the name Henk Janssen is as common in Holland as John Smith is here."

"Go on."

"We found an association for Dutch exiles in Stockwell. We checked the register and couldn't find Janssen or Pieter Hendriks."

"Perhaps they didn't register with the association. There's no obligation on any Dutchman to do so."

Madge came in with a tray of tea. She offered to pour.

"Leave it," said the major.

Madge scuttled out and closed the door.

Kurt showed the major the photograph of the Dutch refugees taken at Tilbury docks. He pointed out Henk Janssen's face.

"I'll give this to the police," said the major. "It will help them to find him."

The tea tray sat untouched on the table. "Would you like me to pour the tea?" said Kurt.

"Help yourself," said the major. "I'm okay. I had a cup earlier."

Kurt left it. "May I ask a question?"

"Go ahead."

"As I understand it, the agents in the Double Cross programme are kept apart from each other."

"That is true. The cooks, the guards, the case officers are all kept apart. No support worker is aware of any Double Cross agent or location apart from the one he's assigned to." The major began to look uncomfortable. "Where are you going with this?"

Kurt recalled the Home Facilities guards' grapevine that Clarence had mentioned. He said nothing about that. Perhaps some old army associations were too strong to be broken.

"Greg Ellis found me and made contact in the café in Perrymead Street."

"That's a serious breach," said the major.

"The point is that he was able to find me. I asked him how, and he said he followed John."

"John?"

"The courier."

The major blanched. "Christ, that's a gaping hole in our system."

"Ellis provides a link between Perrymead Street and wherever Ellis was originally based. If we can establish a similar link between the safe house at Frome Road and number 12 Perrymead Street, that would give us a further connection between the murders and the Gingerbread spy."

A dumbstruck major nodded.

"On that basis, Ellis is where we should start," said Kurt.

Major Robertson hammered his desk with the flat of his hand. "You are determined to throw suspicion on Greg Ellis. I've told you before, Ellis is above suspicion."

Kurt remained impassive. Major Robertson had some personal prejudice in favour of Ellis. Kurt was not about to probe that, but he had a trump card to play.

"What about John, the dispatch courier?"

"What about him?" The major was tight-lipped.

"He had contact with more than one safe house. Could he be the Gingerbread agent?"

"That's ridiculous! These wild speculations are getting us nowhere. Please concentrate your efforts on tracing the missing cleaner."

"May I ask why Ellis's agent was blown?"

"That's not something I'm prepared to discuss," said the major.

"Was it something that would throw suspicion on Ellis?"

"Absolutely not. I've told you, Ellis is above suspicion."

It was time for Kurt to play his trump card. "When Carter and I visited the Dutch exiles association today, we found no trace of the cleaners, as I said, but I found a record of a refugee called Gregor Els. Could this be Gregory Ellis?"

"More than likely, yes. Ellis is a refugee from the Netherlands. He has made no secret of it. He may have changed his name when he arrived in order to blend in. That's not unusual."

"May I ask how the two cleaners, Hendriks and Janssen, were recruited? Were they recommended by someone?"

"I have no idea, but both men would have been thoroughly vetted."

Kurt gave Major Robertson his steely-eyed look. "How reliable is the vetting procedure? Was Ellis vetted?"

The major replied quietly, "Forget about Ellis. He is beyond suspicion. His name has been put forward to replace a member of the London Controlling Section recently lost to bad health. And I've asked him to take over as case officer for your man, Arnold, in the interim."

#

The rain continued to pour down, cascading from fractured downpipes and blocked gutters onto the hapless Londoners in the streets below. Kurt ran to Charing Cross station and boarded a Tube bound for Walham Green. Glad of the solitude and the opportunity to get his thoughts in order, he opened his soggy newspaper. Pollinger's picture had drifted to page five. He read the accompanying article. Sightings from all over the country, from the south coast to York, had all proved false. The agent was still at large.

Kurt opened the door to an empty flat, and immediately remembered that he had agreed to meet Lina in Chez Phillipe's at 6 p.m. He checked his watch. It was after 7. She would murder him when they met again!

Chapter 63

Monday March 13, 1944

Lina finished her meal in a black mood. She was having a bad week. The Luftwaffe raids had continued all week, forcing her to remain in her tiny office in the horrid, cold basement. Jan de Groot had stood her up on Wednesday, and at the same time someone had broken in and searched the flat. And now Kevin had failed to turn up for their meal. To cap it all, she had been caught in a downpour on the way from the Underground station to the restaurant. Her hat was ruined. And she had not enjoyed eating on her own. The food was not up to Chez Phillipe's usual high standard.

The only bright point of the day had been when Joost offered her a lift from the hospital to Victoria Underground station in his fancy silver car. She would have been soaked to the skin if she'd had to walk it. They had a whole conversation in their native tongue in the car.

He told her he was born and brought up in Rotterdam. When the Germans razed the town, he lost all of his family, and barely escaped with the clothes on his back. He was lucky that he had completed his studies the previous year and had no problem finding a good job in Britain.

Lina calculated his age. If he was 18 when he started his studies, he would have been 25 by the time he finished, in 1939. That would make him 30 now, the same age as Kevin. He didn't look that old. She'd been itching to ask if he was married, but she couldn't ask him directly, and she never found a way to work it into the conversation.

She had told him a little about herself, how she was studying to be a nurse in Rhenen when the Germans came, and had to leave the country in the middle of her second year. She too had lost most of her family. Her father and two of her brothers had been killed. Only her mother was still living in Eindhoven.

"You must be awfully young," he said.

She blushed when he said that. "I'm nearly 25."

She didn't tell him about her oldest brother, Dirk, who had an addiction to advocaat and disappeared when the bombs began to fall. She was convinced he was still alive and holed up somewhere.

Men were so unreliable! The only thing you could depend on was that they would let you down, one way or another, sooner or later. She was sure Kevin would have a good excuse for this evening, but was she going to take that from him again? How many times had he let her down? It was bad enough that he had travelled to Ireland to pick up the threads of his earlier love life, but then he'd gone on to Portugal on some wild goose chase and met up with another girl there. The guy was beyond incorrigible.

She resolved to kick him out. She would be polite, but firm, and ask him to leave her flat. It was just a shame that she had lost contact with the charming Jan de Groot. Perhaps he would reappear with an explanation for why he failed to make their second date.

Chapter 64

The bindings holding his hands had loosened. It wasn't much, but it gave him something to work on, something to occupy his mind, at least. Hour after hour, he wrestled with the knots, refusing to accept defeat. Surely, if he kept at it he would break free, eventually.

The task seemed impossible, the chafing on his wrists almost more than he could bear, and there were times when he might have given up. But he kept trying, and gradually he began to make progress.

Finally, his hands were free. He stripped the bag from his head, expecting – hoping – to see some light, but there was none. He was still engulfed in total blackness.

He tore the gag from his mouth and untied his legs. Once he was free of all his bonds, he set about finding the wall. Working by feel, he worked his way around the four walls in search of a door. He found it, but it was locked. Then he found a light switch and tried it, nothing happened.

He hammered on the door and called out, "Help me! I'm locked in. Let me out!"

His cries echoed around him, but no one came. Dejected, he steered his way to the chair and sat down. It was hopeless. He had no idea if it was day or night. Did that matter? Would someone hear him either way?

Then he remembered the pipes above his head...

Chapter 65

Tuesday March 14, 1944

By the following evening, the storm over London had passed. The dark grey blanket of the day before had been replaced by broken clouds, lined with gold. Kurt made his way to Perrymead Street, and took up a position in a shop entrance on the opposite side of the road to number 12.

Within a half-hour, Greg Ellis arrived in his car and entered the house. Kurt caught a glimpse of Harry, the guard, as the door opened. A few minutes later, Mrs Partridge, the cook, arrived, and Harry let her in. Another half-hour after that, John, the courier, strolled up the road carrying a copy of the *Daily Mirror* and took his station in the Pelican Café.

Next, Ellis emerged from the house carrying a newspaper, skipped across the road and went into the café to complete the handover of incoming signals.

Ellis left the café first, jumped in his car, and drove away. Kurt went into the café, and took a seat opposite John. The initial expression on the courier's face was one of alarm, but he masked it quickly with his usual look of upper class disinterest.

"What are you doing here?" he said. "I can't talk to you."

The waitress appeared at the table with her notepad and pencil.

Kurt smiled at her. "Just an extra cup please, Miss."

She hurried to the counter.

"What do you want, O'Reilly? This is not your station any more. And haven't you been decommissioned?"

"I'm no longer a case officer, if that's what you mean, but I'm still working for Overseas Logistics."

The waitress returned with a fresh cup and saucer.

Kurt helped himself to a cup of John's tea.

"In what capacity, may I ask?" said the courier.

"I'm working on something for Thomas. I have a single question for you. How many other pick-ups do you do each day?"

John's brow furrowed. "You've asked me that before."

"And you refused to answer."

The courier shrugged. "This is now my only pick-up."

"But you used to have more than one."

"I have new orders. Why are you so interested in my pick-ups?"

"How many did you have before your new orders?"

"It varied. Usually three, sometimes more." He sipped his tea, pinkie pointing north, peering at Kurt over the rim of his cup.

"I'd like the addresses."

John put his cup back in its saucer. There was a noticeable tremor in his hand. "I'm not giving you that information. If you're really working with Thomas, ask him."

John picked up his hat and left the table without another word. He paid the bill and left.

Kurt had intended to follow John on his rounds, but now that he had only one pick-up, that line of enquiry had been closed. Of course, asking the major for the addresses of John's erstwhile pick-ups was not an option, since Kurt was investigating Greg Ellis – also known as Gregor Els – who was innocent as a baby in the major's eyes.

He was trying to decide what to do next, when the cook emerged from the house and set off along the pavement. He hurried after her.

Drawing alongside, he smiled at her. "Good afternoon, Mrs Partridge."

"Kevin, what are you doing here? I thought we'd lost you."

"I'm not involved with Arnold any more. I just wondered how he is."

"Arnold's well enough. He moans about my food all the time, but that's nothing new."

Kurt laughed. "I thought I'd have a word with Clarence about what has happened. Is he back on duty?"

She shook her head. "Clarence has been replaced."

"I didn't know that. Who has taken over his shift?"

"Someone called Jack."

"Jack Reed?"

"I believe so, yes."

"And who's the new cleaner? I heard the new man, Janssen, didn't last long."

"We had him for two weeks. He was a hopeless cleaner." She rolled her eyes. "And to tell the truth I don't think he was entirely trustworthy."

"Oh?"

"Things went missing. You know, small things, like bags of sugar, ornaments – things like that."

"And you're sure he was the thief?"

"As sure as anyone could be, but I never caught him in the act."

"Have they found a replacement?"

She pouted. "Not yet. I've been doing my best to keep the place clean, but that's not my job. My time is limited. I have to get home to look after my invalided mother."

"I understand. I'm sure you'll get a new cleaner soon. I'll mention it to the people in the office next time I'm there."

She thanked him. They shook hands, and went their separate ways.

#

When Kurt returned to the flat, he found an envelope on the mat that someone had pushed through the letter box. It was addressed to Kurt Müller and bore no stamp. He tore it open. He could count on the fingers of one hand the people in London who knew his real name.

The instructions inside the envelope were short and to the point and written in such a way that only Kurt would understand them:

'Your friends would like to hear from you. They have been reading Dickens's first novel. They can be found at 3517 High Street.'

He was to establish contact with the SD in Berlin, using Charles Dickens's *Pickwick Papers* to generate his daily code matrix. His transmission should use the frequency 3517 MHz.

Rattlesnake, *KPS*, had been activated!

He was sure the major would seize this opportunity to further confuse the enemy about the Allied invasion plans. Kurt didn't have access to a transmitter, of course, but he was certain that Major Robertson would provide him with one when the time was right.

The thought of dealing directly with the head of SD-Ausland made him lightheaded. The thought that Schellenberg knew where he lived made him nauseous. He made a pot of tea. There was no milk. He took his one remaining bottle of whiskey from the mantelpiece and added a couple of fingers to his cup. He finished the pot of tea, adding more and more whiskey to each cup...

Chapter 66

Tuesday March 14, 1944

Lina sat in her office in the hospital basement completing paperwork for the disposition of the remaining seriously injured patients. She hated the place as much as ever, and longed to be assigned to real nursing duties.

All the indications were that the Luftwaffe raids were running out of steam. The number of aircraft arriving each night was lower than the night before, with fewer bombs hitting London. Some nights there were none at all. Those were the worst, for Lina had to remain in her underground dungeon with little or nothing to do. She had pleaded with Matron to let her take her place in the wards on those nights, but Matron had refused. Nothing was said, but Lina guessed that Matron saw her as a disrupting influence, best kept away from the other nurses. The injustice stung. And how would she ever attain fully qualified status without hands-on nursing experience?

Kevin's erratic comings and goings continued. From one day to the next, she never knew when he would make an appearance. Cooking meals for him had become impossible. His moods were even more erratic. For a man on temporary suspension, he was always busy, although she had no idea what he was doing and he wouldn't say. Whatever it was, he was totally absorbed by it. He had so little time for her. He probably wouldn't be the least bit inconvenienced when she told him to leave.

Jan de Groot had not surfaced either. Lina put that episode down to experience. The guy was the worst kind of philanderer. She should never have fallen for his guiles. She resolved to put him from her mind, once and for all. And then she had a sudden thought. What if Jan was the one who broke in and searched the flat? He knew where she lived, and he knew the flat would be empty while she was waiting for him in Leicester Square! But what could he have been looking for?

The basement continued to make strange, unexplained noises, clicking and rattling of the pipes, for the most part, but there were still the sounds of disembodied breathing accompanied by unaccountable light breezes. And there was that smellS

She shivered.

Why was she still here? Was she so dedicated to nursing that she was prepared to suffer fear and humiliation night after night? Could she find a nursing position in another hospital? And if she did, would she be any better off? Perhaps she would be treated the same way by the English nurses whatever hospital she worked in.

What was that?

One of the rattling sounds had changed. It was more of a rhythmical tapping sound, as if someone was tapping out a message on the pipes. She put down her pen and concentrated all her attention on the sound.

Tap, tap, tap-tap-tap. A pause, then five more taps and another pause. This was followed by a long sequence that might have been Morse code.

Still half convinced that the basement was haunted, Lina steeled herself, and set off to investigate.

The way the tapping carried along the pipes, it was difficult to be sure which direction it was coming from, and she took a few wrong turns before she was sure she was going in the right direction. The sounds led her to the end of a corridor and a solid door that she felt sure would be locked.

It wasn't locked, but opening it proved a challenge, as the door was made of metal and nearly too heavy for her. She squeezed through, and wedged the door open before continuing.

She found herself in a disused section of the basement, even colder than her office and with no lights. She nearly panicked, nearly turned back, but her curiosity drove her onward.

The tapping was definitely louder here. She fancied she could hear the actual tapping rather than the ringing sound carried along the pipes. She was also convinced that the tapping was coming from someone alive, someone in trouble, someone who needed her help.

She pressed on into the darkness, and stopped at a door. Whoever was tapping on the pipes was behind that door, she was certain of it. She banged on the door. "Hello, is there someone in there?"

"Yes, I'm locked in. Can you open the door?" It was a man's voice, a German by his accent.

She tried the handle, but the door was locked.

"There's no key," she said. "I'll get help."

She turned back the way she'd come, and almost immediately, someone came through the heavy door carrying a lighted torch.

"Thank heaven you've come," said Lina. "There's someone locked in this room, but I don't have a key."

Chapter 67

Wednesday March 15, 1944

Kurt woke from a disturbed sleep with a pounding head, the smell of Irish whiskey in his nose, the oily taste in his mouth. Lina wasn't in the bed, and he had no recollection of her coming in last night. Had she come in after he'd gone to bed and got up early in the morning without waking him? That would be most unusual, but he had been drunk as a skunk.

He stubbed his toe on the empty whiskey bottle and put it in the sink.

Brushing his teeth deadened the taste in his mouth, but he burped whiskey fumes. He combed his unruly hair and splashed cold water on his face. He considered making breakfast and nearly threw up at the thought of powdered egg.

The Tube journey to Bedford Street did nothing to restore his good health. His head hurt. The side-to-side movements of the carriage made his stomach heave, and his eyes wouldn't focus properly.

Madge Butterworth ignored his sickly smile. Could she smell whiskey off his clothes from across the room? She directed him into Major Robertson's office without comment.

"Schellenberg has made contact, Major," said Kurt without preamble. "I received an envelope in the flat last night containing instructions for coding and a frequency for transmission."

"What was the postmark?"

"There wasn't one. It was delivered by hand."

Major Robertson gave that some thought. "Who knows where you live?"

"Greg Ellis," said Kurt. "He took me for a spin in his car and dropped me home afterwards. That was the day after the double murders."

"Anyone else?"

"No, I don't think so, but I could have been followed home, I suppose."

The major got up from his chair and stood by the window. "Schellenberg's spy has been transmitting. We picked up a signal last night."

Kurt's heartbeat began to race. "Have we been able to decode his signal? And have the RDF boys managed to trace him?"

"Partially, yes. The boffins are working on the coding, top priority. The bits and pieces that we have been able to decode are devilishly accurate, and suggest his information is coming from an incredibly high level source. As for the RDF units, they triangulated the latest transmission to the outskirts of Watford, but he wasn't active long enough for them to catch him."

"Watford, that's a help. They should be ready for him the next time."

The major shook his head. "He's a veritable will-o-the-wisp. He never transmits from the same place twice. RAF surveillance aircraft are keeping a close eye on troop movements in Belgium and France. If the invasion plans have been compromised, we will know about it soon enough." He turned to face Kurt. "In the meantime, I have taken steps to undermine Gingerbread's credibility. We have used agents that the Abwehr must know are blown to transmit material confirming Gingerbread's intelligence."

"That's not going to work, Major. I told you, the Abwehr pass on everything to the OKW, verbatim. The OKW will take your confirming intelligence at face value."

The major dropped heavily into his chair and said nothing for several moments. When he spoke again, the expression on his face was one of weary resignation. "We need to find this spy, Kurt. As long as he's out there we can no longer rely on Operation Fortitude. The whole invasion plan is in extreme jeopardy."

"Where do you suggest we start?" said Kurt.

"We need to concentrate on the most recent occupants of the house at Perrymead Street. The boffins have devised a plan that may work. Tonight's dispatch will incorporate a repetitive sequence that they will be able to decode. If Gingerbread transmits it, we will know for certain that he must be in that house."

"Does that include Clarence?"

"He's in the clear. He was securely locked up in a police cell while

Gingerbread was transmitting last night. And before you suggest Greg Ellis again, let me tell you he was with me in a pub most of the night, so it couldn't have been him."

That was a blow to Kurt. Ellis – or Els – was still his number one suspect. "How long will he continue as Arnold's case officer?"

Major Robertson hesitated before answering, "Greg Ellis is now a full member of the LCS, but he has agreed to continue as Arnold's case officer for a few days. Jack Reed has taken over from Clarence on the early guard shift."

"So your main suspects are Arnold and Harry and Reed?"

"Yes, and Janssen. I'm putting you on watch at the house." He tossed a key to Kurt. "We've rented a vacant flat above the Pelican Café. If either Harry or Reed comes out, follow him."

"What if they both come out?" said Kurt.

"Carter will be with you," the major replied.

Chapter 68

The flat above the café was colder than the morgue, and it smelled of mould. But they had an uninterrupted view of the safe house. Ellis's beautiful, red MG was parked at the kerb outside, looking newly washed.

MI5 had supplied a cot, three wooden chairs to sit on, a black telephone and a dog-eared pack of playing cards, sitting on a rickety table. Carter sat at the table. He shuffled the cards and dealt out a hand of solitaire.

At 8 p.m. Greg Ellis emerged with a newspaper under his arm, and crossed the road to the café. John, the courier, arrived within five minutes. Ten minutes later, both men reappeared. John left the scene, while Ellis returned to the house.

Three minutes later, Ellis re-emerged and set off down the street on foot, in the same direction as the courier.

"He's left his car," said Carter. "Why would he leave his car?"

"He's following John." Kurt strode to the door. "Stay here, keep watch."

Carter threw him his startled chicken look "Where are you going?"

"I'm going to follow Ellis. Keep watch until I get back."

Kurt left the flat before Carter could object. Ellis was well out of sight, and he had to run to find him. Keeping a distance of 50 yards behind him, he followed Ellis to Earls Court Underground station.

Kurt sprinted to the station. He bought a ticket and scoured the station in search of Ellis, but there were too many interconnecting Tube lines, too many routes, too many platforms.

He swore. Following someone through London was no job for one man; it required a team of two or three. He returned to the lookout in Perrymead Street.

"What was that all about?" said Carter.

"I followed Ellis as far as the Tube at Earls Court. I lost him."

"Are we supposed to be following Ellis?"

Kurt said nothing to that.

They resumed their watch. A black cat emerged from number 10 and wandered down the road. Nothing else stirred.

Kurt and Carter cut the deck of cards to decide who would take the first watch. Carter lost. He sat at the table and dealt another hand of solitaire. Kurt lay down on the cot and fell asleep immediately.

Carter woke him at midnight. "Harry Locke has come out. Jack Reed has gone in. What's he doing in there?"

"Jack's covering the early shift while Clarence is in custody," said Kurt. "Do you want to follow Harry or will I?"

"Leave that to me," said Carter. "I need the exercise, and it's your turn to take over the watch, anyhow."

Carter left, and Kurt took his place on one of the wooden chairs and picked up the cards.

Three-quarters of an hour went by. Nothing stirred, not even a cat. Kurt dropped the cards in disgust. The king of diamonds was missing from the deck, making it impossible to play any form of solitaire. Probably someone's idea of a joke. Kurt's eyelids drooped. He caught himself falling asleep, stood up and did a few exercises.

Carter came back with the news that Harry had walked the three miles to his home without incident.

Kurt wasn't surprised. He said, "You can call it a night. Go home. Get some sleep."

"You're going home?"

"Soon, but first I want to go over there to talk to Jack Reed."

Carter looked alarmed. "Is that wise?"

Kurt reminded Carter how he had introduced himself on the mailboat.

"Touché," said Carter.

Kurt crossed the road and knocked on the door. Reed opened it.

"Put the kettle on, Jack," said Kurt, pushing past Reed, and heading for the kitchen.

Reed followed him. "What do you want, Kevin?"

"I'm working on special assignment. I have a few questions. Where's Arnold?"

"He's in his room. He's not a happy bunny."

Kurt grinned. "That's normal for Arnold."

Soon, they were sitting face to face at the kitchen table sharing two steaming cups of coffee. Kurt started by asking Reed if he believed Pollinger killed the guard and the cook at his previous safe house.

Reed said, "The answer to that question is an emphatic 'no'. He may look like a Nazi thug, but Pollinger was not a violent man."

Kurt noticed the switch from present to past tense. His next question was, "How do you think he has managed to avoid the police for so long? How long has it been now?"

"Nineteen days. With every policeman in the country looking for him, an accent you could cut with an axe, and his picture in the papers every day, he could never have lasted this long on his own."

"I agree," said Kurt. "It's inconceivable that he could be out in the open in London. He must be holed up somewhere."

"So someone must be helping him," said Reed.

"Okay, but who?"

Reed spread his hands in a gesture of total bewilderment. "I have no idea."

"Two men were seen leaving the house. It's safe to assume that Pollinger was one, but who was the other one? Was he the murderer? Pollinger had no reason to kill his guard and his cook. Assuming the second man was the killer, could he have abducted Pollinger and be holding him somewhere?"

"But why would anyone want to abduct him?" said Reed. "Pollinger would have no useful intelligence to impart, either about the plans for the invasion or about the Double Cross programme itself. How could he? He's been with the programme since it began. He was one of the first Abwehr agents turned."

"You've been with him since the beginning?"

"Yes." Reed paused. "I fear he could be lying dead in a ditch somewhere."

"Why would anyone want to kill him?"

The expression on Reed's face was an eloquent testament to his affection for the missing double agent. He made no reply.

Chapter 69

Thursday March 16, 1944

The flat at Radipole Road was dark and empty. Kurt's first reaction was one of annoyance. Where was Lina? Could she be working late again? That was entirely possible. There had been heavy Luftwaffe raids over London for the past two nights.

It was an hour before another possibility occurred to him. Could she have left him? The last time he'd spoken to Lina she had been angry with him. She had threatened to kick him out. Could she have left? That seemed unlikely in the extreme. The flat was rented in her name, after all.

He slept badly on his own, suffering a nightmare where his head exploded like Sofia's. He woke bathed in sweat, in the small hours of the morning. The sky was alight with searchlights and the drone of Luftwaffe bombers could be heard in the distance, together with the thump of their bombs and the answering rattle of ack-ack. He had slept through an air raid warning. Could Lina be in trouble? Could she have been killed or injured by a Luftwaffe bomb?

By 8 a.m. Kurt was at the entrance to Millbank Military Hospital. Two ambulance crews were offloading injured people on stretchers. A porter tried to prevent him from entering, but Kurt wouldn't be stopped.

By 8:10 a.m. he was standing in Matron's office, demanding to speak with Nurse Lina Smit.

Matron waved a hand. "I'm afraid I can't help you. We haven't seen Nurse Lina for two days now, and I have to say her absence has been extremely inconvenient."

"You didn't bother to go looking for her? Did it not occur to you that she might be injured or killed by a bomb?"

Matron flushed. "That is not my responsibility. I have quite enough on my plate running a busy hospital in the middle of repeated air raids. Now I'll thank you to leave my office."

Kurt was out of ideas. He could search for Lina in all the hospitals within reach of the flat, but that would take forever, and he was certain they would all be far too busy to help him identify one victim. He would have to wait and hope Lina found her way home.

He walked from Millbank to Overseas Logistics, Bedford Street and pressed the buzzer.

"Who is it?" Madge's voice.

"It's only me. Is the major there?"

There was a short delay before Madge buzzed him in. He climbed the stairs.

"The major's out of town," she said, "but Mr Masterman would like a word."

Kurt opened the major's door. The major's window had been blown out and the glass replaced with a sheet of plywood. J. C. Masterman sat behind Major Robertson's desk. "Whitehall took quite a battering last night," he said. "Tell me you have some good news."

Kurt took his usual seat. "I'm afraid not, sir." He hesitated, uncertain about how much Masterman knew.

"I am fully briefed," said Masterman. "I understand you and Carter kept a watch on the comings and goings at Perrymead Street?"

"Yes, sir. We were there all night. Nothing much happened. Carter followed the guard to his home."

"And you followed Ellis."

Carter's been telling tales out of school again!

"I followed Greg Ellis, yes, but I lost him at Earls Court Tube station."

"Didn't the major tell you to forget about Ellis?"

"He did, sir, but I'm convinced he's mixed up with this Gingerbread somehow."

"Right, well I'm giving you a direct order. Ellis is not a suspect. You will not follow him under any circumstances. Is that clear?"

"Yes, sir."

"You recall that my team put together a clever repeat sequence in the last signal that we gave Arnold, in the hope that Gingerbread would encode and send it? Well, Gingerbread ignored it. He sent a much longer signal instead. The RDF units picked up the transmission in the neighbourhood of Cheshunt. The boffins couldn't decipher all of it, but what we have tells us that the signal was as damaging to our operation as it could be. Fortitude has been blown wide open."

"I'm sorry to hear that, sir," said Kurt.

"There's even worse news, I'm afraid. RAF surveillance aircraft have spotted unmistakable signs that the Germans are preparing to move masses of troops from their current positions. It seems Gingerbread's intelligence reports are being believed and acted upon at the highest levels in Berlin." Masterman took a deep breath. "Our only hope now is to find this Gingerbread and turn him before it's too late."

Kurt waited a few moments before responding, giving the Twenty Committee man's words the respect they deserved. "Could you tell me who recommended the cleaner, Janssen, to the programme?"

"I'm not sure. Is that important?"

"Janssen gave a false address, and probably a false name as well. But we have established that he was a Dutch refugee. I believe Hendriks was Dutch too, and the major said that Greg Ellis is one as well. Could it be that Ellis put forward those two names?"

Chapter 70

Masterman pressed the intercom, and Madge Butterworth entered.

"I want to know where we got the names of the two cleaners for Perrymead Street, Hendriks and Janssen. Check the files, would you?"

Madge bobbed her head and left.

Masterman adjusted the paperweight on the major's desk. "I hear you've been talking to Jack Reed. What did he have to contribute?"

Carter again!

"He confirmed what I suspected, that his man, Pollinger, is unlikely to have committed the two murders. I can only surmise that someone else gained entry, killed the guard and the cook, and abducted Pollinger."

"Clarence Newton is Scotland Yard's main suspect for those crimes."

Kurt shook his head. "I don't believe that. I believe this was the work of Gingerbread."

Masterman's brow furrowed. "Why abduct one of our double agents? Pollinger knows nothing of value to the SD."

Kurt had no answer to that.

"So who do you think this Gingerbread might be?"

"Greg Ellis," said Kurt without hesitation. "He's mobile. He has a car. And there was a break-in to my flat while I was away. Ellis is the only one who knows where I live."

"Was anything taken? And I hope your young woman wasn't injured."

"Nothing was taken, and the flat was empty at the time."

Masterman paused to absorb this new information. "Ellis was in a pub with me and the major in the West End during the spy's transmission from Watford. How could he be in two places at once?"

"He may have an accomplice."

"But why would Ellis be involved in the abduction of a double agent? He knows that Pollinger knows nothing of value."

Kurt had no answer. Luckily, Madge Butterworth came in at that moment to inform Mr Masterman that the two Dutch cleaners had been recommended by Gregory Ellis.

Masterman thanked her. He waited until she had left the room and closed the door. "Very well, Kurt, I will freeze Ellis's involvement in the London Controlling Section until we get to the bottom of this matter."

The phrase, 'closing the stable door' sprang into Kurt's mind, but he said nothing.

"I want you and Carter to follow him when he leaves Perrymead Street this evening. Don't lose him this time."

"It may take more than two of us, sir, and he knows both of us. Could we have a third man, someone Ellis doesn't know? Someone with transport. Ellis has a car."

Masterman picked up the telephone and asked Madge to put him through to Scotland Yard.

Chapter 71

Friday March 17, 1944

Detective Constable Charles Brick of Scotland Yard was well named. Six foot five, with a strong beard and feet the size of Rhine barges, he reminded Kurt of Wagner's Wotan.

"Call me Chuck," he said in a deep voice.

"I'm Kevin," said Kurt, surrendering his hand to the big man's grip. "This is Carter."

Between them, Kurt and Carter briefed the constable.

"This Ellis is a suspect for the two murders?" said Chuck.

Kurt and Carter responded together.

"Yes," said Kurt.

"No," said Carter.

Chuck grinned. "I'm glad we cleared that up."

Kurt said, "Ellis has a car. I'm not sure how we're supposed to follow him if he uses it."

"That won't be a problem. I have a bicycle," said the constable. "How about a game of cards while we wait?"

Carter said, "The pack's no good. There's no king of diamonds."

Chuck, shuffled the pack like a Las Vegas dealer. "That doesn't matter, as long as we all know. What shall we play?"

They emptied the small change from their pockets onto the table, and the three of them settled down to a friendly game of 3-card brag.

"It's not a game I'm familiar with," boomed Chuck as he scooped up the first pot.

#

By 8 p.m. Carter was down to his last three coins, Kurt had run out of change, and Chuck had enough in his pile to make a significant contribution to his police pension fund.

The red MG arrived and parked in front of number 12.

"There's our man now," said Carter.

Greg Ellis climbed out and went into the house.

Forty minutes later, Ellis emerged with a newspaper, and crossed the road to the café. John arrived and completed the pick-up. Then John came out of the café and headed up the road. Ellis left the café and followed John on foot.

"He's has left his car behind again," said Carter.

Kurt strode to the door. "You come with me, Chuck. Carter, stay here and watch for Harry."

Carter picked up the cards and dealt a hand of solitaire. Chuck shovelled his winnings into a trouser pocket, and he and Kurt set out after Ellis.

"You go on ahead," said Kurt. "Get as close to him as you can, I don't want to lose him in the Underground again."

Chuck set off on his bicycle and was soon well ahead, closing on their quarry.

When Ellis disappeared into the Tube station at Earls Court, Chuck was within touching distance. Kurt was 40 yards back. He sprinted to catch up, passing the constable's abandoned bicycle at the entrance to the Tube station.

The station was packed with early evening travellers going about their business, criss-crossing every which way. It took Kurt a few moments to find him, but Chuck's head was visible above a stream of people heading for the District line.

Kurt reached the platform as a train was arriving. The doors opened, hundreds of people disembarked and hundreds more took their places in the carriages. It was only Chuck's height that enabled Kurt to find him in the crowd. Chuck boarded the train, and Kurt did the same.

Chuck got out at Victoria. Then Kurt spotted Ellis moving toward the exit with the constable close behind. He lost sight of them again until he emerged onto the street to see the constable striding away in the distance heading northeast.

Kurt broke into a run.

The constable turned right onto Vauxhall Bridge Road, and continued south toward the river. Kurt could see Ellis again, in the distance. Constable Brick increased his pace, and Kurt did the same, closing the gap between them.

Close to Vauxhall Bridge, Ellis turned left onto Millbank, the constable followed him, and Kurt followed the constable.

Part 5 – Gingerbread

Chapter 72

Friday March 17, 1944

Ellis arrived at the Millbank Hospital and went inside. Kurt and Chuck followed him.

The hospital was a chaos of people, ambulance men, nurses, doctors, patients on trolleys, porters, and members of the general public.

Constable Brick stopped a passing porter. "Did you see a man come in through the entrance, this tall, wearing a trench coat and hat?"

The porter laughed in his face and walked away.

Kurt took Chuck to Matron's office, where a queue had formed.

The constable pushed his way to the front. He flashed his warrant card. "Constable Charles Brick of Scotland Yard. We followed a man here, this tall, well dressed. It's vital that we find him."

Matron gaped at him. "You have a name for this man?"

"His name's Greg Ellis," said Kurt.

"Don't I know you?" said Matron. "You're Lina's beau."

Kurt nodded. "Yes. Has she turned up yet?"

"I don't know." And Matron was swamped by the multitude. She called out over their heads, "Try her office in the basement."

Kurt and the constable returned to the throng. They joined a queue at the doors of the elevator. When the doors opened, they got on board with a dozen other people. The elevator went up, dropping off passengers and picking up new ones at each floor. Finally, it arrived back at the ground floor and descended to the basement.

Kurt and Chuck got out.

The basement was deathly quiet. It looked deserted.

"Which way?" said Chuck.

"I don't know. I suggest we split up. I'll go right, you go left. We'll meet back here in ten minutes."

The basement was eerily quiet – and cold as the grave. It was hard to believe so much noise, so much frenetic activity, was going on just one floor above his head.

Kurt hoped to find Lina. Her knowledge of the hospital would help to shorten the search. He called out her name. There was no answer, just a trace of an echo from the bare walls.

He walked along a dimly-lit corridor, peering in through every door he came to. He found an office with a desk and piles of files, and recognised the handwriting on a notepad. It was Lina's office, no question about it, but there was no sign of Lina. He pressed on. After ten minutes, he was thinking about returning to the elevator, when he came to an intersection where two corridors crossed. He turned the corner and bumped into Greg Ellis.

Ellis looked dazed. "What are you doing here?" he said.

"I was just about to ask you the same question. I was looking for you," Kurt replied. "Where do you keep your transmitter?"

Ellis laughed nervously. "I don't have a transmitter. What are you driving at?"

"We know you're an SD spy. We know you've been sending secrets to the enemy."

That shocked Ellis out of his dazed state. "You're mad. I would never betray my country to the enemy."

"Your country being the Netherlands?"

"Yes, I'm Dutch, and proud of it. I escaped when the Germans invaded my country in 1940."

"What are you doing in this hospital?"

"I followed Jan here, but I lost him in the crowd."

"Who's Jan?" said Kurt.

Ellis ran a hand across his brow. "You know him as John, the courier, but his real name is Jan de Groot."

"Are you saying John is Dutch, like you?"

Ellis frowned. "He's Dutch, but not like me. Jan is a traitor, a member of the Nazi Party of Holland, the NSB. I have been watching him for days. I can prove that he was involved in firing those flares that nearly got our beloved Queen Wilhelmina killed in her residence."

"That is hard to believe," said Kurt

"What? That John is a traitor?"

"That he's Dutch. His accent was very convincing. Why didn't you go to the police with your evidence?"

"I know there were two NSB men involved in the crime. I was hoping Jan would lead me to his accomplice."

"Okay, so what brought you down here, to the basement?"

Ellis scratched his head. "I'm not sure. I had a strange feeling..."

"What sort of feeling?"

"Déjà vu? I feel as though I've been here before."

"And have you?"

Ellis shook his head. "I don't remember."

Chapter 73

Kurt took Ellis back to the elevator, where Constable Chuck Brick was waiting. Kurt introduced Ellis and the constable. He explained to the policeman that they were now searching for someone called Jan de Groot.

They split up. Ellis took the elevator to the first floor to search the wards. Chuck wasn't convinced that he could be trusted and went with him.

Kurt found a telephone, and rang the office. He asked to speak to the major.

"He's not here," said Madge. "He's in conference. Would you care to leave a message?"

"No thanks, but please tell him I'm with Greg Ellis in Millbank Military Hospital."

"Who's injured? You or Greg?"

"Neither of us. The trail has led us here."

"Tell me Greg's in the clear."

That question gave him goosebumps. How well-informed was Madge? Was she closer to Major Robertson than everyone supposed?

"Yes Madge, he's in the clear."

"That is good news." She sounded breathless. "I'll tell the major when I see him. He will be pleased."

Kurt ended the call and resumed his search of the basement, calling out Lina's name from time to time. All he found was a maze of corridors and empty rooms, a storeroom with spare beds and another piled high with blankets and other hospital supplies. At the end of one corridor, he came across the morgue, with dead bodies laid out in rows on tables.

Now, he wished he wasn't alone. Afraid to call her name in a room with 15 bodies, in case somebody answered, he held his tongue.

He struck out in a new direction, wandering up and down the corridors at random. He found nothing. When he stumbled upon the morgue for the second time, he realised the foolishness of what he was doing, and took the elevator to the ground floor.

He stopped a passing nurse. "Where can I find a layout of the building?"

The nurse directed him to the office of the head of maintenance. The office was vacant, but a quick rummage through the drawers revealed complete floor plans of the building. He removed a plan of the basement, laid it out on a table, and ran his eyes over it.

He recognised some of the areas he'd searched already. The morgue was at the north end. At the south end of the building the plan showed an area hatched out.

The head of maintenance burst into the office, a slight individual in his fifties. "Who are you? What are you doing with that?"

"My name's Kevin O'Reilly. I'm with a police team searching for a killer. We followed him to this hospital."

"Right, what do you need?"

Kurt was surprised by the man's helpful attitude.

"I have two men searching the wards. I thought I'd concentrate on the basement. What can you tell me about this area here?" He pointed to the hatched out area on the plan.

"That's where the old coal boilers are located. When the hospital switched from coal to oil, at the turn of the century, they put in new boilers – here." He pointed to the plan.

"Are the old boilers accessible?"

"That whole area is locked up."

"Tell me you have a key," said Kurt.

The maintenance man was called Grant. He grabbed a bunch of keys and a torch and led Kurt back to the basement. They strode down a long corridor that got progressively darker.

"When the light bulbs blow down here, we don't bother replacing them," said Grant.

They came to a door at the end of the corridor. While Grant sorted through his keys looking for the right one, Kurt tried the door handle. The door swung open with an eerie creak.

"That's strange," said Grant. "It should be locked."

He stepped inside, and Kurt followed him.

\#

A dark corridor opened up before them, dimly visible in the light from the open door. Then the access door swung closed with a loud thump, and they were in total darkness. Kurt was gripped by a moment of panic.

Grant switched on his torch. "The boilers are down there, near the centre. These other rooms are all empty."

Kurt tried the handle of one of the doors. It was locked. "Can you open it?"

Grant shone the torch on his keys. "Yes, but it could take a while to find the right key."

Kurt held the torch while Grant worked his way through his bunch of keys. When the door was opened, the torch revealed an empty room. They moved on to the next door.

Grant found the fuse box on the wall, and switched the main breaker. After that, they had light from the few bulbs that were still working in the corridors.

After 30 minutes, they had opened eight doors and found nothing. They checked out the boiler rooms, with the same result.

"This is pointless," said Grant. "Why did you think we might find someone down here?"

Kurt heard a sound. "What was that?"

They listened. Kurt heard the sound again. A swishing sound, like a shoe on linoleum.

"Probably a rat," said Grant. "They sweep their tails on the floor. They communicate with one another that way, you know."

Kurt shivered. He called out, "Hello, is anyone there?"

There was no answer.

"We need to check all the other rooms."

They opened the doors to three more empty rooms. As Grant was trying his keys on a fourth, Kurt heard the sound again, coming from inside the room. Then he heard another sound, a muffled moan. "That was no rat's tail," he said.

Grant found the right key.

A smell of urine and human waste assaulted them as soon as the door opened. A sweep of the room with the torch revealed someone tied up in a corner, head covered by a bag.

"He's alive," said Kurt.

Grant tried the light switch, but it didn't work.

Kurt sprang forward and whipped the bag from the person's head.

"Lina!" Kurt removed the gag from her mouth and untied her hands.

"You know each other?" said Grant.

Lina gasped. "What kept you? I thought you'd never find me."

"How long have you been here?"

She shook her head. "I need water."

Grant left the room and returned with a glass of water. She gulped it down.

"I heard a noise. I went to investigate. Someone came. I thought he might help, but he grabbed me and tied me up."

"You didn't see who it was?"

"I know who it was. Help me up. I need to clean myself up, and I'm starving. I think the bastard intended to leave me here to die of hunger and thirst."

Chapter 74

Kurt helped her to her feet. "Who tied you up?"

"His name's Jan de Groot. He's a Dutch refugee, and he's a snake," she hissed.

John the courier is the Gingerbread spy!

That made sense. He would have known the location of several safe houses. Pollinger's house must have been one of his pick-ups.

Kurt said, "My colleague reckons he was one of those responsible for directing the Luftwaffe to Queen Wilhelmina's residence."

"Why does that not surprise me?" said Lina, wearily.

"Tell me about the noise you were following," said Kurt.

"It sounded like Morse code, tapping on the pipes. But I haven't heard it for a while."

"Where was it coming from?"

"I don't know. Somewhere in this part of the basement."

"Hello. Kevin, where are you?"

Kurt recognised Ellis's voice. "We're down here."

Ellis and the policeman arrived.

"It looks like Jan is our man," said Kurt to Ellis. "We need to find him."

Ellis put an arm across his nose. "It's a bit ripe in here. Has someone soiled themselves?"

Kurt ignored him. Lina didn't seem to have heard him.

Kurt said to Grant, "Take Lina out of here. Leave the torch and the keys with me."

Grant handed over his torch and keys. Tucking his shoulder under Lina's armpit, he helped her through the access door and back toward the elevator.

Kurt, Ellis and Chuck continued the search. Two more doors opened to reveal empty rooms. They found Pollinger in the third room, sitting on a chair, trussed up with a bag on his head, like Lina. Unlike Lina, he had not soiled himself.

Kurt untied him.

Pollinger pointed to the wall by the door. "*Licht*. Turn on the light."

Chuck found the switch and turned it on. The room flooded with blinding light, revealing the extent of Pollinger's newly grown beard. Kurt helped him to his feet.

"You heard my message on the pipes?"

"Not us, Herr Schumann, but somebody did."

"You know my name?"

Chuck stepped forward. "Tell me why you killed your guard and your cook."

"That wasn't me. That was the man who took me from the house. It was horrible." Pollinger shuddered. "He slit their throats. There was so much blood. He brought me here."

"Who slit their throats?" said Chuck, impatiently.

"One of the two men that have been interrogating me. I don't know his name."

Two men!

Kurt held up a hand to silence Chuck. "What questions have they been asking you?"

"Questions about the planned invasion, and they wanted to know how many Abwehr agents have been turned by the British."

"What did you tell them?"

"What could I tell them? I know nothing. I made things up. I told them that the main invasion force will land in Rotterdam, with barges down the Rhine."

"They believed you?"

"I don't think so. They used *Hypnose* the last time. What is the English word?"

"Hypnosis."

"*Ja*. I cannot remember what I told them that time."

"Oh my God!" said Ellis. I need to report back to the major." He leapt to his feet and hurried away to find a telephone.

"What's got into him?" said Constable Brick.

Pollinger looked alarmed. "What did I say?"

It was clear to Kurt that something was seriously wrong. He watched Ellis barge through the canteen door. "I don't know."

The policeman resumed his questioning of Pollinger. "What can you tell us about the two men?"

Pollinger shrugged. "One was taller than the other. Both were about your age, about 30. They spoke good German..."

"How did they address each other? Did you catch a name?"

"One was called Jan."

"Was he the one who killed Dennison and Mrs Pettigrew?"

"No, that was the other one."

"His name?"

Pollinger shook his head. "I never heard his name."

"They fed you?" said Kurt.

"They gave me water, but very little to eat."

"They gave you access to a toilet?"

"*Ja.*" His bottom lip quivered under his beard. "It was not easy for me, tied up in the dark. Without light, it is difficult to measure the passage of time."

Chapter 75

Lina thanked Grant for his help as he left her at the door to the staff changing rooms. Stripping off her filthy clothes, she scrubbed herself clean and washed her hair. Cleansed and refreshed, she found some clean underwear in her locker, and put it on.

She was reaching for a fresh uniform when she heard a noise in the toilets. She went to investigate.

"Hello, who's there?"

There was no answer. Suddenly afraid and aware of her near nakedness, she shivered and turned back. But before she made it to the changing room, a figure emerged from one of the cubicles and grabbed her around the neck.

"You minx, how did you escape?" She recognised the voice and caught a glimpse of him in the mirror.

Jan's arm tightened around her neck.

Enraged by his betrayal, not just of her, but of her beloved queen, she summoned all her strength and drove him backward, where he smashed into the wall. His hands slipped from her neck. She picked up a bedpan, and swiped at his head. He ducked, turned and ran to the door.

"Stop him!" she shouted as he charged outside.

Passing in his wheelchair, Dan stuck his plastered leg in front of the fleeing Dutchman and brought him crashing to the ground.

Lina hit Jan over the head with her bedpan before he could regain his feet. He crumpled to the ground, and Martin, the second porter, put a knee between his shoulder blades, pinning him to the floor.

"He's a traitor. Hold him. Call the police," said Lina, before ducking back inside the changing room to put on her uniform.

#

Lina found Kevin in the canteen. Lunchtime was over, but the catering staff assembled a reasonable meal for her from the leftovers in the serving trays.

She was ravenous. As she stuffed food into her mouth, she told Kevin about her encounter with Jan in the nurses' changing room.

"You hit him with a bedpan?"

"Knocked him out, cold. The porters are holding him until the police can take him to jail."

He kissed her on the head. "You're amazing."

She smiled. "Didn't you notice that I wasn't in the flat?"

"Yes, of course I noticed. I thought you were working late."

"For two nights?"

"After the first day, I thought you'd left me."

"Leaving all my stuff behind? My clothes, my hats?"

"Tell me how you knew Jan de Groot," he said.

"I met him here. We had a meal together."

"You met him in the hospital?"

"At the entrance. We collided. He spoke to me in Dutch."

"When was this?"

"I don't know. When you were away."

"You had a meal together? Is that all you did?"

She blinked. She knew she was a poor liar, but she pressed on. "Yes, of course. We arranged a second date, but he never showed up."

"I was only away for a couple of weeks." He looked hurt.

"It was nothing," she said. "I suspect he broke in and searched the flat while I was waiting for him outside a cinema in Leicester Square. As I said before, he's a snake."

He said, "He won't cause any more mischief."

Ellis joined them. "I hear the hospital porters have captured Gingerbread, and Constable Brick has taken Pollinger in for questioning. I've told the major everything. He wants to see us both in his office first thing in the morning."

Matron came into the canteen. She hurried over to the table, and stood frowning down at Lina.

"Grant tells me you were tied up in the basement. If you're fully recovered I'd like you to resume your duties."

"Yes, Matron."

"You can't imagine how difficult it has been without you." It sounded like an accusation.

"It wasn't her fault, Matron," said Kevin. "I hope you don't think she was on some sort of holiday. Lina was held captive with no food or water for how long?"

"Nearly three days."

"She was trussed up like a Christmas turkey when we found her."
Matron grunted. "But you're ready to go back to work, now, yes?"

"Yes, Matron."

"Good. Joost needs your help. He's planning a session with Victor."

"And he wants me to help?" Lina was amazed. Joost had never asked for her help before.

"He asked for you. Now run along. You don't want to keep him waiting." Matron strode from the canteen.

Lina stood up. "See you later, Kevin."

"Victor who?" said Ellis.

"Colonel Victor Macintyre. He's seriously disturbed. Our psychologist has been working wonders with him." She hurried off to Joost's rooms.

#

Ellis waited until Lina had left the canteen before speaking. "Victor Macintyre was a member of the LCS. He had some sort of breakdown. I replaced him. He would have detailed knowledge of the original deception plan, the original version of Operation Fortitude." Ellis looked as crestfallen as Kurt had ever seen him.

"But the new version is quite different, isn't it?"

"I assume so. I was never informed about the old one. We need to check out this psychologist, Joost whatshisname. Psychologists use hypnosis, don't they?"

"Yes, I'm sure they do."

"There was something else the major said. Gingerbread has been transmitting again. The RDF units picked up a long signal sent from somewhere near Croydon this afternoon."

"Have the boffins deciphered it yet?"

"They're working on it. But I'm very much afraid we may have a serious problem. I don't remember much about yesterday. I remember following Jan. He must have led me here. I believe I may have been hypnotised and I could have given the whole game away. I remember a fob watch swinging on a chain."

"You don't know that," said Kurt. "Let's wait and see what Gingerbread has told his masters."

The revelation made Kurt weak at the knees. Since he joined the LCS, Ellis was fully briefed on Operation Fortitude. What he could have said under hypnosis didn't bear thinking about.

They asked for directions to Joost's rooms on the ground floor. Kurt tried the door. It was locked.

"How do you want to handle this?" said Ellis.

"We smash the door in," Kurt replied.

Ellis put his shoulder to the door, and they burst in.

Chapter 76

The scene that greeted Kurt looked no different to any doctor's consulting rooms. An elderly patient sat with Nurse Lina facing the psychologist.

What took the breath from Kurt's lungs was the sight of the psychologist. It was Pieter Hendriks, the first cleaner from the house in Perrymead Street.

Pieter Hendriks/Joost van Dijk got to his feet. He waved his arms about. "What is the meaning of this intrusion? Can't you see I'm with a patient? Get out and close the door."

The psychologist had a wild look about him, his eyes blazing, his mouth a thin line. It was a look that Kurt had seen before, the look of a man backed into a corner, facing impossible odds, but determined to stand his ground – the look of a Nazi fanatic, married to his credo.

Kurt snarled at him, "The game is over, Doctor, if you really are a doctor."

"I am a clinical psychologist, of course. Now get out of my consulting rooms, both of you."

Lina leapt up and stood beside him. "Kevin, what do you mean? Doctor van Dijk is a legend in this hospital. He has worked miracles on his patients." She looked confused.

Van Dijk patted her on the shoulder. "Thank you, Lina."

Victor Macintyre was on his feet then, yelling, "We are under attack. Prepare to repel boarders!"

Lina went to him, took him by the arm and spoke to him in calming tones.

Ellis stood facing the psychologist, fists clenched. "You are Dutch. Tell me why you and Jan de Groot targeted Queen Wilhelmina. How could you guide the German bombers to our beloved queen?"

Joost curled a lip. "The Dutch monarchy is doomed. They are decadent, a burden on the people of the Netherlands."

"I love them," said Lina. "They are loved by millions."

"They are irrelevant, Lina. The new order will sweep them away."

"You should be ashamed of yourself," said Ellis. "It's you and your Nazi friends who will be swept away." He lunged at van Dijk, but Kurt hauled him back.

Kurt said, "What were you hoping to gain by taking a position with Home Facilities?"

"I've no idea what you mean," said van Dijk.

"Using the false name Pieter Hendriks, you took a job as a cleaner. You cannot deny it."

"You're out of your mind," said the psychologist. "Why would I take a job as a cleaner?"

"To gather information for the Third Reich!"

Ellis said, "You extracted highly secret information from me under hypnosis."

"That's nonsense," van Dijk retorted. "Can you prove it?"

Kurt said, "You extracted information from your patients. For that alone you are guilty of serious medical misconduct. And once we find your transmitter, we will be able to prove everything. You are a German spy."

A twisted smile spread over the psychologist's face. "I owe a lot to Victor, here. He gave me all the intelligence he had, but I knew it wasn't enough."

Victor's face turned bright red. Lina held on tight to his arm to keep him anchored to his chair.

"So you abducted an Abwehr agent from the Double Cross programme. You interrogated him."

"Schumann wasted a lot of our time."

Lina said, "Who's Schumann? Is he one of our patients?"

Her question remained unanswered.

"Schumann knows nothing," said Kurt. "You killed a guard and an innocent cook for no benefit."

Van Dijk said, "You must blame Jan de Groot for that." His first half-admission of guilt.

"I don't think so. Jan wouldn't have gained access. Dennison knew you from his time as a patient in this hospital. He must have let you in. You slaughtered him in cold blood."

Van Dijk said nothing.

"Did you have to kill the cook, Mrs Pettigrew?"

The psychologist grabbed Lina's arm and pulled her to him. A knife appeared in his hand.

"Let her go, Hendriks or van Dijk, or whatever your name is," said

Kurt. "The game's up. Put away the knife and give yourself up."

Joost smiled his crooked smile again. "The British can do nothing to me, Kurt. My work here is done. The intelligence I have sent to Berlin today will ensure the failure of the invasion, and will result in the fall of the corrupt organization that is the Abwehr."

Kurt feared the truth of what the SD spy was saying. Operation Fortitude was irreparably damaged, the upcoming invasion of Europe would be a disaster for the Allies. And the intelligence coup would give Schellenberg all the ammunition he needed to destroy his enemies and take control over the Abwehr. The Black Orchestra would cease to exist as a resistance unit within the Abwehr.

"Who's Kurt?" said Lina.

Van Dijk pulled Lina closer to him. He put an arm across her shoulders and held the point of the knife at the side of her neck. "Now stand away from the door. Lina and I are leaving."

Kurt stepped aside, but Ellis stood his ground.

"You are under arrest for two murders," said Ellis. "Drop the weapon. Let the nurse go."

Van Dijk glared at him. "You cannot stop me, Els. If you lay a finger on me, I swear I will slit her throat."

It was clear that he meant what he said. A spot of blood appeared on Lina's neck.

Kurt placed a hand on Ellis's chest and pushed him to the side. "Let him go, Greg."

As soon as van Dijk reached his car in the car park, he released Lina. She struck him once on the upper arm with a closed fist before he got into the car. Van Dijk barely noticed the blow, but her courage lifted Kurt's spirits.

Dan the porter wrote down the registration number of the car, and pushed his wheelchair to Matron's office to alert Scotland Yard.

Kurt ran to Lina as the car drove away, but Ellis got there first. She was shaking. He held her tight, then walked her back inside the hospital, talking to her in Dutch.

"You were very brave," said Ellis, stepping away from Lina to allow Kurt to take over.

She shook her head. "What on earth was that all about? Joost really is a wonderful psychologist. You wouldn't believe the amazing results he has had with shell-shocked patients."

"He is a German spy," said Kurt gently. "He fooled everyone."

"He was always so kind to me. I will miss him. But he hates our queen. How is that possible for a Dutchman?"

Ellis said, "He's a Nazi, a member of the NSB. They have no respect for anyone; no sympathy for any philosophy except their own twisted ideology."

Kurt said, "Forget about him, Lina. The police will catch him soon enough."

A junior doctor tended to the wound in Lina's neck. It required nothing more than a touch of iodine and a Band-Aid.

Chapter 77

"Who was that man? Ellis, was that his name?" Lina asked Kevin when they were back in their flat.

"Greg Ellis. He also calls himself Gregor Els. He's a colleague of mine. Why do you ask?"

"No reason. Did you see his dinky red car?"

"Yes." He grinned. "I've even been for a spin in it."

"What will they do with Joost when they catch him?"

"He'll be taken to a secure facility for interrogation by British Intelligence."

"And then what?"

"That depends on how well the interrogation goes."

"You mean he could be executed?"

"Yes, Lina, he may be executed. He is a German spy, after all, and he killed two innocent people."

Lina chopped up some vegetables and tossed them into a pot on the gas ring. She needed to keep her hands busy to stop them from shaking.

"I've been thinking, Lina..."

"Me too," she said. "All the time I was tied up in the dark in the basement, I could think of nothing but you and me. We've been good together, we've had fun and we've had our ups and downs. On balance, I have no regrets, but we were never really a couple."

She paused for a reaction. He said nothing.

"I mean, couples build their lives together. They get married and have children. Those were never options for us."

She looked at him again, but the blank expression on his face told her nothing. "What were you going to say?"

"It's not important. Carry on."

She sliced a carrot and added it to the pot. Then she took a deep breath and told him. "I finally came to the conclusion that we should split up. I know what you're going to say, but time has run out on us. We have to face the fact that we have no future together. You belong with Gudrun and nobody else."

Still, he said nothing. The silence stretched like an abyss between them.

"Say something, Kevin, please," she whispered.

"You know I'm very fond of you, but you're right – Gudrun has my heart. I'd hate for us to split up, but if that's really what you want..."

"It is. Let's be honest, I know nothing about you. Nothing. Can I believe anything you told me about your past? And you've told me nothing about your work. Are you really an Irishman? It seems I don't even know your real name."

"Your vegetables are burning," he said.

Chapter 78

Saturday March 18, 1944

The following morning, Kurt and Ellis presented themselves to Major Robertson in his Bedford Street office.

"Congratulations are in order," said the major. "That was a splendid outcome all round. Gingerbread didn't get far. The police stopped his car on the A41 near St Albans. He and his sidekick are both behind bars."

Kurt was taken aback by the major's upbeat manner.

Ellis gave voice to Kurt's thoughts. "Don't we have a crisis on our hands, sir? Hasn't Operation Fortitude been torpedoed by Gingerbread's last transmission?"

"Yes, of course, the operation has been holed well below the waterline." The frozen smile on the major's face was more menace than mirth. "You must explain to me later how you managed to allow an enemy agent to interrogate you under hypnosis."

Ellis's eye flashed around the room before settling on his boots.

Kurt said, "And what about the SD? Have we not given the Nazis the ammunition they need to get rid of General von Neumann and take over the Abwehr completely?"

"Yes, so it would seem. But nil desperandum, gentlemen. We have the means to repair the damage and refloat the good ship Fortitude." He paused for dramatic effect. "Your new friend, Herr Schellenberg, is expecting you to send him a list of Abwehr double agents, is he not?" He handed a file across the desk to Kurt. "We mustn't disappoint him. In this file you will find a list of the call-signs of the Abwehr double agents in London."

"All of them?" said Kurt.

"No, not all of them. What you have there is the call-signs of 25 carefully chosen agents. I would like you to transmit the list to Herr Schellenberg, using your new call-sign. What was it, again?"

"*KPS* – Rattlesnake." Kurt examined the signal. He found

Arnold's call-sign. The last call-sign on the list was *LBK* – Gingerbread. "Schellenberg is unlikely to believe this list."

"Perhaps, but it will place a doubt in his mind."

"He may simply ignore the signal," said Kurt.

"I've thought of that. You did say that Schellenberg expects you to send the list to the Abwehr 24 hours after you've sent it to him?"

"Yes, sir."

"If you do that, he will not be able to ignore the signal or to hide it from his superiors, since the Abwehr will pass it up the line of command. Any and all intelligence previously sent by Gingerbread will be discredited, and any move that Schellenberg makes on the Abwehr will be easily repulsed."

Kurt nodded enthusiastically. "That could work. But I'm going to need a transmitter and a copy of *Pickwick Papers* by Charles Dickens."

Kurt was dismissed. Ellis remained behind to explain his hypnosis episode.

#

Back at the flat, Kurt found a note from Lina.

I have a few days off. I'll be staying overnight with my friend Kathy. I'd like you out of the flat by Tuesday. I've started packing your things. You'll find a suitcase in the bedroom.

Lina xx

Short and to the point! He thought the two kisses were an ironic addition. So Kathy was a friend now?

How was he going to move out by Tuesday? He hadn't the first clue where could he go.

Chapter 79

Sunday March 19, 1944
RSHA PrinzAbrecht Strasse 8, Berlin

Walter Schellenberg checked his appearance in the mirror. He was usually happy to put on his SS uniform for his meetings with the Reichsführer-SS, but not today. Today, he faced Himmler's wrath, and possibly the end of his career. He straightened his tie, moistened a finger and ran it over the iron cross hanging from his breast pocket.

His duel with the Abwehr had been like a chess match. Move and countermove, he and von Neumann had played the game for two years. In that time, Hans Oster had been sent to Flossenbürg in disgrace and Admiral Canaris was suspended from duty. But still, the final checkmate eluded him. And now, it seemed he was about to lose the whole game. All his hard work would come crashing down around him, like the ruins to be seen everywhere in the centre of Berlin.

He took the stairs to the top floor and was admitted to Herr Himmler's office without the usual delay. Erwin von Neumann was already seated, facing the Reichsführer. Schellenberg gave him no sign of recognition, apart from an almost imperceptible heel click, before taking the second seat.

Heinrich Himmler was engrossed in something on his desk. His two visitors waited. After a few moments, he looked up, fixed a gimlet eye on Schellenberg, and spoke. "As I understand it, Walter, you have an agent operating in London independent of the Abwehr, an agent who provided intelligence that you passed on to the military high command. I also understand that the OKW acted on this intelligence, moving significant numbers of troops and heavy equipment south and west toward Cherbourg, away from the Pas-de-Calais area."

He paused to take a breath. Schellenberg might have interrupted at this point, but the look in Himmler's eyes told him to hold his tongue.

"General von Neumann tells me he has received word that this rogue agent of yours – call-sign Gingerbread – has been captured by the British, so that any intelligence he transmits must be treated entirely as misinformation supplied by the British to fool our high command."

Himmler paused to allow Schellenberg to respond, but he found he had nothing to say.

"General Keitel informs me that these pointless manoeuvres have cost the Wehrmacht a small fortune. They could have cost considerably more, but fortunately the general acted upon his own natural restraint, taking account of the widely held view that the Pas-de-Calais is the only logical choice for the invasion. As it is, they cost in the region of..." He consulted the papers on his desk. "1.6 million reichsmarks. What do you have to say for yourself?"

Schellenberg tugged on his tunic. He cleared his throat. "Herr Reichsführer, the agent in question has been operating deep undercover in London for several years. He is a loyal member of the National Socialist Workers Party of Holland, a stout supporter of the Führer, and I have every faith in him."

"Are you denying that he is under the influence of the British? General von Neumann has assured me that this is the case."

"No, sir, I am sure that Gingerbread has been captured by the British. What I question is whether he was captured before or after the transmission that revealed the British and American plan to concentrate their invasion forces on the Normandy beaches."

Himmler sat back in his chair. "What are you saying? Are you saying we should leave things as they are with vital troops diverted to Normandy on the chance that your man's intelligence was sound to begin with?"

General von Neumann gave a snort of derision.

Himmler continued, "No, Walter, we cannot act on anything your man tells us. Erwin here has already notified the OKW of the error, and I am assured that the troops and equipment will be returned to their original positions."

"If I may say a few words," said von Neumann. Himmler indicated his permission with a wave of his hand.

The general fixed Schellenberg with his gaze. "Placing and running agents overseas is a difficult and delicate business, as anyone in the Abwehr will tell you. We have been training agents and placing them behind enemy lines for years. The SD, on the other hand, has little or no expertise in this area. This episode only serves to prove the foolishness of dabbling in an area outside your knowledge. I would urge you, Walter, to surrender to the Abwehr any other agents you may have operating overseas."

This was no more than Schellenberg had expected, but still his hackles were raised. A dressing down by a superior, like Heinrich Himmler – or even Ernst Kaltenbrunner – was acceptable, but not from an equal, and certainly not in front of the Reichsführer.

"As you know very well, Erwin, we have been operating agents overseas since well before the start of the War. There is nothing particularly difficult or delicate about it."

"Poorly," said von Neumann.

"Can you rely on your own record? I could point out that the Abwehr is known for the poor quality of its training. The signal that exposed my agent in London also named 25 Abwehr agents that are operating under control of the British."

Himmler held up a hand to silence them both. "Enough of the bickering. Tell me what you intend to do about this mess."

Schellenberg replied, "Every single scrap of information received by those 25 Abwehr agents will now have to be unearthed and scrutinized."

"That could take months," said von Neumann. "You can do that if you wish. The Abwehr will continue to supply solid, reliable intelligence to our armed forces in preparation for the Allied invasion."

"Your whole operation is tainted," said Schellenberg.

"Don't be ridiculous," von Neumann replied. "Only 25 of our agents have been captured, we still have nearly 100 operating in London, free of British interference."

"That's enough," said Himmler. "Get out of my office, both of you."

Chapter 80

Monday March 20, 1944
Tar Robertson's office

Major Robertson's beaming smile told Kurt that Operation Fortitude was back on the rails. "RAF surveillance aircraft have detected unmistakable signs that the earlier German troop movements are being reversed. And now that we have identified 25 Abwehr men operating as double agents, our deception operation is stronger than ever. We have the means to misdirect and misinform the enemy on a scale never attempted before."

Kurt returned his smile.

"I don't suppose you've considered the implications for yourself," the major said.

"I realise that Rattlesnake will have to continue transmitting."

Major Robertson nodded. "As of today, you are a double agent. You will be set up in a safe house with your own case officer."

"Do I need a case officer, sir?"

"I'm not having a double agent in the programme without a case officer."

"With guards, a cook and a cleaner?"

"Guards won't be necessary, and I expect you to do your own cooking and cleaning. I've appointed Humphrey Carter as your case officer. You know him, and I think you get on well together."

Kurt groaned inwardly while nodding with enthusiasm.

"The house is in Frome Road, north London, number 27. You should get yourself over there by close of business tonight." The major tossed a bunch of keys across the desk. Kurt caught them.

Kurt's accommodation problem had been solved at a stroke, but he wasn't at all sure about sleeping in a house where there had been a gruesome double murder. "What about Joost van Dijk? Did you find his transmitter? And will he be charged with the double murder?"

"His transmitter was hidden in his car, where his spare tyre should have been. He's under interrogation in the London Cage. Tin Eye Stephens will decide his immediate fate. If he offers him the option of joining the programme and if van Dijk accepts, his trial for the murders will have to wait until the end of the War."

"And his accomplice, Jan de Groot?"

The major's gaze fell to his desk. "John is due for summary execution. His was an egregious betrayal."

"What about Henk Janssen?"

"The police are still searching for him. It appears he is nothing but a petty thief. Now that the police know that, and they have his picture, he will be apprehended soon enough."

Madge Butterworth came in with the customary tray of tea. She smiled at Kurt.

When Madge had left, the major poured out two cups of tea. "I've had a telephone call from Scotland Yard. A dead body has been found in a field beside the rail line from Poole in Dorset to London."

Kurt lifted his teacup to his lips, holding it in two hands, to dampen a sudden tremor.

"The police have identified the dead man as a member of the Russian diplomatic mission, name of Polanikov. They wondered if we might be able to shed some light on the matter."

The major paused for a response. Kurt said, "An unfortunate accident by the sound of it. Falls from trains are not uncommon, I believe."

"This one had a bullet hole in his forehead. You travelled from Poole to London recently, didn't you?"

"Yes, Major, but I know nothing about any dead Russians."

"I'm told he was dressed as a ticket inspector."

"How bizarre," said Kurt. "He was probably up to no good."

"Probably."

Kurt replaced his cup carefully on its saucer. "Greg Ellis—"

"Greg Ellis is in the clear. How many times do I have to tell you that? He's now a full member of the LCS."

"I just wondered how he knew my real name," said Kurt.

"He doesn't. Only Miss Butterworth and I know that."

"And yet, he called me Kurt in an unguarded moment."

The major chewed that over for a moment. Then he pressed his intercom. "Madge, please step into my office."

Madge opened the door and came in.

"Is it true that you and Greg Ellis have been stepping out together?"

"Yes, Major, but not any more. We had a falling out about a month ago." Her downcast look could have indicated regret, but Kurt suspected she was smothering an urge to smile.

"I see. Well, Kurt tells me that Greg used his real name in conversation. Is it possible he picked that up from you?"

Madge blushed bright red. "No, no, Major. Not unless I spoke in my sleep. If it did happen, I'm sorry."

"It's Kurt you need to apologise to," said the major.

"I'm sorry, Kurt," she said.

"That's all, thank you, Madge," said the major, and Madge left the room.

"What will become of Pollinger?" said Kurt.

"He'll be put back to work under a new case officer."

"In a different house?"

"Naturally, we could hardly expect him to operate in the house where he witnessed the brutal killing of his guard and his cook."

But you've no problem placing me in there, thought Kurt.

"Is there anything else?" said the major.

Kurt sipped his tea. "Has there been any progress in the search for the Russian mole in London?"

"Philby's on the case," said the major. "He has already identified the German agent operating in the Russian embassy in Madrid."

"Has he been removed?"

"He has been taken care of, yes."

Kurt wondered what that meant. "And what about the NKVD agent in London?"

"As I said, Kim Philby is on his trail. More tea?"

Chapter 81

Kurt took the Tube back to Walham Green and made his way to the flat. As he turned the corner at the end of Radipole Road, he spotted a red MG Midget accelerating away toward the city centre.

He let himself in to the flat, and found Lina standing by the kitchen sink, her arms folded across her chest.

"I've come for my things," he said.

She pointed to his suitcase behind the front door. "I've packed everything for you. It's all in there."

"Thank you."

"Are you going to be all right? Have you found somewhere to stay?"

"I'll be fine," said Kurt. "How are you going to cope, living on your own?"

"I expect I'll find someone," she said. "How about you?"

"I have Gudrun and Anna."

"Yes," she said in a barely audible voice.

"Was that Greg Ellis I saw outside in his red car?"

Her eyes narrowed. "His name's Gregor Els. He's from Holland, and he has become a friend."

"Nothing more than a friend?"

"Time to leave, Kurt," she said.

#

Kurt took the Tube to Turnpike Lane, made his way to Frome Road, and let himself into number 27.

The house was empty. He turned on the light in the front parlour. The carpet had been removed, leaving a suspicious dark stain on the floorboards. He shuddered and checked the rest of the rooms. He found no more signs of the recent violent deaths.

There was tea, coffee and sugar in the kitchen larder, but no milk. He made a cup of coffee and drank it black with two spoonfuls of sugar. He found a writing pad on a shelf and took it with him upstairs.

He thought about Sofia Beckman. Her violent death was etched in his memory. Surely he had contributed to her death. His request for a list of British workers in pre-war Madrid had alerted the Russians. His mind turned to the Good Samaritan in Lisbon. He still had no idea why Flavio, a total stranger, came to his aid when he most needed it. He owed a debt of gratitude to Flavio that he might never get a chance to repay. Then he thought about his trip to Ireland, how his love for Gudrun – and Anna – had been rekindled. He had been such a fool, and such a coward.

Pollinger's bedroom was easily identified. The bedclothes were still on the unmade bed, as if he had left it that morning. Kurt searched the linen press for clean sheets and remade the bed. He checked the wardrobe and the chest of drawers, half expecting to find Pollinger's clothes. They were empty.

He lifted the suitcase onto the bed and opened it. Inside, he found Gudrun's postcard on top of his clothing. Under the postcard was the envelope he had asked the nurse in Dublin to post for him. He propped Gudrun's postcard in front of the mirror on the dressing table. Then he opened the envelope and pulled out the paper inside. He unfolded it, and placed it on the dressing table. Anna's picture of a banana and a bunch of grapes brought a broad smile to his face.

He unpacked the suitcase, and put his clothes in the wardrobe and chest of drawers. Then he sat at the dressing table and began to write. He wrote in English. A letter in German would never be delivered. It was sure to be intercepted by the Royal Mail.

27 Frome Road, London N22
March 20, 1944

My dearest Gudrun,

As you will see, I have a new address. I moved in here this evening. The house is cold and empty, and I miss you terribly. I am still working for Thomas. He never ceases to find me things to do here in London.

When we met at the end of February and early March, I think you guessed that I had not been living alone over here. I confess that I have been living with a nurse called Lina for a few months. She's from Holland. I hope you'll believe me when I say that I never stopped loving you. I was simply overcome by loneliness and I gave in to temptation. I hope you can forgive me.

That episode is over now, and I'm living in total isolation here in this new location.

I promise I will not stray again, and will save all my love for you and Anna for when this horrible war is finally over.

All my love to you, Anna and Mother.

And I hope I'll be with you for good one of these days.

K

He reread the letter twice and addressed the envelope. Before placing the letter in the envelope, he read it a third time.

Then he tore it up and started again.

27 Frome Road, London N22
March 20, 1944

My dearest Gudrun,

As you see, I have a new address. I moved in here this evening. The house is cold and empty, and I miss you terribly. I am still working for Thomas. He never ceases to find me things to do here in London.

When we met at the end of February and early March, I realised how much I love you, and how I long to be with you and Anna.

Tell Anna I have her banana and grapes here to keep me company and remind me of her.

Let's hope and pray that his horrible war will end soon.

I will write more often. Maybe you could write to me at this address. That way, the time will pass quicker until we meet again.

All my love to you, Anna and Mother

K

THE END

Thanks for reading my book. Word of mouth is essential for any author to succeed. If you enjoyed the book, tell your friends and please consider leaving a review on Amazon. Reviews really help.

ACKNOWLEDGEMENTS

Thanks to all my proofreaders, Helen Baggott, Marion Kummerow, Paul T. Lynch, Peter O'Boyle, Susan Offord Jones, Jason Orpwood, Fred Stowell, Pam Toner and Pamela Wilkinson. I am indebted to LionheART Publishing for formatting the paper version, to Anya Kelleye for an inspired cover design, to the Flyingboat museum at Foynes for information about the wartime service to Lisbon, and to Flavio the real life Good Samaritan in Lisbon airport. A special thanks to Pam, Roisin, Kaitlin and Joshua for the Gingerbread men.

About JJ TONER

I am a full time writer. I write short stories and novels. I live in Ireland with my wife and youngest son. Look for me on my website http://www.JJToner.com/

Other Books by JJ Toner

The Black Orchestra, The first in the WW2 spy thriller series
The Wings of the Eagle, The second in the Black Orchestra series
A Postcard from Hamburg, The third in the Black Orchestra
series

These three books are also available as audio books

The Serpent's Egg, A Red Orchestra spy thriller

eBooks

Zugzwang, a Kommissar Saxon mystery
Queen Sacrifice, the second Kommissar Saxon story

Houdini's Handcuffs, a police thriller featuring DI Ben Jordan
Find Emily, the second DI Jordan thriller

Science Fiction

EGGS and Other Stories
Murder by Android
Rogue Android